The subject of *Scenes from Married Life* is very rare in novels, a happy marriage. The central character is the young man, hero of *Scenes from Provincial Life*, who, in 1939, was sleeping with his girl but avoiding marrying her: now, in 1949, not so young, he is still unmarried and by his knowing friends written off as a permanent bachelor. Has Joe missed the boat? A third of the way through this novel he triumphantly catches it, with a delicious schoolteacher called Elspeth. And then what? 'It's easier to *get* married,' says his most knowing friend of all, a lady psychiatrist, 'than to *be* married.'

*Scenes from Married Life* is set in London, in the world of men's clubs, government offices and suburban houses. Joe is now a temporary civil servant and a novelist of some reputation; but his career-problem, like his non-insiderish temperament, persists — will he manage to keep his job, and will he manage to get his next small masterpiece published?

What Mr. Cooper has to say is funny, truthful, touching, ironic and, in its particular flavour, all his own. The incidents in the story are comic and the writer's purpose is serious. The main theme is an account of two people, amiable and intelligent but pretty individual, making their marriage work; the second theme is an account of two other people doing the same: Robert, Joe's old friend and novelist colleague in the Civil Service, and Annette, the sweet daughter of a Civil Service boss.

From patient, amused, good-natured observation of the human comedy, Mr. Cooper makes an individual contribution to the natural history of the human heart.

# SCENES FROM MARRIED LIFE

BY

## WILLIAM COOPER

MACMILLAN LONDON

This book is dedicated to
My Wife

ISBN 0 333 34445 6

First published 1961 by
Macmillan London Limited
London and Basingstoke

Associated companies in Auckland, Dallas,
Delhi, Dublin, Hong Kong, Johannesburg,
Lagos, Manzini, Melbourne, Nairobi,
New York, Singapore, Tokyo, Washington
and Zaria

This edition published 1982, reprinted 1982

Printed and bound in Great Britain
at The Pitman Press, Bath.

# CONTENTS

## Part I

## Part II

## Part III

# Contents

# PART I

## CHAPTER I

## ON A NO. 14 BUS

'P.S.A.,' said Sybil, in a tone of amiable comment. She was looking through the window of the bus and I had my arm round her.

Startled, I followed her glance. The bus was going along Piccadilly — I was on my way to seeing her off at Euston — and I judged that her glance was directed towards one of those huge-windowed shops which in London appear to be indispensable for selling motor-cars, though there is no evidence that fewer motor-cars are sold per financially eligible head of population in say Aberdeen without them. P.S.A.? Or was it B.S.A.? That rang a bell — it was the make of bicycle I had ridden when I was a schoolmaster before the war. A ridiculous idea. There could be no B.S.A.s among Hillmans and Austins and Bentleys, in fact there was no connection between them other than in my imagination, where, when a provincial schoolmaster astride a B.S.A., I had imagined myself writing a novel which could sell enough copies to buy me a Bentley, or for that matter an Austin, even just a small Austin.

I could see no letters P.S.A., nor B.S.A. In fact I could see no three-letter group anywhere on anything.

'What on earth does P.S.A. stand for?' I asked.

Sybil half-turned to me and said: 'Pleasant Sunday Afternoon, of course.'

I burst into laughter. It was appreciative laughter. Just before getting on to this bus, Sybil and I had been in bed together. My appreciation was enormous.

Sybil was an unusually pretty girl. She looked remarkably like Marlene Dietrich — Marlene Dietrich when young,

3

though Sybil was now about thirty-two. Sybil was aware of the resemblance and plucked her eyebrows accordingly. Above her wide-open blue eyes, they rose in two hyperfine arches, which, when she was talking to you, wiggled in a remarkable manner. I was fascinated by them: I could never understand why they did it.

'I thought you must have seen the letters on a shop-front,' I said. 'I was looking for them everywhere.'

At this Sybil turned away thoughtfully. The fact which I might have remembered, thereby saving myself some trouble, was that Sybil was so short-sighted she could scarcely see the shops. There was a pause while we went round Piccadilly Circus, and then she turned back to me and, with her eyebrows wiggling, said:

'Joe, do you think I ought to wear contact lenses?'

Like a fool, I replied: 'I should have thought a pair of specs would have done just as well.' Having bits of glass against one's eyeballs seemed to me creepy.

Sybil's expression was not a hurt one: it was an uncomprehending one. Contact lenses were something she could envisage: spectacles were not. I realised why not, by reference to a concept which originated from a friend of mine named Robert, who knew Sybil well. Robert was convinced that in her inveterate perusal of women's magazines Sybil had succumbed to the propaganda that any woman can be beautiful by following certain rules of make-up — 'Glamour Tips' was what Robert was convinced they were called, and he believed that there was a fixed apocalyptic number, actually forty-four, of them. Robert, I realised, would have understood at once why Sybil looked uncomprehending — not that he did not understand everything at once, being that sort of man: I revered him for it. Robert would have understood that contact lenses were numbered among Sybil's Forty-four Glamour Tips, whereas spectacles were not.

'Perhaps you ought to have contact lenses,' I said, to get on the rails again.

4

'Yes,' said Sybil. 'I can't see very much when I'm out.'

'How much can you see?' I said, thinking of her when she was in.

Sybil looked through the window again. She read out the name of the play that was then on at the Globe Theatre, *The Lady Is Not For Burning* — the year was 1949. As the letters were a foot high and only a pavement's width away, I said:

'If you look at the people on the other side of the road, can you tell which sex they are?'

Without hesitation, and with what seemed to me a touch of characteristic complacency, Sybil said:

'If it's fairly clearly marked.'

I laughed, and then something, perhaps actually looking at the people on the other side of the road, made me speculate on how the world looked to Sybil. Very, very different from how it looked to me. The difference visually was obvious — whatever my moral defects were, I had pretty good eyesight — but that was only the beginning. Not only did Sybil see the world differently from me with the outer eye: the truth was that after knowing her for years I had no idea *what* she saw with the inner one.

I had known Sybil off and on for fifteen years. She worked as a librarian in the provincial town that I came from. I repeat, as a librarian. Sybil looked so like Marlene Dietrich that you might have thought she would never have had a book in her hand, that nobody would ever even have shown her one. Not a bit of it. Once during a lull when we were in bed she recited the whole of one of Hamlet's soliloquies — and not the '*To be, or not to be*' one, either. I was amazed.

Sybil was a mystery to me. After knowing her for fifteen years I had to confess that I had not the faintest idea what moved her immortal soul, what made her tick. Nor had Robert. We used to discuss it with persistence and chagrin. You may think I was in a better position to solve the mystery

5

because she had slept with me and not with Robert. Well, no, you are wrong there, I think.

Anyway, the generalisation that you will penetrate the mysteries of somebody's nature if she sleeps with you is a shaky one at the best of times, and in the case of Sybil it was simply non-operative. There she lay, for example, happily reciting one of Hamlet's soliloquies. Amazing, but not exegetical.

'What does Sybil want out of life?' Robert would ask me. When propounding a question to which neither he nor I knew the answer, Robert always safeguarded his own self-esteem by aiming the question at me.

I told him I had heard her say she would like to be a film star.

Because it was out of the question for her to become a film star, Robert looked at me as if he thought I were reporting her untruthfully. It was not possible for Robert to believe that aspiration could exist so independently of action: in Sybil they existed together without the slightest mutual influence — they appeared not to cause each other a scrap of bother. Sybil went on her way imperturbably. Sometimes I thought conceitedness might have been the source of her imperturbability, but she never seemed particularly conceited.

Then Robert and I argued about whether Sybil wanted to be married again. Robert wanted to know if she wanted to marry me, and when I said I saw no signs of it, that between Sybil and me marriage somehow did not come into it, he looked neither satisfied with my reply nor dissatisfied. He said: 'H'm.'

Sybil and I were friends who had slept together off and on for years, the off spells corresponding on my side to the times when I was in love with someone, and on her side to the spell when she was married. The latter, alas, was short. In 1943 she married a willowy, dashing young man in the Parachute Regiment, and he was killed at Arnhem. After that she went

on working in her library, helping to support her mother.
There were always men about the place who wanted to
marry her, and no one was more in need of a guiding hand,
literally, than Sybil. Sybil standing on the pavement looking
for a bus-stop was a sight so heart-rending that any man
who saw her longed to drive up in an expensive car and carry
her away. Yet she did not marry.

Marriage and widowhood had made no difference in
Sybil's attitude to me: failure to marry and confirmation in
bachelordom had obviously made no difference in my
attitude to her. Sitting in the No. 14 bus that November
Sunday evening, we might just as well have been sitting in a
provincial tram soon after we first met. Oddly self-possessed
yet diffident, in some ways ineffably remote — not to mention others in which she was deliciously contiguous — with
beautiful eyes picking up next to nothing and eyebrows
wiggling like antennae, she gave me no clue whatsoever to
what made her tick. She never had. She never would.

That Sunday evening was almost the last time I ever saw
Sybil, so that I have had ten years to recollect her in tran-
quillity. Still no clue.

The bus fetched up at Euston and we went into the
station. Euston is dark at the best of times and, on this
particular evening, night had come early, coldly and
wintrily, wafting into our nostrils fog flavoured with sulphur
dioxide. We were in no hurry. We went through the classical
entrance into the forecourt, where the lights were burning
without seeming to make the slightest difference to the degree
of illumination. A faint shadow had crossed both our minds,
for a glance at the clock had reminded us that although time
was passing it was still too early to get a drink.

How often I had entered this station, just before seven
o'clock of a Sunday evening! *Autre temps, autre femmes,* I
reminded myself in a sprightly way — that suddenly fell
flat . . . I was reminded of *autres temps,* some years back, when
I had thought I was all set to get married.

7

'Damn this station!' I must have said it aloud, because Sybil said:

'Yes. It isn't as nice as Paddington.'

We went on to the platform and found that the train was in. It was always in. I put Sybil's case on a seat and then we strolled down the platform. The faint fishy, appley smell was too poignant to be borne, I thought. I really wished I might never be seeing anybody off from this station, from this particular platform, ever again. I said to Sybil all the same:

'How soon can you come and see me again?'

'Not till after Christmas, more's the pity!'

A porter beginning to slam the doors at the top end of the train took us by surprise. It was time for Sybil to get into the carriage.

When the train had gone out I made for the bar, which was now open, and ordered a large whisky. It may sound as if I had fallen into a bout of *tristezza* consequent on the pleasures of the afternoon, but to my mind it was consequent on something of much longer duration, and not pleasurable either. To ward it off I drank the whisky quickly and ordered another. I paused. And then inspiration suddenly hit me in the way a large whisky does.

There was something wrong with my life, and my predicament at this moment expressed it perfectly. Having just seen off Sybil, what had I got to go home to? An empty flat. At my age — I was thirty-nine — what had all other men got to go home to? A cosy house with a wife in it and some kiddies. What a corny dream-picture! I thought, and yet what an attractive one! (For the moment I disregarded the fact that if there had been a wife and some kiddies in my flat I should have been lucky to get out for a solitary whisky, let alone to see off at Euston, *con tristezza* or *con allegria*, some such girl as Sybil.)

A romantic bitterness about my fate temporarily overcame me, in the deserted bar. When I was young I had not

8

wanted to get married. And now? At that question my spirits slipped a notch lower. I began my second whisky.

As my colleagues in the Civil Service would have put it, I 'reviewed the situation'. What a situation! And what an awful review! For fifteen years I had slept with someone whom I comprehended so little that somehow marriage just never came into it. Like ships that pass in the night, Sybil and I, for all the passing and re-passing which practically amounted to a regular service, were still a couple of ships, lone in the night. I was still lone in the night. Was it, could it possibly be, that there was something wrong not with my life but with *me*? When I thought that, I felt something deep in my psyche like the fall of ice-cream on teeth that have just been scaled.

'Joe,' I said to myself as I drank some more of the whisky, 'it's bad, very bad.' I meant the prognosis was bad.

Mine was indeed a predicament — in Robert's idiom, a predicament and a half.

Remembering Robert made me decide to explain my latest view of my predicament to him. Of course he knew all about it, as he knew about everything else. The trouble with our predicaments, especially when they are painful, incapable of resolution, even tragic, is that we are just a bit proud of them, just a bit attached to them. Though Robert knew all about mine already, I had every intention of explaining my latest view of it even if I bored the hide off him.

I made my way out of the station and caught a No. 14 bus going in the opposite direction to the one I had come on.

'Terminus,' I said to the conductor heavily, but meaning it literally. I was living at Putney.

## CHAPTER II

## TALKS WITH A FAT MAN

HARRY was one of those active fat men who are really more muscular and less fat than they look, though that is not saying much in the case of Harry, whose shape came as near as makes no matter to a globe. And like the terrestrial globe, he seemed to be always spinning. When he approached you, moving bulkily on light, strong feet, a whirling gust of air preceded him — it was the outskirts of a vortex at the centre of which you saw Harry, sweating profusely and fixing you with a beady, eager, inquisitive look.

Harry was a distant cousin of mine. (Exactly how distant was something that he and I — unlike members of the aristocracy, to whom, with titles and large sums of money in the offing, such calculations seem to come like second nature — had never bothered to work out.) Though our families saw little of each other, Harry and I, between the ages of fifteen and eighteen, when he was going to a country grammar school and I to a town secondary school, had been companions for pursuits involving bicycles, box-cameras, air-guns, tents and suchlike; pursuits frequently commended by parents for promoting healthy adventurous instincts in boys, and often undertaken by boys chiefly as a means of getting away from parents.

I still possess a small terracotta Roman bowl, artfully stuck together with Seccotine, that Harry and I ought to have handed in to the local museum of antiquities. I also keep an old photograph of both of us, taken by another boy and somewhat imperfectly 'fixed' by the look of it, in which Harry misleadingly appears as lithe, broad-chested, and quite unglobe-like. Globedom, as in those dried Japanese flowers which you drop into a glass of water, was then securely hidden in the comely packet of Harry's particular type of physique — a type which he and I nowadays referred to with professional facetiousness as the Pyknic Practical Joke. The joke was comic enough when played by the Deity on Harry, but was seen by us at its most comic when played on a young man who married a beautiful, lithe, broad-chested girl, in whom was hidden, as in one of those Japanese flowers, etc. etc. etc.

Harry, I may say, was surviving the joke with over-high blood-pressure but admirable grace. I found him more fun now than I had done twenty years ago, not because his nature had changed, but because I suppose I had meanwhile learnt how to find people entertaining. Boys have a dim time of it because they have so far learnt only how to find each other useful. Anyway, I was glad when Harry reappeared in my life.

One day the telephone in my office rang — by this time I had become a Principal in the Civil Service — and it was Harry. Our boyhood companionship had lapsed when I went up to Oxford to read science and Harry went to Manchester to start becoming a doctor. Throughout the last twenty years I do not suppose I had seen him more than half a dozen times. My sense of family was strong but of the passive, non-visiting, non-corresponding kind. It was not activated by a feeling that if I did visit and correspond I should be overwhelmed by moral approval of my goings-on. Harry's and my family was sprinkled with Methodist ministers, my father being one of them.

I felt nothing but pleasure when Harry rang me up that day to say he had got a job in the Medical Research Council and had bought a house in Putney. I was ready to take up our friendship just where we had left off.

But the first time Harry and I met again, I realised that it was pure illusion on my part to think that anything had been left off where he was concerned. There was no lapse, no blank, no absence whatsoever of contact from his side. Harry seemed to have a complete dossier of everything I had done during the last twenty years.

At this point in my story I have to make my chief revelation about Harry's nature. About Sybil I remarked that I had not the faintest idea what moved her immortal soul, what made her tick. There was no such mystery about Harry. His mainspring was visible to everyone. What moved Harry's immortal soul can be named in one word — curiosity. I have never in my life known anyone to come anywhere near Harry's level for being moved so constantly, so powerfully, so magnificently by curiosity. It shone in the beadiness of his bright hazel eyes; it whirled in the warm gust of air that preceded him; curiosity, fat, energetic and insatiable.

'Good gracious!' I exclaimed when I first saw him come into the room — we met at my club — not having expected him to be anything like so globular. His waist measurement must be his biggest, I thought with stupefaction.

Harry looked at me shrewdly for a moment, and said in his quick, fluent, high-pitched voice:

'You're greyer than your photographs show, aren't you, Joe?'

I could not think where he had seen a photograph of me. As for being grey — it is very hard to realise how much older one is looking. Whenever I was at the barber's and a wad of hair fell in my lap, I always had a job not to exclaim: 'Is that *mine*?'

Harry, I observed, had not much hair at all now. He had a globe-shaped head, over the top of which his fine-textured, straight, mouse-coloured hair could scarcely be said to hide the pink of his scalp. He had a shining, intelligent face, in the middle of which sat a snub nose. With the years' accretion of flesh round them, his eyes looked smaller than they used to, not quite puffy, not quite baggy, but somewhere in between the two. He took out a handkerchief and wiped a few drops of sweat off his forehead before he sat down.

'I suppose,' he said, when he had sat down, 'getting turned down in marriage, that last time, must have taken a lot out of you?'

'How in God's name do you know all about that?' I said. After all, I had hardly told my parents anything about it, and I presumed our family was his source of intelligence.

Harry said: 'Oh, I pieced it together . . .' His tone might have been thought apologetic as well as explanatory. But his complexion gave him away. I noticed the sudden tinge of a blush. It was a blush of triumph, of pure triumph.

I stared at him.

'I was sorry to hear about your bad luck.' While he was saying this, his eyes seemed to enlarge with sympathy, and he looked at me with intimate concern.

Harry's feeling was not in the least put on for the occasion. His curiosity was linked with unusual empathy. Looking at him now I realised that when we were boys I might have been unaware of what he was like but I had not been mistaken in choosing him for a friend.

'It's the sort of thing that happens to one,' I muttered, looking down.

'I wonder . . .' he said. His tone stayed on its high, honeyed pitch. 'Don't you think you attract that kind of bad luck?'

I looked up pretty quickly at that.

'There's the internal evidence of your novels, you know,' he said. And again he was unable to keep the triumphant look off his face.

'I don't write my novels to provide the likes of you with internal evidence,' I said, trying to hide my huffiness by grinning.

'I think,' he said, without the slightest flicker in his friendly concern, 'they're very good novels. Especially your last one.'

I should like to know what I could say to that.

Anyway, all this happened a year or more before the evening I described when I saw Sybil off at Euston. It is relevant because instead of going home to my empty flat that night, I went round to Harry's house, which was only a quarter of an hour's walk away. It was Harry and his wife, Barbara, who had persuaded me to quit the dilapidated square in Pimlico where my most recent disaster in love had happened to me, and to start life afresh in Putney. Energetically they had found me a flat and supervised my removal. I was grateful to them. I did like the change. Also, I had been constantly troubled by the prospect of my Pimlico landlady giving me notice.

I strolled along the dark, bosky by-roads from the bus-stop, feeling encouraged by the prospect of being offered something to eat at Harry's. I was hungry.

Harry opened the front door to me, silhouetted like a globe against the light from inside the hall. A whirl of air left me standing as his high voice receded down a corridor.

'Come into the kitchen, Joe. Barbara's out, so I'm getting my own supper.'

In the kitchen I could readily see that for myself. There stood Harry, with drops of sweat on his forehead and an apron tied round his equator, preparing an omelette. On the top of the table were a piece of Gruyère cheese from which a teacupful had been grated, a saucerful of chopped chives, and the broken shells of no less than four eggs.

'Are the children still up?' I asked, looking at all this.

'No,' said Harry, taking a cardboard crate of eggs out of the refrigerator. 'Can you eat more than two of these? They're rather small.'

In a moment the smell of hot butter rose from the stove, and the sweat began to run down into Harry's eyes. His movements were deft and quick.

'I'm hungry,' I said.

14

'I expect you must be,' said Harry, and added lightly, *en passant*: 'Did the train leave on time?'

I could not help laughing, but as he was busy with the omelette he did not notice.

'Platform 17, I suppose,' he said.

'No,' said I. '12.'

Harry spun round, and his astonished look of 'How-could-they-have-changed-the-platform-without-my-knowing?' rewarded me in full. Had the omelette not been sizzling deliciously in the enormous frying-pan that he was holding in front of him, I think he would have whirled off to the telephone instantly to ring up Euston. Suddenly an elephantine glint came into his eye.

'I know why it was!' he said. And he produced on the spot an inordinately convincing explanation of the change.

Having already had my full reward, I considered this was pure bonus. (It had been Platform 17, of course.) I said:

'Let's eat, Harry!'

Harry divided the omelette, and while I took out of the oven a long French loaf that had been warming up, Harry drew two glasses of cold water from the tap over the sink — he drank very little alcohol, under the impression that so doing would keep his blood-pressure down.

We began to eat.

In view of his questions about Sybil's train, you may think Harry's curiosity would have led him to begin quizzing me about the events of the week-end. That would have been a journeyman's method. Harry was a virtuoso. His method was to pick up a detail here, a detail there — the more improbable the quarter the better — to throw in now and then a shrewd guess or a sharp bit of deduction, and then to 'piece them together'. It was only then that professional pride allowed him to ask a direct question, just to prove to himself that he already knew the answer anyway.

Harry did not mention Sybil again that evening. What we began to talk about, while we were eating the omelette, was my job. I have remarked that I was a Principal in the Civil Service. I worked under Robert, who was an Under Secretary, and most of my job was interviewing people. I saw large numbers of them, and, for both human interest as well as professional use, I needed some scheme for classifying them. Nobody can look with detachment at a large number of his fellow human beings without noticing that when two people of approximately the same physical shape turn up they show resemblances to each other in temperament. Some particular kinds of temperament go with some particular kinds of physical shape. Part of the fascination of my job, the claim it had on my imagination, was the search for a generalisation, detailed and well-ordered, about these things.

Harry was interested, professionally as a doctor, privately as Harry — curiosity moved both of us, in this field at least, with the same power. Our discussions lasted us well into the stage of the meal when we were eating delicious cold apple-pie.

However, Harry's curiosity could not be confined indefinitely. I suppose I might admit the discussion had come to an end, but during the following pause I was still thinking about it. Suddenly, sweetly out of the blue, Harry dropped a question. About Robert.

Now my having told you Robert was my boss, my intimate friend of twenty years' standing and my literary comrade-in-arms as novelist — we were fighting to liberate ourselves through Art from the Civil Service, Robert having already half-won the battle and gone on to part-time — has not told you all. It has not made clear how important to me Robert's continued presence in the Civil Service was. Robert was the creator of his own job and of mine. I had reason to believe that if he resigned his job, mine would disappear.

The question Harry dropped, sweetly from the blue while he stood by the stove making our coffee, was:

'Is it true Robert's going to resign from the Civil Service at the beginning of next year?'

## CHAPTER III

## LUNCH IN A TEA-SHOP

THE effect of sleeping on a troublesome idea is, as every sound man knows, to flatten it a bit. One puts it, like a crumpled pair of trousers, under one's mattress, and oh! the difference when one brings it out next morning. If one is lucky. But then sound men *are* lucky.

Next morning, in the ordinary light of day as contrasted with the dazzling night of Harry's imagination, I saw that Robert simply could not be intending to leave me in the lurch. In my opinion, though not in his, Robert had many faults; but lack of responsibility for his friends was not among them. I had been momentarily swept off my feet by one of Harry's *ballons d'essai* — it suddenly occurred to me that if one ever actually saw a *ballon d'essai*, it would probably look like Harry.

So I got up that Monday morning feeling refreshed by the week-end and looking forward to my work. I did not want my job to disappear. I liked it. I was fascinated by it. Also it kept me from starving.

Robert and I were employed in a department of government that got scientific research done on a big scale. Large numbers of scientists and engineers were involved; and looking after those we had, together with trying to lay our hands on more, was a task and a half. During the war, when anybody who could do a job well got a chance to do it, Robert had taken that task and a half upon himself with great success — and, I should like to add, with my devoted assistance.

If you know the Civil Service only in peace-time you would expect such a task to fall to the lot of the department's establishments division. Though our department had a perfectly competent establishments division, with a brace of perfectly competent Under Secretaries at its head, Robert had got agreement after the war for continuing his job as head of a separate, semi-autonomous directorate. Though his directorate was closely linked with our establishments division, and one of their Under Secretaries was technically Robert's boss, we were, well, not *of* them. Robert, as a novelist, was a creative artist: there was indeed more than a touch of creative art about his Civil Service set-up.

The set-up had obvious advantages for us, but it required hypnosis to make any advantages for our establishments division obvious to that division. Many of them asked themselves how Robert managed it. In the first place he was a man of hypnotic personality. In the second, he had made himself a pretty high reputation and none of his immediate seniors was anxious to take the responsibility of losing him to the Service. Nevertheless, at the end of 1949, when the Service had shaken down to something more like its pre-war regular self — had shaken down far enough for many a regular Under Secretary to have completely forgotten that he was in his present post through irregular entry or promotion during the war — the touch of creative art about our present set-up was becoming over-apparent. And one has to remember that although Mankind has always had Art about the place, there is no evidence that Mankind could not have got on without it. My job of interviewing scientists and engineers and making decisions about their futures was one that quite a few people in our establishments division would have liked. And I have to admit that I had only Robert to hypnotise them into agreeing it were not better so. You see why it was very important indeed to me that Robert should not resign for the time being.

All the same, when I set off for work that Monday morning, Harry's question was not high on my list of things to talk to Robert about at lunch-time. I was thinking mostly —

and not unnaturally, if it comes to that — about Sybil. It was a bright November day and I strode down Putney Hill cheerfully singing under my breath. After all, I had come to Putney to start life afresh. Something brought the tune of 'Sweet Lass of Richmond Hill' into my mind, and I tried to fit in words to denote myself.

'Brave Lad of Putney Hill' commended itself insistently because it was so obvious. Yet its Housmanesque ring, I thought, was so wrong. I was neither young nor bucolic, and offhand I could not recall any occasion that had shown me to be brave. I passed the traffic lights and the Zeeta café, and noticed the usual haze drifting up from the river. The buses flashed a particularly inviting red, while their bile-shaded luminescent posters were more evocative than ever of nausea. Suddenly I caught sight of myself in Marks & Spencer's window, and my unconscious mind got the better of me:

'Smart Chap of Putney Hill!'

Unbidden — I would certainly have turned my back on them had I known they were coming — the words attached themselves to the tune, and the image of a Smart Chap attached itself, horribly, to me. It was not what I thought I was trying to look like at all. 'I don't look like a gentleman,' I thought. 'All well and good, because I'm not a gentleman. But a smart chap! . . . There are all sorts of other things one could look like. But no, not that!'

I passed Marks & Spencer's pretty quickly, I can tell you. And it was with relief that I heard a high-pitched, honeyed voice calling behind me:

'Joe!'

It was Harry, overtaking me. We often met at this time of day and travelled to work together.

'You're looking very dapper this morning,' he said.

I did not reply. I simply did not reply. And on the way to London we discussed neither my appearance nor the question of Robert's plans for getting out of the Civil Service.

We read our newspapers. But all the same, he did, merely by his presence, provoke my concern. I decided that I would put the matter higher on my list of things to say to Robert at lunch-time after all.

Robert and I usually had lunch together and we usually went to a tea-shop. Practically all our colleagues went to our canteen, with an air of loyally all keeping together — as if they were not together enough in their offices! — and in the canteen chewed over indiscriminately, but with apparent satisfaction, a mixture of bad cooking and office shop. Robert and I frequented a café where there was not the slightest likelihood of our meeting any of them.

Our behaviour was, of course, completely contrary to the Social Ethic, which tells you to be as other men are. Now in my experience men are more tolerant than they are often made out to be. They do not mind your not being as they are. What they will not tolerate is its *showing*. And here I must point out a great difference between Robert and me. When Robert and I sloped off at 12.45 to our tea-shop, *something showed in me*. There was no doubt about it. But in Robert? Did our colleagues realise that if I had not been there he would guilefully have excused himself from chewing over toad-in-the-hole and shop? They did not. That is the way life is.

I will tell you about me. At the end of the war, when Robert set up his directorate, we had been asked if we would care to be made permanent civil servants. In two minds, but politely, I had filled up a form I was given for the purpose. And in due course I got a reply, Roneo'd on a slip of paper of not specially high quality, measuring about four inches by six, and beginning thus:

MISC/INEL
Dear Sir,
    The Civil Service Commissioners desire me to say that having considered your application for admission etc. . . .

And ending thus:

> They must, therefore, with regret declare you ineligible to compete and cancel your application accordingly.
>                    Yours faithfully,

It was a mistake, of course. Of course it was a mistake. I got an immediate apology from someone higher up the hierarchy than anyone I had had an apology from before. But was it a mistake? Had something *showed* already?

MISC/INEL. Miscellaneous/Ineligible, it stood for. The letter I thought I might, as a literary artist taking on the style of a petty official, have invented. But not MISC/INEL. That was beyond me. That was the invention of an artist in his own right: it had the stamp of uncounterfeitable originality, the characteristic of striking through to a deeper truth than its creator comprehended. MISC/INEL. It could not be a mistake. Through that slip of not very high quality paper, measuring about four inches by six, I saw my epitaph, composed by a delegated member of the company of men and inscribed on everlasting, distinctly expensive marble.

Here lies the body of

### JOSEPH LUNN

Who though admittedly
A Great Writer A True Friend
A Perfect Husband and Father
Must in The End be classed

### MISC/INEL

Actually the MISC/INEL letter settled my flirtation with permanency. My two minds about becoming a permanent civil servant became one, and that one said No. I asked myself what on earth I had been thinking about. I wanted to be a writer. If it came to that, by God, I was a writer.

The battle that I referred to earlier, the battle for the day
when I would be nothing else but a writer, was on.

So much for that. Back to the story —

'Give my regards to Robert,' said Harry, as I got out of
the bus — and then, never short of a *ballon d'essai*, he loosed
off: 'Not forgetting Annette, of course.'

He wanted to know whether Robert was going to marry
Annette or not. I said: 'Sure, I will,' in an American accent.

When I got to the office, there was Robert sitting on the
edge of my desk, reading a proof-copy of my next novel. He
glanced up as I came in and I saw that his face was pink.

'This is very good,' he said, although he must already have
read the book five times. He had a characteristic muffled,
lofty intonation that gave enormous weight to everything
he said, but the pinkness of his complexion gave evidence of
something other than weight. Robert was prudish, but that
is not to say he was not just the faintest bit lewd. He shut
the book, and looked at me with eyes that were sparkling.
'It's very good indeed.'

If that is not the sort of literary comrade-in-arms you want,
I would like to know what is. What a friend! And what a
book he was reading!

'How was Sybil?' he said.

'Very well,' said I. 'How was Annette?'

'Very well.' He glanced away, through the window —
not that he could see anything through it, as it faced on a
dreary well: modestly Euclidean, I have always felt that an
internal circumference, so to speak, would be shorter than
an external one; yet our office-architect had contrived to put
at least twice as many windows looking inwards as outwards.

Robert said: 'We went to the Zoo,' in a tone which
stressed the cultural, rather than the erotic nature of the
expedition.

'Oh,' said I, 'we stayed in.' I let it go at that.

There was a pause for reflection, very satisfactory reflection.

22

Robert, sitting on one haunch, was swinging his foot to and fro. He looked like Franklin D. Roosevelt. I am sorry to have to say, within the space of describing three of my friends, that two of them looked like world-figures, and I will not do it again with any of the others. But it would be absurd for me to let Sybil's resemblance to Marlene Dietrich stop me saying Robert looked like F.D.R., because he did. F.D.R. without the gap teeth. Robert had a massiveness of body and of head that nevertheless gave the impression of a certain lightness. Like the best kind of cake, he was big without being heavy.

It was the same with Robert's temperament. Essentially he was a man of *gravitas*. His temperament was massive and complex, deep-sounding and made for great endurance. From the time when I first got to know him, when he was my Tutor at Oxford, I had sensed his *gravitas*. Yet it was *gravitas* leavened, I am happy to say, by extraordinary wiliness and charm, and by the occasional flash of unpredictable private fun that put you in mind of a waggon-load of monkeys — than which, incidentally, Robert was much cleverer. Much. Robert was as clever as, if not cleverer than, a waggon-load of high civil servants.

It will be apparent to you that I was still in the attitude towards Robert of an undergraduate bowled over by his Tutor, an attitude causing constant irritation to my nearest and dearest, but a source of great satisfaction, not to mention use, to me.

On we go. But not very far. My telephone rang. It was our P.A. (short for personal assistant) saying our Senior Executive Officer wanted to speak to me. While she was putting him through, Robert said:

'Who is it?'

I told him. 'He's got on to me because he wanted to speak to you and you weren't in your room.' I held out the receiver towards him. 'You can speak to him here.'

'He probably wants you in any case.'

23

I hesitated at this display of extra-sensory perception. He who hesitates sees the other man nip gravely out of the room before he can get another breath.

The day's work had begun. I had some people to interview, and Robert had his usual Monday morning commitment, which was a conference with the Under Secretary, Murray-Hamilton, who was technically his boss, and Murray-Hamilton's Assistant Secretary, Spinks. (Perhaps I ought to explain the titles. In the worlds of commerce and industry, your secretary is your subordinate: in the Civil Service, not on your life. Rating in the hierarchy goes up thus: Assistant Principal, Principal, Assistant Secretary, Under Secretary, Deputy Secretary, *Secretary*!)

I was glad to be in my own shoes and not in Robert's. By a mischance that was tiresome to say the least of it, Murray-Hamilton and Spinks strongly disapproved of me. The last thing I would have proposed for my own good was a morning with those two: I did everything I could to keep out of their way. Yet I say this with some ambivalence of feeling. I disapproved of Spinks — 'Stinker Spinks,' I called him to myself — but there was nothing remarkable about that as he was pretty thoroughly disliked by everybody in the department. On the other hand I approved of, even liked Murray-Hamilton. He was first-rate at his job and furthermore he had — what was unusual among senior civil servants — a brooding, reflective look . . . I had not the faintest idea what he was brooding or reflecting about, but I felt drawn to him by his look.

When I met Robert at lunch-time, he did not show signs of having spent the morning with marked enjoyment. He sauntered along the Strand beside me in an abstracted mood, and at a street corner he bought an *Evening News*, which he began to read as he walked along. The pavement was crowded and he covered the rest of the journey by a sort of 'drunkard's walk', bouncing obliquely off passers-by. The morning sunshine was dimmed by now, and a thin mist, very

November-like, seemed to be clinging round the roofs of the tallest buildings. We went into our tea-shop and ordered our usual ladylike snack.

Throughout the meal Robert read his newspaper, so I got no opportunity to refer to any of the topics I had waiting. And when finally he put it down — Robert did not fold up a newspaper when he had finished with it: he just quietly dropped it over the arm of his chair — I saw the heavy, thoughtful look he usually wore when he was irritated or displeased.

'What's the matter?' I asked.

'Nothing of any particular interest.'

I watched him, waiting. His large, light grey eyes appeared to be focussed on his cup of coffee and he was frowning. Suddenly he said:

'Actually there is.' And then he looked away from me. 'I'm fed up with being sniped at by these people.'

He meant Murray-Hamilton and Spinks. I said:

'What about?'

He turned to me.

'You.'

There was a pause.

'What have I done now?' I said.

Robert promptly leaned over and picked up his newspaper again.

'Just general,' he muttered in a tight-lipped way that indicated he was not going to say anything else.

He started to read again.

## CHAPTER IV

## DINNER WITH TWO DOCTORS

Harry's wife, Barbara, was a doctor, too. She was intelligent, good-looking, and well-disposed towards me. In manifestation of the latter she had a way of giving me a look that indicated I-know-you-better-than-you-know-yourself.

I told myself I could have taken it more readily from a man than a woman. After all, I conceded, I actually had taken it from at least one man over a period of twenty years, namely from Robert. Of course you may think there was something wrong with me rather than with Barbara — you certainly may if you happen to be a woman. But that does not alter the fact that I found the look hard to take, above all when Barbara gave it me while declaring:

'*You*'ll never get married.'

You see what I mean?

Harry had married slightly above him, both socially, which may or may not be all to the good, and financially, which is beyond all doubt beneficent. Harry and I were quite simply petty bourgeois: Barbara's father, now dead, had been a provincial lawyer of considerable substance, and a portion of this substance had already come down to Barbara — that was how she and Harry came to have such a large house. Her mother, who stayed with them sometimes, was even slightly grand in her manner: she used to take Barbara to race-meetings, which to me, in spite of seeing the Irish dregs of Shepherd's Bush pour out of trains from Newbury at Paddington, always smacked of the idle rich.

At this particular time Harry and Barbara had been married eleven years and had begotten three children. Barbara was about the same age as Harry — they had first met when they were medical students. She was a brisk, energetic woman, with the sort of trimness of body that active women often have, though she was now thickening at the middle. She had a longish face, whose length she enhanced by sweeping her hair up at the sides. Her complexion was unusually fine and very fresh in colour, slightly freckled, and her eyes were a clear, light hazel. They were large, clear, knowing eyes.

'Barbara's a strange girl,' Harry used to say to me.

The first time he said it I was amazed. Active, strong-minded, confident and direct was what she seemed to me. Above all, direct. But when he had said it to me on several occasions, I got over my amazement to the extent of being able to note what *his* emotion was. The look in his eyes was not as usual shrewd and inquisitive: it was sentimental, indulgent . . . Barbara seemed strange to him, I realised, because he *wanted* her to seem strange.

The explanation? Harry was, I think, born to be a faithful and devoted husband — I had in my time come across quite a few men who were clearly born to be the reverse and Harry reminded me of none of them. I turned over in my mind the idea that Harry's curiosity played the absorbing part in his life that sexual adventurousness played in theirs. His wife, to Harry, had simply got to be someone around whom his curiosity could play. Whereas to me she looked like a woman destined to be a local councillor and a Justice of the Peace, to Harry she had got to look as mysterious and enigmatic as the Mona Lisa.

'Barbara's a strange girl,' he said. He was always looking away from me when he said it, clearly meditating on good-ness knows what subtleties of mind and convolutions of temperament in his loved one.

I nodded my head. The revelation was mad, but oddly

appealing to me. I could not help liking him all the more for it.

So there you have Harry and Barbara. Oh yes, I have not told you yet that Barbara, as well as running a house and being a mother, also had a part-time job at a children's clinic on the other side of London. I had a feeling that although she found no difficulty in knowing adults better than they knew themselves, children did present her with certain problems. Whether that made things better or worse for the children was a question upon which I used to speculate.

The occasion when Barbara gave me her I-know-you-better-than-you-know-yourself look and simultaneously said ' *You*'ll never get married' was the first time I went to dinner with her and Harry after I had gone to live at Putney — uprooted from dilapidated Pimlico, mark you, with her exhortation and Harry's assistance, in order to re-build my dilapidated life. Even if Barbara did know me better than I knew myself, might not she spare me, I wondered, the knowledge of my doom? Might not she and Fate keep it to themselves, as Fate did when operating on its own? Apparently not.

Still, I liked Barbara. And I liked her cooking. I really looked forward to dinner with her and Harry.

The next time I went to dinner at their house after the night Harry asked me if it was true that Robert was going to resign from the Civil Service, Barbara was going to cook a duck. I was very partial to duck. All previous looks and questions were forgiven and forgotten.

Over dinner Harry and I got down, as usual, to a fine professional discussion about classifications of physiques and temperaments. We were recently completely *épris* — if you can use that word about scientists — by the ideas of an American named Sheldon. He seemed to us a master man, not without reason: he had got over the two hurdles which had previously floored everybody else at the start of their operations in 'typing' physiques, namely how to measure up a physique reliably, and how to cope with the obvious fact that it was not a 'type' anyway but something in between.

Harry and I could scarcely wait to start trying out the ideas for ourselves. You cleared the first hurdle by photographing the physique you were proposing to 'type' in a pre-defined posture from the front, side and back, and then you made your comparative measurements from the photographs. You cleared the second by regarding this individual physique as a blend, in different proportions, of your chosen 'types' — the rounded fat man, the cubical muscular man, and the linear skinny man. From your comparative measurements you could make a quantitative assessment of the blend. Quantitative! The thing was beginning to look like a science.

But that was only the half of it. The same idea was paralleled on the side of temperament: in the particular temperament you were proposing to type, you made a similar quantitative assessment of the blend of three 'type' temperaments, these 'type' temperaments being the temperaments that characteristically went with the 'type' physiques. The whole thing tied up, was our verdict.

'It's maddening,' said I, 'that *we* didn't think of it.'

'It's like all the best revolutionary concepts,' said Harry. 'So obvious, so simple!'

You can see how *épris* we were.

At Harry's dinner-table we were concerned not so much with the phon and antiphon of praise as with the prospect of getting down to business on our own. We were agreed that we had got to devise some means of trying out Sheldon's 'somato-typing'.

'If only you could get the M.R.C. to set you up with a research unit!' I said to Harry.

Harry looked at me with baggy bright eyes.

'But surely you,' he said, 'in your job, have all the people we need for it. You've got them all there, simply on tap.'

29

I looked back at him. And well I might! You see, when one refers to physiques in medical society, one is not thinking of their being clothed. I imagined our engineers and scientists being invited, after I had questioned them on their technical life-stories, to go into an adjoining room to be photographed in the stark — from three viewpoints!

'Do you want to get me hounded out of the Civil Service altogether?' I said. I was not thinking what would happen if the *Daily Pictorial* got on to it. I only needed to go as far as thinking what would happen if Murray-Hamilton and Spinks heard of it.

For a moment Harry held his large round head on one side. Barbara intervened.

'Couldn't it be combined with a medical examination?' Sometimes Barbara, instead of saying the most peculiar thing, baffled one by saying the most sensible.

'Not in this set-up,' I said firmly.

Barbara gave Harry a glance, but I did not feel inclined to explain to her.

We had finished our dinner and Barbara said: 'Shall we have our coffee in the drawing-room?'

We went into the drawing-room. The house was Edwardian, massive and ugly but spacious. Harry and Barbara had done it up very agreeably in the first post-war fashion, which was called 'contemporary'. This evening a fire was sparkling in the grate; lamps were glowing in the right places for comfort; and Barbara, wearing a black dress and a big topaz and diamond brooch which set off the colour of her eyes, looked unusually handsome. I said to her:

'That roast duck, Barbara, was simply——' and I made a gesture such as I thought I had seen Italians make in restaurants to indicate that food was delicious.

Barbara laughed. And then she blushed.

I drank my coffee thinking how pleasant life was.

In a desultory way we began to gossip. I scarcely noticed it when Harry first mentioned Sybil. He said he supposed she was coming up to London at Christmas, and I was feeling too relaxed to tell him he was a few days wrong. He was sitting fatly in an armchair whose legs splayed outwards. He was smiling.

'I suppose Robert asks you if you're going to marry her,' he said.

I grinned.

Barbara leaned forward and said to him:

'Does Robert really ask that, do you think?'

'I was saying I *supposed* he did,' said Harry. 'After all, Joe's mother asks me every time I see her.' He glanced at me sideways to see how I took this gambit.

I took it with stupefaction: I knew that it would be unlike Harry not to go and see my mother whenever he went to his own home, but that he was on these terms with her was something that I had not even considered.

Harry was quick to see the effect. He went on with a happy smile:

'Only last week she asked me if you were going to marry "your Sybil".'

This instantly conveyed verisimilitude. The prefix 'your' conveyed without a doubt that my mother had said it, since it evoked the particular tone — unintentional, I ought to say — with which my mother always seemed, to my sensitive ears, to refer to any of my young women.

'Did *she* think I would marry Sybil?' I enquired.

Harry shook his big, globe-shaped head. 'I think she's thought for some time now that you've missed the boat.'

'Missed the boat!'

Harry leaned his head against the back of his chair, and said nothing. Barbara said nothing: there was clearly no need for Barbara to say anything.

After a while, Harry said pensively:

31

'I like Sybil.' He paused. 'I never understand her.'

I said: 'Nor do I, for that matter. I don't really know her even after fifteen years.'

'And that,' said Barbara promptly, 'doesn't affect your relationship with her?'

You will recall my predicament as I saw it on that night of self-revelation in the bar at Euston. I said to Barbara:

'Not an atom!'

Barbara regarded me.

'There's a very definite split, there,' she said, 'between comprehension and function.'

'I see what you mean,' I said. Suddenly I was delighted, as a lewd transformation of her words occurred to me. 'You mean between knowing and doing.'

Barbara looked mystified. 'Perhaps,' she said firmly.

I turned to Harry. I could see that he was thinking about something else. He said:

'I suppose Robert has in mind whether you're thinking of marrying Sybil——'

I interrupted: 'I'm not thinking of marrying Sybil!'

'—because of his plans to marry Annette.'

'*Is* he going to marry Annette?' said I.

Harry looked at me triumphantly and sympathetically. He said, in a high sweet voice:

'Well, *isn't* he?'

I said nothing now. You see, when Harry told me Robert was going to leave the Civil Service, I was disturbed for the practical reasons that I have since explained. When he told me Robert was going to marry Annette, the disturbance was just as serious but much less worthy of a decent man. Robert and I were comrades in the unmarried state, and my first response to Harry's remark was to foresee another kind of desertion.

I picked up my coffee-cup and held it towards Barbara, asking if I could have some more coffee. And I looked at

32

Harry, wondering if he knew exactly what sort of dismay his inquisitiveness caused me. He was a clever man, and I had a strong suspicion that he did know. By nature Harry was generous, kindly, devoted — a good man. Yet I could not help thinking that he was also a devil.

## CHAPTER V

## A COCKTAIL PARTY AT ANNETTE'S

Annette was a sweet girl. Her father was a high civil servant, a very high civil servant indeed.

At that time, Annette was living in her father's flat. She had just come down from doing a D.Phil. in Oxford. Yes, she was quite young, about twenty-five, I suppose, against Robert's forty-four — he was five years older than me. She was young, pretty and clever. The reason I have said she was sweet was that, granted that there is a strain of the cruel, the uncharitable and the ill-disposed in all of us, in Annette it was unusually weak. She was charitable, nicely balanced, quickly stirred to sympathy; in a word — sweet. Robert was very fond of her, and that did not surprise me.

Annette was living in her father's flat while she made up her mind what career to go in for. She was taking her time, partly because she was serious about it and partly because — here, alas, I display my own uncharitableness — in my opinion she had fallen in love with Robert. A feminist would say that a woman's falling in love ought not to make her less serious about choosing a career. I say that if it did not make Annette less serious, certainly it made her slower. Annette's choice seemed to me to show distinct signs of hanging fire that were not to be associated with intellectual or moral difficulties over deciding between becoming say an Oxford don or a Wapping schoolmistress. It did not worry me, of course. Nor did it appear to worry Annette: she seemed pretty happy.

Robert and I went to a cocktail party at Annette's. (It was called 'drinks at six-thirtyish' — the word 'cocktail' was going out.) Robert seemed pretty happy as well. He had been on another cultural expedition to the Zoo with Annette at the week-end. Though Annette's father retired to his house in Berkshire from Friday to Monday, Annette stayed in London, having the flat to herself.

Robert and I went straight to the party from the office. It was a wretched, sleeting night, and the flat was in an area just north of Hyde Park that was salubrious but inaccessible by bus.

'We'd better have a taxi,' I said. 'I'll pay half.'

'No. Why should you?' said Robert. I told you he was pretty happy.

Annette opened the door to us. Before she had come to live in the flat her father had had a servant, but Annette had insisted on dispensing with her.

'Hello, darling,' said Robert, and gave her a hug of noticeable warmth before taking off his overcoat.

Annette stood back — she was a short, sturdy girl — and looked up at him. Her eyes were shining with amusement and pleasure.

'You can't pretend he isn't spontaneous, in spite of all they say about him,' I said to her.

Annette shook her head. Her hair was straight and cut plainly in a bell-shaped bob: when she shook her head one expected to hear a sweet lucid peal. She took hold of Robert's hand for a moment.

'Come in,' she said.

I thought: 'Well, there you are . . .' and took off my overcoat.

We went into the living-room, which was L-shaped, the walls of the foot of the L being covered with books, and the walls of the stem, which included the windows and the fire-place, being panelled with a light-coloured wood. Annette's father was both a scholar and a traveller, and the objects of decoration in the room were chiefly small pieces of classical statuary. Between the windows there was a statue of a

35

woman, headless and draped, which I should like to have owned.

The party was for Annette's friends, and though Robert and I were the only two civil servants there, also the only two novelists, we were not the only two men who were more than ten years older than Annette. A very satisfactory state of affairs, I thought: the world was all the better a place for the existence of girls like Annette. There were, of course, some young women of Annette's age. I saw a girl I had met there before, a painter from behind the Fulham Road, and one of Annette's Oxford girl-friends who did philosophy too. Still better a place! I recognised some of the men — they were chiefly academic persons, philosophers, some sociologists, and a young scientist whom I had once interviewed for a job. I noted that Harry was not there, or, as I put it to myself, had for once not managed to get in.

Perhaps I ought to have explained before that there was a connection between Harry and Annette. Harry had discovered that Annette's brother, who was a doctor, had been a house-surgeon at the hospital where Barbara had done her clinical training. Though Harry and Barbara now looked on him with the special contempt they reserved for anybody who had become a gynaecologist, this did not diminish Harry's use for the connection or his satisfaction with having unearthed it. I may say that for Harry this passed as a strong connection. When he saw that Annette was a figure in my life and Robert's, he would have found a connection, even if it was that the housemaid Annette had dispensed with happened to be the illegitimate grand-niece of the organist at the church where my father preached his first sermon.

Half an hour later, to make a change from talking to people, I went over to have another look at the statue that fascinated me. I put out my forefinger and drew it lightly, for the sensuous experience, down the folds in the drapery. Then I looked at my forefinger, the receptor of that experience. It was black with dust. There was a good thick layer of dust on the top of the table on which the statue was standing. There was also a pile of books, new books. I picked up the top one and opened it — a review slip fell out and floated down to the floor.

'Are you really going to read that?' It was Annette who spoke. She was standing beside me, laughing.

I retrieved the review slip and put the book back on the pile. It was a philosophical work.

'Is it any good?' I asked.

'I haven't read it yet. I'm going to review it.'

I looked at her with curiosity, as one does at any young person who is going to be entrusted with passing a professional opinion upon a matter of serious import. My interest switched from curiosity to approval. Annette was pretty and her complexion was beyond compare. She never wore any make-up, and there, in all its incomparableness, was her complexion exposed as it might be to one's forefinger. Fine, clear, high-coloured, and glossy with the sheen that comes from heartily washing it with soap. Her lips, without lipstick, were simply red. I did not know why Annette saw fit never to use make-up, but I never felt inclined to question the result. I brought my mind back to her books.

'Have they all seen,' I asked, referring to the authors, 'the great truth that metaphysics is bunk?'

This was my standard joke, for what it was worth, when I was talking to Annette. She belonged to an up-to-date school of philosophers whom I habitually referred to as the 'metaphysics-is-bunk' school, out of what Barbara would have called a distinctly ambivalent attitude. Though I felt that any school of philosophers ought to be treated with irreverence, I was far from sure that I did not think metaphysics was bunk myself.

I had never got over a crucial moment in my young manhood, when, hearing my father proclaim his favourite text, 'God is Love', for the I-don't-know-how-manyth time, I

37

suddenly realised that it did not mean anything to me and I could not see what it could mean. This was a shock. 'God is Love' — I kept thinking and thinking about it, focussing on the word *is*, which now appeared so incredibly between the other two. The only circumstances, I kept thinking pig-headedly, in which God and Love can have *is* between them is not if God is a person and Love is what we all mean by love, but if God and Love are words, merely words.

I had never got over it. Some words were only words: my father's favourite text was a piece of literary algebra. Of course I had been subsequently shown the error of my thought, but it had permanently coloured my approach to metaphysics.

'We don't say metaphysics is bunk,' Annette said. She laughed as if she were amused by my joke, but did not hesitate to correct me just the same. 'We just think there aren't any platonic essences that many of the words we use in metaphysics would have to correspond to — if they were going to have the meaning we've chosen to give them.'

'H'm,' I said, not committing myself to agreeing with her — or understanding her, for that matter. Yet, you can see how, when I was talking to Annette, though I might have been shown the error of my thought I was not entirely convinced by the demonstration.

'Such words as Truth,' I said, doing my best to fall into the swing of things.

'Such words as Truth.' She shook her head, and her bell of hair swung to and fro.

At that, something made me think of my father's second favourite text: 'God is Truth.' Oh dear!

However, I have to say that it was a comfort of sorts to have a young woman like Annette, clever as paint and much admired in academic circles, to assure me that some of the words of which I had never been able to grasp the common use, such as my father's, could with advantage cease to be used in that way.

'Now, what are you two talking about?' Robert interrupted us.

'Scarcely anything,' I said. 'We've only just started.'

Annette looked up at Robert. I could have removed myself to the other end of the room without her noticing. Robert returned her look. I thought they must be intending to get married.

At that moment I noticed Annette's father in the doorway. He glanced round the room as if he were not certain whether to join the party. I heard Robert say:

'Darling, there's your father.'

'Oh yes,' said Annette.

One might have expected that Annette would hasten across to her father and that Robert would remain with me. On the contrary, it was Robert who lost no time in going across to Annette's father. Annette stayed where she was.

'I hope somebody will give Daddy a drink,' she said.

I laughed at her idea of a hostess's functions. Annette was oddly shy about some things, and entertaining was one of them. She liked having parties and got as far as inviting the guests, but at that point she seemed to get paralysed. I did not understand why, though I felt it might be connected with shyness. And yet, was it? Was it really shyness that made her go without make-up and appear at this kind of party wearing a shapeless woolly jumper and skirt?

'Oughtn't you to go and give him one?' I asked.

'It's all right — Emma's giving him some sherry.' Emma was the painter from behind the Fulham Road. Her name was Margaret, but she was always called Emma. She was a big girl, wearing a sweater and trousers, these, paint-stained, being the current uniform of her set. There was a scruffy-looking man with her in an identical outfit. I had never seen them dressed, at any time of day, in anything different; and pointing to the two of them, I said to Annette:

'Do they take those things off to go to bed?' thinking they looked as if they slept in them.

'Emma doesn't go to bed with *him*,' said Annette. 'I mean, not now. Or at least only now and then.'

'Oh,' I said. 'Oh.'

It was only asking for difficulties, to try and explain now what I had originally wanted to know, so I paused, and then said:

'There seem to be some sociologists here.'

Annette said: 'I don't think I should really like to work with sociologists.' She explained thoughtfully: 'The trouble with all the social sciences is that their laws are reducible to laws of individual psychology. It means they lack the autonomy that the physical sciences have.'

'Oh,' I said. I had been trained in the physical sciences — in physics, to be precise. Her remark sounded favourable to me, so I said 'Oh' again, more enthusiastically.

I looked at her, and found that she was looking at me. Her eyes were a clear bright brown. Her cheeks were glowing.

'Annette,' I said, 'you're a sweet girl.'

She said shyly:

'I do want to marry Robert. Do you think there's any chance?'

## CHAPTER VI

# THE RECURRING SITUATION

D ID I think there was any chance of Robert marrying her — well might Annette ask! I told her, Yes, of course, but I did not see fit to prolong the conversation by discussing the length of the odds. As Robert had reached the age of forty-four without getting married, it was obvious that he was not the sort of man who takes to matrimony like a duck to water. And though he stood in no danger of being written-off, like me, he did lay himself open, clearly, to the charge of being reluctant. Poor old Robert.

In fact there was more to it than common reluctance, in Robert's case. We had discussed it a good many times. In the past he had fallen so deeply in love as to overcome common reluctance. But on each occasion the girl had been so odd, so eccentric, or even so crazy, that somehow the upshot, partly through her own actions and partly through a final move for self-preservation on Robert's part, had been no marriage.

Suspicious, that! you might say. Why did he not fall in love with someone who was sufficiently ordinary, sufficiently uncrazy — after all, there were lots of pretty girls who came into that category — to be marriageable? The only answer Robert seemed able to find was that they, the ordinary, uncrazy ones, did not seem to him so fascinating.

In the present situation, though, the fact seemed to me that Annette, while eccentric enough to be fascinating, was sufficiently uncrazy as not to be likely to hit him on the head with a bottle of whisky or take an overdose of aspirins — two of the deterrents to matrimony which had come his way in the past. There was definitely a chance for Annette, I thought.

It appeared, the following day, that Robert thought the same thing. He came into my office first thing in the morning, and sat on the corner of my desk.

'That was a very good party, last night,' he said.

I said it was.

He paused, and then said in a different tone:

'I don't know what to do. Ought I to marry Annette?'

I did not reply. Throughout our lives we had often asked each other's advice on matters of this kind. We had never taken it.

I was thinking what to say. We had never taken each other's advice in the exact form in which it was given: what we did was something tangential, something based on what the other advised, but modified by our own impulses, sensible or otherwise.

'She's a sweet girl,' I said.

Robert said: 'Of all the women I've known, she's easily the sweetest.'

'What's holding you back?'

He shrugged his shoulders and did not answer for a long time. I just waited. He said:

'It's hard to say. Some sort of instinct about the future. It's rather hard to place it exactly. Annette's easily the sweetest girl I've ever known, but that doesn't mean that in some ways she's not very' — he tried to find the right word — 'self-concerned. For instance, she attaches much more importance to some of the decisions, in particular the moral decisions, she makes than I ever should.'

'Isn't this part of the current fashion among philosophers?'

'If you mean is it something that has nothing to do with her natural inclinations, I think the answer is No. I think the fashion suits her rather well.'

I thought it over, and said:

'But isn't this all a bit theoretical? I don't see why it should cause any special practical difficulties.'

'Nor can I. And yet something tells me it will.'

'Then don't marry her!' I said, knowing this was the last thing he wanted me to say — his last sentence had ended in 'will'.

Robert laughed and stood up.

'Do you happen to have that file about revised salary scales?' he said in a completely different tone, lofty and rather official. 'It would be a bit of a help if you'd clear it pretty rapidly.'

I was delighted by the change. It was one of Robert's gifts to have at his finger-tips, so to speak, the capacity for chameleon-like transformation.

'Spinks is asking for it,' he went on. 'He seems to think you're holding it up.'

'I'm *not* holding it up!' I said. 'It only came in yesterday.'

Robert shrugged his shoulders and went out of the room.

'Really!' I shouted at the door as he pulled it to behind him.

I began my day's work by dealing immediately with the file about revised salary scales. And, in case you would like to know, I wished Spinks could get sacked.

During the next few days I did not see very much of Robert. It was on the following Sunday afternoon that he turned up unexpectedly at the club to which we both belonged. He knew that I was likely to be there, because on Sundays I usually spent the day at the club to save having to get my own meals at my flat. I lunched with about half a dozen members who enjoyed bachelordom in various degrees of confirmation ranging from that of elderly specimens of my own species to that of middle-aged married men whose wives had left them. Afterwards I took my manuscript to the library to work, and they mostly went into the reading-room to sleep.

At tea-time I had come down to a small central room that

was the Piazza San Marco of the club, normally astir with gossipers having tea or drinks but to-day deserted. It would have been cosy had there not been so many doors always open for people to go through to other rooms. Lights were shining over pictures lent by members of the club, but the chandelier in the middle of the room had not been switched on. I was sitting beside the fire, munching a piece of anchovy toast and reading the novel reviews in the previous Friday's *Times Literary Supplement*. Someone came in and I looked up. It was Robert.

I exclaimed with surprise.

'I thought I'd find you here,' he said, sitting down at the other end of the sofa I was sitting on.

I held up the *Times Literary Supplement* and said:

'You'll observe that I'm keeping up with literature.'

Expecting that, as usual when he found himself having a casual meal with me, he would pick up a newspaper and read, I began, for once, to read myself. A servant brought in a tray with Robert's tea on it and put it on a small table in front of him. Robert poured a cup of tea and then said:

'I'd like you to put that down for a moment, if you will.'

He was looking both solemn and excited. He said:

'I came to see you because I wanted you to be the first person to know that Annette and I are going to get married. We decided last night.'

'That's excellent!' I cried, and shook him by the hand. 'I'm delighted. I hope you'll be as happy, as happy as anybody can be!'

I really was delighted. And I really did feel, suddenly, unutterably wretched. I was devoted to him, I had been whole-heartedly wretched on his behalf when he was having disastrous love affairs — in fact the occasions of the whisky bottle and the overdose of aspirins had been not funny but bitterly serious — but now, when he was going to be happy, I was not whole-heartedly delighted. Envy, the most unpleasing and the most common of emotions, suddenly caught me. In the midst of thinking how glad I was for him, I wished, yes, I wished it were *I* instead of him.

Robert was watching me. I remembered well his once having observed epigrammatically that it was easier to sympathise with one's friends in their defeats than in their victories.

'I thought you would,' I said, meaning 'would marry Annette'.

He laughed. His laughter sounded confident, relieved and faintly rueful. 'There's a difference between thinking one will and actually doing it.' His glance seemed to become more penetrating. 'As you'll discover for yourself.'

Of course he knew I must be wishing it were I. I said:

'Robert, do you think I *shall*?'

'Think you shall what?'

'Do it?'

He did not answer me immediately. Then he said: 'That depends on you. On what you make up your mind to.'

'Make up my mind to?' I said. 'Surely one doesn't make up one's mind to something, just like that. . . . It's got to arise from one's nature. . . .'

An elderly member with a stick made his way slowly through the room, greeting us as he passed. We smiled at him — in the ordinary way we should have encouraged the poor old man to stop — and then we waited for him to go.

As soon as he was through one of the far doorways, I said to Robert:

'One's behaviour falls into a pattern that arises from one's nature. The reason the pattern gets fixed is because one's nature is pretty fixed, though we don't like to think it is.'

I was referring to a theory Robert and I had of human behaviour, which depended on what we called the Recurring Situation. It was particularly easy to identify in people's sexual lives. Time after time we had seen our friends, not to mention ourselves, embark on a sexual gambit which might superficially look as if it were something new, but which, as time went on, led to a familiar situation — if it were not leading to it in the natural course of events, the instigator of it seemed to force it, himself, into the familiar shape. We got the impression that for many men there was a characteristic situation to which, from whatever point they started, they always tended.

Sitting beside the fire in the club that Sunday afternoon, Robert and I did not discuss all this because we had discussed it at length many a time before. We had accepted our own behaviour as examples of our theory. Certainly Robert had arrived often enough at the situation of being deeply in love with a woman who was — it seemed to him — just that bit too crazy for him to risk marrying her.

In my own case, the recurring situation was twofold: I always found myself either wanting to marry someone who would not marry me or not wanting to marry someone who would. There was no future in my recurring situation, either way.

'I'm not sure it's so completely fixed,' said Robert.

'What?'

'Either the pattern or one's nature. One can be too rigid about these things.'

'Indeed!' I said, rather as if I were in favour of rigidity.

'Yes,' said Robert.

He suddenly gave me a quick, odd glance that made me pull up. I stared at him and then tried to laugh.

'You're not trying to take my recurring situation away from me, are you?' I said.

Robert shrugged his shoulders.

When I was first describing my predicament, I observed how many of us, poor fish that we are, are rather attached to our predicaments, are even a bit proud of them. We also, I might have added, tend to find them something stable in our lives. Take them away — even, as it might appear for our own good — and we are left faced with . . . we know not what. It is the same with the recurring pattern. We

46

want to get out of it, and yet also we want to stay in it. I do
not pretend to be able to explain my own ambivalence —
nor the ambivalence of most of the human race, for that
matter. Double, double, we are all double. . . .

'I have always granted,' said Robert, 'that there is a
recurring pattern. But there are times when it's possible
to break out of it.'

Even if his reply might be going to take the ground from
under my feet, I said:

'How?'

'By an act of will.'

An act of *will*! 'Like all the best revolutionary concepts, so
simple, so obvious . . .'

I did not say anything. I knew it was true. An act of
will could get me out of my recurring pattern. I felt as if
the ground really had been taken from under my feet. And
yet at the same moment I was feeling something opposite. It
was a thrill of — what? I had not the slightest doubt what
it was a thrill of. It was of hope.

# PART II

## CHAPTER I

# CHRISTMAS EVE IN THE CIVIL SERVICE

THE first and only occasion Spinks set foot in my office —
you can imagine I never went out of my way to invite
him across just for the sake of his *beaux yeux* — was on
the afternoon when we shut down that year for Christmas.
Every Christmas Eve Murray-Hamilton and Spinks did the
rounds of their own people and then of ours on a visit of
goodwill. The members of staff most affected by the prospect
of the visit were the messengers, though I could never see
why, since the only duty that fell upon their cadre was that
two of them should hold the lift doors open while Murray-
Hamilton and Spinks got out. But affected they were: their
bush telegraph, which in the summer circulated up-to-the-
minute Test Match scores, hummed all afternoon with
the current movements, from room to room, of the touring
party.

It was unusual for Spinks to deliver the goodwill message
to me in my own office. At this stage of the Christmas Eve's
proceedings, Robert and I were usually at the tea-party
which our own people held in the room where most of them
worked. This room was referred to by Robert and me as
the big room, and by some of its racier inhabitants, I gleaned
from passing the time of day with them in the lavatory, as the
snake-pit. The room and what went on in it interested me,
but my communication with its inhabitants was supposed to
be on paper, or if it was a personal matter, through our Senior
Executive Officer, who was their boss. At this rate, had it
not been for the lavatory, which was small and over-
crowded, I should never have identified some of our clerks,

let alone — for hygiene is a great leveller — have picked up some of their racier observations.

Perhaps in fairness to the service, I ought to interpolate that Spinks's minion responsible for 'accommodation' was shocked when I made him note how small, over-crowded and dirty our lavatory was, shocked that Robert and I had to use the same one as our clerks.

Anyway, there was the snake-pit having a party and Robert and I sitting in our own offices not invited. And this year it was not a tea-party, far from it. The inhabitants had collected money for drink, and by keeping the collection to themselves had set up a neat basis for excluding outsiders. And why was it, I speculated, as I listened to the sounds of entertainment echo down the corridor, that the inhabitants of the snake-pit wanted to exclude outsiders? There were two possible explanations. The first was that they thought Robert and I were stinkers. The second — this was more than an explanation: it was fact — was that our Senior Executive Officer had got at loggerheads with them.

The chief messenger put his head round the door, which I had left open.

'Mr. Murray-Hamilton and Mr. Spinks have got separated, sir. Over in Registry. That'll be, Mr. Spinks is coming on first. And then Mr. Murray-Hamilton sort of after him.'

Thinking of the lift doors, I said: 'Twice as much work for you.'

A burst of riotous noise came from down the corridor. He wagged his head towards it.

'If Mr. Murray-Hamilton and Mr. Spinks don't get here before long, they'll be dancing down there.'

'Dancing? Will they really?' I said. I was very fond of dancing. Also of drink, too.

'Ar,' he said. Having been leaning a little forward, he now shifted his weight comfortably over his heels. Then he said:

'Have you seen the decorations this year, sir?'

'Yes. I glanced in.'

'Not so good as last year's,' he said.

'Not so necessary,' said I, thinking of last year's tea-party and this year's saturnalia.

'Ar.'

Our conversation went on for a few minutes in this vein, counterpointed by sounds from down the corridor. When he had said they would be dancing in the big room, he had meant it metaphorically, but in point of fact somebody had brought a portable gramophone. We heard music.

'Shall I leave the door open, sir?' he said, when he thought it was time to go back and take his place in the bush-telegraph.

'Do. I should like to hear the music.'

I wondered if they really would dance, and what sort of dancing it would be. When I have referred to saturnalia in the big room, I may have given the wrong impression about its inhabitants. Every year, after the Senior Executive Officer had brought in to Robert their annual reports, Robert said without fail to me in an awed tone:

'You'd be surprised how old some of them are.'

I was not in the least surprised, since the S.E.O. reminded me of it every time I found something to complain about in the work of the office. We had what I agreed was a higher proportion than might be expected of clerks who were past retiring age. In fact I sometimes thought there was evidence for what the S.E.O. was always suggesting, that Spinks's side of the organisation used our side as a dumping ground for crocks and misfits in general. We had our share of them: a walk through the big room confirmed that. Had we more than our share?

'It's one of the results of full employment, Froggatt,' I said. (That was the S.E.O.'s name.)

His expression combined deference with disbelief. He argued that Spinks's side of the organisation were dumping crocks and misfits on us so as to use our resulting inefficiency as a reason for taking us over themselves — the argument had its points, of course.

So the saturnalia that was going on in the big room, under the shade of brightly coloured paper chains, tinsel balls, and squares of cardboard (inscribed with peculiar mottoes) that floated in the air like mobiles, was not an affair of nymphs and satyrs — not unless you are prepared to face the fact that some of us stay nymphs and satyrs till we have one foot in the grave.

'*I'd like to get you,*' sounded the music,
'*On a slow boat to China . . .*'

'It would have to be damned slow for some of you,' I thought, having in mind not the aged ones, who were rather nippy, but some of the forty-year-old clock-watchers, who were more bone idle than I could have imagined. Slow! If they had not had all the office-hours in which to do their football pools they would never have got them in in time.

I looked at my watch. Half past five. The sooner Spinks and Murray-Hamilton came in with their Christmas handshake the sooner I could go home. There was no more work to be done — or anything else, for that matter. I wondered whether to go into Robert's room, but thought I had better not as he was doing some re-writing of his next novel. I might have gone into the small room where our P.A. and one or two of her colleagues worked, but I thought they would be busy clearing up the remains of the Christmas tea-party they had loyally given for Robert and me and Froggatt and the H.E.O.'s, in default of our being invited to the saturnalia. I had my own next novel to work on, but somehow I was never able to get going in the office, being inhibited either by files coming in or the likelihood of files coming in — remember that unlike Robert, who was part-time, I was full-time.

The chief messenger's head came round the door-cheek.

'Mr. Spinks has just left the other side, sir. They say he's got Mr. Jacques with him.'

54

I cannot say the news affected my spirits one way or the other. At that particular moment it did not occur to me that the visit could either have any effect or lead to any action. I did not object to the addition of Jacques, for I liked him. He was the minion I referred to a moment ago as responsible to Spinks for 'accommodation'. It seemed to me that, as a civil servant, his talent for execution was well eclipsed by his talent for sycophancy. He was a tall stringy man with large eyes and a pleasant voice; and like all successful sycophants, he was born with a genuine desire to please: if I had to choose between that and a genuine desire to kick people in the teeth, I chose that. Also I judged that while Jacques sucked up to Spinks with natural abandon, he did not in the least care for him as a man.

'Thank you,' I said to the chief messenger. 'Perhaps you might shut the door now. You know . . . it will give them something to open.'

'Ar,' he said with a non-comprehending grin. I regretted the door's being shut, because from down the corridor came the sound of the gramophone playing, amid delighted shrieks:

*'A-hunting we will go! . . .'*

'What *can* they be doing to that?' I said to him.

He shook his head. 'I don't know, sir.' He was not interested, other than in the sounds as a manifestation, I thought, of the difference between how the upper and the lower orders behaved.

I was left alone, quiet, in my rather large room. I had switched on only half the lights, so as to enhance the dirtiness of the walls which must once have been painted by the Ministry of Works in a shade known to them, I believed, as primrose. My picture on the far wall was crooked, which puzzled me, since the office-cleaners never touched it. Below it the tablecloth formed a long rectangle of dead navy-blue — it was a piece of felt that had been used during the war for black-out curtains: Robert had got rid of his, leaving his table-top bare, but I kept mine as a souvenir.

I sat swinging around in my chair, waiting for the visit.

Spinks and Jacques came in. They looked hearty and bright, and had clearly been fortified on their way at somebody else's party. They brought in a distinctly Christmassy air, and suddenly we all shook hands in one of those waves of *bonhomie* that sometimes sweep unpredictably through a group of men who hate each other's guts.

'I didn't expect to find you in here,' said Spinks, glancing round my office.

'We had a small sedate tea-party on our own,' I said, and explained that we had not been invited to the non-tea-party down the corridor.

I do not intend to describe Spinks, certainly not in any way which might lead anyone in the Civil Service to think this is supposed to be him. I will content myself with saying that he did not look the detestable man he was. Had you met him you might have presumed he was a man whose wife and children were probably fond of him: they were. It would have been a shock to hear that he was the most detested man in our part of the world: he was.

'This is your office?' he said.

As he was also one of the cleverest men in our part of the world, I thought he must either be drunk or so little interested that he did not care what he was saying. He did not look in the least drunk. Jacques, I was happy to see, did look drunk — he rocked slightly and said:

'It's dark in here.' He caught my eye. 'We must do something about it.' His glance moved critically round the walls. 'A coat of paint . . .'

I knew that he would not get them a coat of paint, but I thought it was amiable of him to have said it. You see why I liked him. Spinks was looking at my bookshelf.

'Are these your books?'

'Yes.' They were a very odd collection of throw-outs from my flat, ranging from a second copy of *The Tale of Genji* to a first copy of *The Admiralty Handbook of Wireless Telegraphy*.

At this it appeared that the Christmas visit was over. Spinks and Jacques smiled at each other and then at me. Then we all shook hands again and said, 'Well, a happy Christmas,' and they went out of the room. It seemed, as an incident, harmless enough, in fact positively innocuous. I hung about until they had gone, and then went and did a similar round of our own people while I waited for Murray-Hamilton. And that was that.

But was it that? One day in the week after we came back after Christmas, Robert and I were strolling along to our tea-shop for lunch, when Robert said:

'By the way, you'd better get one of those trays for your desk, to keep papers in.'

Let me explain. The Civil Service provided a long compartmented tray for the top of one's desk, the compartments usually being labelled In and Out. (The current joke among bosses was to propose four compartments labelled In, Out, Pending, and Too Difficult.) On the grounds that our P.A. always brought in my work in the morning, always took it out when I had done it, and hung on to anything that was pending till the morning when she could bring it in ready for me to do, I had got rid of the tray. A dust-collector, I thought it.

'What on earth for?' I said.

'I know you do a lot of work, but it makes it look as if you don't.' He was not looking at me.

'To whom does it make it look as if I don't?' I asked. For once I thought Robert could put up with having his evasiveness on this kind of topic punctured.

'Just tell me *whom*!' I said.

Robert put his head down. After a pause he said in a muffled, distant voice:

'As it were Spinks.'

I was too enraged to speak. I have to admit that my immediate cause of rage was not so much Spinks's being beastly as his being beastly on Christmas Eve. On Christmas Eve! The fact that Christmas had little significance, either religious or sentimental for me, affected me not at all.

When we got back to the office after lunch I told our P.A. to get me a dust-collector for my desk and then I spent a few minutes considering Spinks.

It seemed to me that the first fact to take into consideration was that Spinks was going to find it hard to get a lot further in the Civil Service than his present mid-grade of Assistant Secretary. Somehow, somewhere among his seniors, a decision had been come to that he was not going to be one of the successes.

This may seem odd. It seemed odd to me. Yet often I felt that the final verdict on a man's career had been pretty well settled, whether he knew it or not, by the time he was forty. A spell in the Cabinet Office, a spell in the Treasury, and the word must have gone round the reaches above him: 'He'll go a lot further,' or 'He won't.' In a way it was not difficult to explain. Firstly, with the Administrative Class being very small compared with the Service as a whole, the number of bosses was small enough for them all to know each other well, and so for the judgment to get around easily. Secondly, the bosses (*a*) were clever men, and (*b*) took to this kind of assessing and judging with enthusiasm. There was nothing to show that they made many mistakes either. Mind you, they were not without the power to help their own prophecies along: the man who was tipped for success got the more exciting jobs, while the man who was tipped for failure was headed towards some backwater of the Service.

If Spinks had not been so beastly to me, I should have been sorry for him. It seemed to me that he must have been tipped for un-success and was perceptive enough to have seen it — remember that in this particular sphere, men's perceptions have a notable record of letting them down: it is very hard indeed to perceive that you are tipped for un-success.

And what about me? By not becoming a permanent civil servant I had not entered the competition. I wanted to stay where I was, working with Robert, till the day of liberation through the art of letters. I was not to be tipped for going further or for not. As I sat at my desk considering Spinks, I perceived that the two alternatives for which I could be tipped were for being allowed to stay where I was or for being pushed out altogether.

I felt rage again. I recalled Robert's being sniped at about me. Granted that I was by nature MISC/INEL, what, I wanted to know, did I *do* that was wrong? After all, it seemed to me, I was paid my salary for choosing and looking after scientists; not for what I was.

Obviously one of the things I did that was wrong, was not having a tray on my desk.

I ask you . . .!

## CHAPTER II

## FALLING IN LOVE

Though Barbara had laid it down as axiomatic that I would not, or could not, get married, she and Harry introduced me from time to time to fresh girls. I was never sure what, if one of them caught my attention, I was supposed to do — I sometimes knew what I wanted to do, but that, of course, was a different matter. I usually met fresh girls when she and Harry gave a party.

Harry and Barbara gave excellent parties. Their drawing-room was big enough to dance in; there was plenty of drink; and the guests covered a wide and entertaining range of society. Their 'party of the year' was on New Year's Eve, when they invited, so they said, everyone they knew, irrespective of social status. Certainly the range in social status of the people who turned up was wide enough to make this explanation seem plausible. There were people from the M.R.C. of rank both some distance above and well below Harry's: there were distinguished doctors and probationer nurses, professors and laboratory assistants; and a smattering of people connected with the arts — a painter or two, two or three writers, and some journalists. Also there was a collection of persons whose profession was not clearly defined, to say the least of it. I used to look forward to New Year's Eve at Harry's.

I had not told Harry and Barbara about my new source of hope. The concept of changing one's fate by an act of will — especially when it referred to my fate not to get married being changed by an act of my will, such as it was — was not likely to impress Barbara. I was not certain how much it impressed me. I felt cautious about it. I contemplated my will, such as it was.

Before I went to the party I had been seeing off Sybil at Euston. As well as coming to London, for a few days before Christmas, she had managed to fit in a few days after. Barbara had asked me if I would like to bring her to the party.

'She's planned to go home,' I said, hoping to dismiss the idea.

'Surely some plans are made to be broken?' said Barbara.

'They form a small category, compared with that of plans that are meant to be kept.'

Barbara gave me a sidelong penetrating look. 'Very well, then,' she said. 'Come alone!'

As that was what I had always intended to do, I felt I might now relax to the extent of assuming a mournful expression.

'Always alone . . .' I murmured, as if I were speaking to myself and not to her.

And yet, when I sat in the bar at Euston after Sybil had gone, I felt genuinely mournful. The recurring pattern had just recurred.

'A Guinness, please,' I said.

If I stopped the pattern, in its most immediate sense, recurring, I was not going to see Sybil again. Sybil sitting in buses trying to distinguish male passers-by from female; Sybil standing at bus-stops clutching her beaver-lamb coat round her; Sybil lying quietly on her back reciting soliloquies, long soliloquies, from the plays of Shakespeare . . . all over, all gone.

I have to say here and now that it never for one moment occurred to me that, if I did get married, it need not necessarily be all over, all gone. To men who did not take getting married seriously, to men who could get married at the drop of a hat, it might have, it would have, appeared differently. Not so to me. I took getting married very seriously indeed.

Few men could have taken it more seriously than I intended to take it.

'And a ham sandwich,' I said, thinking that if I were going to drink a lot at the party it would be well to have food inside me at the start.

'The recurring pattern . . .' I said to myself, lifting the glass of Guinness to my mouth. '*Can* I break it?'

By the time the waitress brought me the ham sandwich I was shaking my head even more mournfully. I was back again at the contemplation of my will. It's going to take a long time, I was thinking. A long, long time. There was not a soul, probably not even Robert, who believed I could do it. I ate the sandwich.

All the same, however long it was going to take me to break the recurring pattern, I decided to go home before the party and spruce myself up. There was no need to let everybody know that life had got me down. I put on my newest suit, and a bow tie to indicate that I was more of an artist than a civil servant. Then I walked briskly, if not hopefully, from the block of flats where I lived to Harry's Edwardian mansion.

It was a warm and drizzly New Year's Eve that year, and every so often the overhanging ornamental trees in people's front gardens let fall large drops of accumulated rainwater, plop among the specks of drizzle, on my head. Lights were shining from almost every window of Harry's house, and as I walked up the drive I could hear the sound of dance-music. There was a clutter of cars in the roadway and drive, and I noticed some bicycles propped against the large cast-iron dog, a greyhound I think it was, which stood heraldically beside the front door.

The eldest of Harry's children, a boy of nine looking extraordinarily pleased with himself at being allowed up so late, took my coat from me and pointed out to me where his mother was. Already cheered up by the party atmosphere, I kissed Barbara.

'You look very nice,' I said. She had altered the way in which her hair was done. Instead of being severely swept up at the sides it hung softly and loosely over her ears. Her skin glowed with high colour, and the confidence in her clear hazel eyes was masked by excitement. Active, strong-minded and knowing, Barbara nevertheless had a girlish love of giving parties.

'You do look nice,' I said. Then I felt the rush of air that preceded Harry's whirling up to join us.

'Come along inside!' he said in a high hallooing voice, while mopping his forehead with a handkerchief. 'We've got some pretty girls for you.'

It crossed my mind that, faithful and respectable husband though Harry might be, the pretty girls were perhaps not invited for the delectation of only his guests.

'We want you to dance,' said Barbara. 'We've collected a lot more records for to-night, jivey ones.'

'Why, how did you know? Jive is my second favourite activity.' I thought it was a very old quip.

Barbara gave me a satisfied look. 'I see the connection!' she said.

I went first of all to the room where they had rigged up a small bar and helped myself to a drink. The room was crowded. Standing just inside the door, where I had missed him when I came in, was Robert, talking to a man whom I saw was Harry's M.R.C. boss. I caught Robert's eye and waved to him. Then, having emptied my glass, I had it filled up again and pushed my way through the drinkers to the drawing-room.

Barbara's description of the records was apt enough. As I reached the door I heard a stirring performance of the 'Chicken Reel' coming out of the radiogram. I supposed that although the record happened to have been made a long time ago, it was Barbara's interest in the 'contemporary' that had led her to get it for a party like this. True, in one corner of the room a couple of young men with their hair

63

done in cow-licks — I took them to be lab-assistants — were jiving with their girls: but the rest of the floor was occupied by persons of higher social status indomitably doing the dance they did on all occasions, a sort of walk.

I put down my glass on the nearest ledge and looked round for a partner. Somebody had got to show the flag for persons of higher social status. There was a girl standing quite close to me, watching the dancers while a heavy-jowled man beside her appeared to be advancing the fact that he did not dance as a reason for surreptitiously groping round her waist. I did not blame him. She was dark-haired and comely. Nor did I see why I should not stop him instantly.

'Why don't you dance?' I said to her.

She gave me a surprised half-glance and then laughed.

'Why not?' she said. With a twist she was out of his reach and lifting her hand for me to take hold of. 'I've been wanting to . . .'

She had a pale complexion and she was dressed in a rosy, coral colour. I wondered, somewhat late in the day, if she could dance.

'Let's go over there,' I said, and led her over to where we could congregate with the lab-assistants and their partners.

It was all right—she could dance. A bit too quick on the lead, I thought, but that did not matter: it showed she was anxious to please. I was not looking at her most of the time we danced, because I had been given to understand that in this sort of dance one was supposed to appear abstracted and independent, if not actually schizophrenic. Of course I did glance at her now and then. I was puzzled: she seemed easy-going and relaxed, and yet she was too quick on the lead. How could that be?

The record ended. Before anyone else could forestall him, one of the lab-assistants, both knowing and determined, turned the record over. On the other side was the 'Dark Town Strutters' Ball'.

'Wonderful!' I said to my partner. 'Now we'll really get hep!'

And we did. Her glowing dress spun out this way and that; her short dark hair flopped over her forehead.

'Now!' I cried, flicking her right hand downward behind her waist and catching it on the other side — giving it a spiral tug upwards could send her spinning twice without having to be let go. It *would* have sent her spinning twice without having to be let go, had she not suddenly staggered.

'Oh!' she cried.

She was nearly on the floor before I managed to grasp her. I lifted her. As her head came slowly upwards we looked each other in the face, close to, for the first time. I saw grey eyes, brilliantly sparkling, looking into mine, long red lips twitching up at the corners in chagrined laughter——

I could go on with the description, but I cannot wait to come to the point. We were looking each other in the face, close to, for the first time. I thought:

This one's the right one for me.

Those were the words. I am sorry, but I just did not think anything else. I can see it was a moment that ought to have brought out the highest poetry in me. Grey eyes sparkling, a beautiful mouth, loose dark hair over her forehead, her body panting against mine as I hauled her up from having let her drop on the floor. Oh! the poetry that ought to have surged through me. What did surge through me?

This one's the right one for me.

Oh! the echoes, if it comes to that, of chapel jokes in my youth about 'waiting for Miss Right to come along'.

The girl said: 'I think one of my heels must have come loose.'

'Oh,' said I.

Was it love at first sight? Certainly it was at first sight. But love? Love, love, love . . . Did I hear nightingales singing, waves crashing, bells tinkling, winds blowing? . . . I cannot say that I did. I just heard one of the flattest sets of words I had ever come across, at regular intervals.

This one's the right one for me.

Her glance went swiftly round the room, and then came back to me. She did not say anything. Laughing made two lines, like brackets round her mouth, flash into existence and out again. The flat set of words might have been signalled to and fro between us — was she thinking I was the right one for her?

'I don't know your name,' I said.

'It's Elspeth.'

I said: 'Mine's Joe.'

To my surprise, she blushed. I said:

'We ought to get somebody to introduce us to each other.' I straightened my tie. 'I'm all for the proprieties.'

'I'm sure we can get somebody to introduce us,' she said. 'If you like.'

We were standing at the edge of the dance-floor, and just then the 'Dark Town Strutters' Ball' stopped. A whirling gust of air caught us.

'What are you two doing?' We turned to find Harry's inquisitive eyes moving shrewdly from one of us to the other.

I said we were looking for somebody to introduce us. A look of great cunning came over Harry's face.

'I'll introduce you,' he said.

I thought: He's guessed! Harry's curiosity was insatiable, but that was not to say it was always wildly off the truth.

'Are you,' I said to Elspeth while we were being introduced, 'by any chance Scottish?'

'No. I'm English.'

Harry was not in the least affected by this attempt at diversion. 'I think you two ought to come and tell Barbara you've met.' He said to me: 'Elspeth is one of Barbara's friends.'

I looked momentarily at Elspeth with fresh eyes. She seemed unconcerned by the revelation. Perhaps, I thought,

66

it might be all right — I did not know what had made me
think I might be in for some opposition from Barbara.

I said: 'Didn't Barbara mean us to meet?'

Harry burst into laughter. 'Of course. That's what we
invited her for.'

Elspeth turned on him. 'Really!' She was blushing
again.

I said to her: 'Don't worry!'

She said to me: 'I'm not, really.'

Harry led us through the doorway into the hall. There we
came straight upon Barbara and her mother, who must have
been keeping an eye on the dancing.

'What happened?' Barbara asked Elspeth.

'We saw you enjoying yourself,' her mother said to me.

Barbara's mother looked like Barbara, only, like many
mothers in comparison with their daughters, more so. Her
jaw was longer and squarer than Barbara's, her complexion
so much higher in colour that it looked permanently
weather-beaten. The look of confidence in her eyes was
opaque. Battle-axe, I thought. She said:

'It's the first time I've seen that kind of dancing.'

Her smile told me instantly that she had viewed my
performance not as showing the flag for persons of a higher
social status but as abandoning it to join persons of a lower
social status. How could I make her see the truth? At that
moment I caught sight of myself in a big looking-glass on the
wall behind her — a smart chap, in a bow tie, grinning. How
indeed?

Barbara said to me: 'We're going up to my room to see if
we can find a pair of my shoes that will fit Elspeth.'

I said: 'But aren't all your shoes the same size?' I had
forgotten that in the romantic hope of making their feet look
smaller or smarter or both, women buy shoes of all shapes
and sizes.

Elspeth and Barbara exchanged feminine smiles instead
of replying to me.

67

Anyway, I thought, watching Elspeth go up, she would have to come down. I could afford to wait. The fact of which I was convinced was not one that could alter with time.

For want of something to do, I turned to Harry and enquired who the man over there with the heavy jowls was.

'That's Barbara's *bookmaker*,' he said triumphantly, and went away.

The man was now standing next to a fair-haired girl, leaning over her shoulder and quietly putting his hand on her waist. His jowls looked heavier than ever.

I was going to point him out to Barbara's mother, but found that she had gone. I saw Robert coming out of the room where the bar was: with him still was Harry's boss. He called to me.

'Joe, will you come over here?'

Harry's boss and I shook hands. I reminded myself of the rule Robert had formulated for me to obey when I met bosses.

'We've been having an interesting discussion,' Harry's boss said. He was about my height, a tough, muscular little man with a leathery, grey face and a croaking voice: he used to make Robert and me think of a shark. We liked him. In the strictest privacy we used to call him The Shark.

I nodded my head. Robert's rule was for my self-preservation.

'Very interesting indeed,' said Robert.

I nodded my head the other way. The rule was, of course, to try not to say *anything*.

Robert began to say: 'It was about——'

'I was telling Robert,' said Harry's boss, not being the man to let anyone else speak for him, 'that you chaps are more fortunate than we are in getting supplies of people to do research.' He stared at me, showing his teeth slightly — just like a shark.

I tried wagging my head this time.

Harry's boss gave Robert a glance, as much as to say, 'Is

68

your friend dumb?' and continued, undismayed by my handicap, with his exposition.

'You'll hear it said that our present budget is too small, that the country ought to be spending more than three and a half millions on medical research. So it ought. But if we had more money we should scarcely know what to do with it. We've got plenty of problems we should like investigated, but chaps of the right quality to investigate them don't exist.' He aimed a question mid-way between me and Robert. 'How would you cope with that one? I should like to hear what you'd say.'

I said nothing. I thought Robert must be pleased with me.

Robert began: 'Lunn and I took steps some years ago to ensure that bigger supplies of research people were *made*.'

Lunn and I! He really was pleased with me. He really must think I was increasing my reputation with The Shark.

I was so encouraged that from then on I never looked back. Until Harry's boss shook hands again — 'That was a very interesting discussion!' — I did not utter. As we separated Robert gave me a frankly congratulatory look.

Within five seconds of our actually having separated, Harry was at my elbow. A honeyed voice said close to my ear:

'The Shark's in good form, to-night, isn't he?'

I caught a bright sideways glance coming past Harry's snub nose and said nothing.

'You know he's going to put in for another half million on our budget?'

I could not help it — I burst into laughter.

Harry looked hurt. For a moment instead of whirling he seemed to be quite stationary. Then he picked up.

'I must go and find Barbara's mother,' he said busily.

I stayed where I was. In a little while I saw Elspeth looking in the crowd for me. I called to her. When she joined me I said: 'Let's go and have a drink!'

'I think I've had enough already.'

'Let's dance, then! Will you be all right?'

'If we don't do anything too sudden.'

'Nothing easier.'

I took her on to the dance-floor. The lab-assistant had been deposed from his charge of the gramophone, and low soothing music was coming from it now. A voice crooned.

*You are*
*The breathless hush of springtime . . .*

'Suits me,' I murmured.

Elspeth did not hear.

We did a gentle circuit of the room, quarter turns all the way. 'Did you know that man was Barbara's bookmaker?' I said.

'No. I'd only just met him. Thank you for rescuing me.'

I had rescued her. I brushed my cheek against her hair.

'What a romantic beginning!' I murmured, this time loudly enough for her to hear.

As I went on brushing my cheek against her hair, I was unable to see her expression. You cannot have everything.

*You are the angel-glow*, crooned the voice, taking a more improbable flight,

*That lights a star . . .*

This one, I thought, is the one for me. Just that. Why try to think about anything else?

I had never felt like this in my life before. I had fallen in love before; I had fallen, I have to admit, into bed; I had fallen into ecstasy; and my goodness I had fallen into error. But I saw all of these things now as things else. In the conviction that this one was the right one for me, I had the feeling, quite new, that I had this time cut all the cackle and come straight to one single, stark, wonderful hoss. It was a traumatic experience, traumatically satisfying. I could have gone on doing the quarter turns all night. Elspeth said:

'You don't really have to be quite so un-sudden as this . . .'

I dutifully swung into a running turn, which ran us backwards into another couple.

*And now that moment divine,* crooned the voice, brought to the foreseeable misfortune contingent upon apostrophising one's love with an inventory, namely having to wind it up,

*When all of the things you are,*
*Are mine.*

The orchestra went on playing the song over again without the voice, and we sank back into the quarter turns.

'Isn't this nice?' I said.

Elspeth nodded her head so far as that was possible, seeing that we were cheek to cheek.

'We must meet again.' It hardly seemed necessary to say that.

She nodded her head again, and that was enough for the time being. We must meet again, again and again.

Soon after this it was midnight, and everyone crowded into the room and we all joined hands for Auld Lang Syne. Then Barbara announced that there was food ready in the kitchen, whereupon everyone crowded out again at twice the speed. I lost touch with Elspeth, and expected to find her in the kitchen. When I got there I saw her trapped on the other side of the room with Harry and Barbara's mother.

Suddenly, quite close to me, I saw Annette.

'Has Robert left you on your own?' I said.

Her eyes were bright, and when she shook her head the bell of hair swung to and fro. She had discarded her shapeless jumper and skirt in favour of a party dress that reminded me of what the girls of fifteen used to wear at our school dances: it was of a shade that used to be called apricot. She was wearing no make-up. She looked charming.

'Who was the girl you were dancing with?' she asked.

'Did I make such an exhibition of myself as that?'

'One always notices anyone who falls down,' said Annette.

I burst into laughter, and Annette looked pleased.

'She's called Elspeth,' I said. 'Why do you want to know?'

'I liked her. I should like to know her.'

I could not resist the indiscretion of saying: 'I hope you'll have plenty of opportunity.'

Annette said: 'Are you going to marry her?'

Her tone was simple, sweet, unoffending. I was taken aback.

'Good God! I don't know . . . I've only just met her. Give me a chance.'

'But, surely that's just what you've had. A chance, I mean.'

I hastily crammed a sausage roll into my mouth.

Annette said: 'I should like you to dance with me before you go. You look as if you know what you're doing. I don't.'

'You could have a few lessons,' I said sharply. I had great faith in lessons.

Annette shook her head and looked away. 'I suppose I'm self-conscious,' she said. I cannot say that she looked specially troubled by the thought.

'Anyway,' she said, 'Robert doesn't dance very much.'

'No.' I was glancing through the crowd to see if there was any sign of Elspeth getting free. And I was distracted by the word 'marry' having been introduced into my thoughts.

Suddenly it occurred to me that Annette appeared to think that I really could get married.

'Yes, let's dance!' I said enthusiastically. 'I'll teach you.'

I danced with Annette. There was now no sign of Elspeth. Perhaps she had gone home. Perhaps she felt a little shaken after all. Perhaps somebody had offered her a lift in a car. After I had handed Annette over to Robert, I made a last tour of the house without finding Elspeth. I decided it was time I went home.

As I said goodnight to Harry, I asked:

'What's happened to Elspeth?'

Harry gave me a quick look. 'I thought she was waiting for *you* to take her home.'

I was on no account going to accept that remark for the start of a conversation with Harry. 'I expect she's already gone,' I said, with such decisiveness that it carried me over the threshold and out into the garden before Harry could try another tack.

The drizzle had stopped, but the bare branches of prunus and lilac still dropped their large drops of water on my head in the darkness. I looked forward to my walk home. I was of the opinion that, unlike most of the guests I had left behind at the party, I was sober.

I thought about Elspeth. I was not dismayed by not having seen her again. I could well do without seeing her again that night, I thought. My conviction that she was the girl for me, the one exactly right for me, was quite enough for me to cope with. For the time being I wanted no more. I walked back up Putney Hill just thinking about it.

## CHAPTER III

## A TABLE AT THE CARLOS

I LET a couple of months go by before I got in touch with Elspeth. What was I waiting for? you may wonder. I will tell you. I was waiting till Sybil's next trip to London was over.

In the days before the war, when I was a schoolmaster, I had had a robust friend who used to prolong his anguish over the passing of an old love until he had got a new love actually ready to get into bed with him.

'I must have continuity,' he used to say — somewhat self-righteously, I used to think.

My own need now was the reverse. I must have *dis*-continuity. It seemed to me as a changed man, as a man now aiming at marriage, improper to get in touch with Elspeth while still 'carrying-on', as my mother would have called it — no doubt did call it, to Harry — with Sybil. As a changed man I was getting curious ideas of propriety, I noticed. But there it was. The recurring pattern had to be broken. I needed discontinuity. And I happened to have previously arranged for Sybil to come up to London in February.

So that accounts for the delay. It also accounts for a final scene in the bar at Euston whose mournfulness exceeded all previous mournfulness. This was, I had decided, really the last time I was going to see Sybil. Is it any wonder I was mournful? Sybil, with the looks of Marlene Dietrich, with the softest of voices and the most touching of myopias, was now gone, gone for good. From now on I was aiming at marriage.

I drank a large whisky and considered the prospect. And
I considered Sybil again, too. Marriage, I thought . . . the
very word was like a knell.

I meant to try and marry Elspeth. I bought myself
another whisky and told myself to put knells out of my
mind, even though this one was metaphorically ringing a
New Year in as well, more obviously, as an Old Year out.

During January and February I kept out of Barbara's
and Harry's way. This was not difficult because for part
of the time I had to go down to one of our major research
establishments and do what was called a staff-review. Instead of being able to dwell on the breathless hush of springtime and the angel-glow that lights stars, I had to bend my
mind to following professional discussions about shock-
waves, aspect-ratios and suchlike; which, I can tell you,
takes a lot more out of you than thinking about love. It
also, I can tell you with the same authority, puts a good deal
more into you, too.

I had noticed, before, the therapeutic value of a stay at
one of our research establishments. If you lead a life of
sexual disorder, there is nothing like a bit of science and
technology for putting you straight. In the first place I
found it interesting to think about shock-waves and aspect-
ratios just out of natural curiosity. In the second place the
people who were doing research on these topics had so little
intention of discussing anything else that they gave me less
than half a chance to maunder privately about my sexual
life. I used to come away from these visits feeling a tireder
but a better man. Perhaps only a little better; certainly a
lot tireder. Still, only a little better, I felt, is *something*. Good
for you, science and technology!

Since nobody else I knew could give me Elspeth's address,
I had to ask Harry for it.

'I thought you'd want to know it,' he said, kindlily,
'sooner or later.'

I thanked him.

He said: 'I suppose you weren't able to take her up straight away because of being out of London.'

'Yes,' I said, delighted by the thought that his spies at Euston must have failed him for once.

'Elspeth was very disappointed, I think, that night. She was waiting to go home with you. She was up in Barbara's room . . .'

He was looking at me with such an innocent expression, and the speech had gone so smoothly, that a pause elapsed before I tripped, in retrospect, over the test phrase. 'She was waiting to go home with you.'

I tripped, before I knew what I was doing, with chagrin and frank astonishment. I had realised that I was a changed man, but I had not realised I was so changed a man as to be shocked by the thought of a girl being ready to go home with me the first time she met me.

'How did she get home?' I asked casually.

Harry answered in his high, fluid voice: 'We put her up for the night here.'

I felt relief.

In the time between telephoning Elspeth and meeting her I reached a conclusion about myself that could scarcely have been more embarrassing. My reaction to the concept of the girl I proposed to marry being prepared to go to bed with me the first time she met me was the typical reaction of my father and the congregation of which I was no longer a member. I could now only conclude that, having discarded my recurring pattern, which, when all was said and done, was my own invention, I was going to fall back into the conventional pattern of the society in which I had been brought up. Not to put too fine a point on it, I must be going to be *respectable*.

I recalled what I chose to regard as my life of revolt. I had seceded from my father's church, in fact I had seceded from all religious belief; and I had practised my recurring pattern. Altogether a pretty fair score in the way of revolt, as both sides admitted. And now at the age of forty I was thrown back in one sphere at least — I saw no sign of dawning religious belief — to the start. I saw the prospect of courting Elspeth as if we were any two members of the choir, any two respectable members of the choir, that is.

A further thought occurred to me before I met Elspeth again. Supposing Harry had not been lying about her? Horrors! When I sat waiting for Elspeth in the foyer of the Carlos Hotel, where I had asked her to dine with me, one of the questions I most wanted to find the answer to was whether Harry had any grounds for his lie.

The Carlos was an hotel I had frequented since about the middle of the war. It was small and, as far as I could gather, very grand — the sort of place that made Claridge's look rather commercialised: I mean, the Carlos would never have had flags outside, or gypsy music, or anything like that. As a result of my dining there alone when there were air-raids going on, some of the servants had got to know me. And considering how good the food was, I decided it was not as expensive as all that. The Carlos, as I had told Elspeth, not without intent to make an impression, was my favourite hotel.

You may think my attitude to the Carlos does not accord with my having said a little while ago that I was simply petty bourgeois. Not a bit of it. I may have cultivated some of the tastes of persons of a higher social class than myself — who would not cultivate the Carlos, if he had the chance? And I may have modelled some of my behaviour on theirs — I had removed most of the provincial accent from my speech, though naturally I could not do anything about removing it from my physiognomy. But I never really felt that my own social class was any different from that to which I had been born.

Perhaps I can make myself clearer by referring to my political attitudes. I had taken it into my head that the Labour Party were out to try and give the lower classes a better time of it, the Conservative Party to see that the upper classes did not lose one jot or tittle thereby. For that reason alone I could never have voted anything but Labour. (I may say that I kept strictly away from political meetings because the sight of M.P.s tended to put me off voting altogether.)

'The Left is motivated by envy and hope,' Robert had once pronounced, 'the Right by nostalgia and fear.'

Awful as the whole human race was, I stood by the side which at least was moved sometimes, in its envy, by hope.

So there you are. I was sitting in a big high-backed armchair in the entrance hall of the Carlos, not feeling like a lord. If anything, I was feeling like Charlie Chaplin sitting in a chair made for Hamlet. I was waiting for Elspeth. Beside me, on a heavy William Kent'ish table with a marble top, there was a vase of flowers. The time of year was spring. The flowers were mimosa. I did not have to wait long for Elspeth, because she was punctual. She came through the revolving doors, hatless and a shade less pale than I had remembered. We shook hands.

She was nervous. And so was I. A handshake, and a formal handshake at that, was somewhat different from the last physical contact we had exchanged — I glanced at her cheek, thinking that my cheek . . . She caught me doing it, and suddenly we were looking each other in the face again as we had done when I hauled her up off the floor.

'Let's have a drink!' I said.

'I don't drink very much . . .'

I said playfully: 'I only suggested one, anyway.'

Fleetingly the lines like brackets round her mouth came and went. She really was nervous, I thought. As we went past the huge vase of mimosa I saw her notice it with surprise and awe.

'What a lot!' she said.

'And who's paying for it?' said I. 'Us, of course.'

78

She succeeded in laughing. I was pretty sure she had never set foot in a place as grand as this before. We both sniffed the mimosa with pleasure, and then I steered her into the big drawing-room, where there were more vases of it. At this she laughed naturally.

While we were having a drink I realised that she looked less pale because on the previous occasion she had been wearing a coral-coloured dress whereas to-night she was in dark green. It suited her: I noticed that her eyes were a transparent blue. No jewellery, no scent. I bet she has not got many dresses, I thought, and found the conjecture touching.

We had a drink, and then another one. Some of her nervousness disappeared, but not the air of mild formality. As you will have gathered, I was on my best behaviour. It became apparent to me that so was Elspeth. Our behaviour at the party, whether it was our worst or not, was a thing of the past, I thought — as also was Harry's deplorable suggestion. I had no doubt that Elspeth was somehow moving along on the same lines as me. Our parents, after they had got over the surprise of our being in the Carlos, would have recognised us as their own son and daughter respectively.

I have said 'our' parents. The way Elspeth and I spent most of our time over dinner was in exchanging information about our careers and our families. Her social origins were not very different from mine.

Elspeth was twenty-five years old and working as a school-teacher in Bethnal Green.

'I'm afraid I didn't go to a university,' she said, blushing, and glancing swiftly round the room as if she were ashamed of something.

I too glanced swiftly round the room. 'I doubt if all these ladies are honours graduates of Girton or Somerville, either.'

She grinned, though she still looked ashamed.

'Where *did* you go?' I asked.

'To a teachers' training college.'

'Did it do you any good?'

'It was very hard work.' She paused. 'So it must.'

I said: 'That's a fine Calvinist sentiment! *Your* father doesn't happen to be a non-conformist minister, does he?'

She laughed. 'No. He's a school-teacher. We're all schoolteachers in my family. You know, at council schools. . . . I've gone the highest, by getting into a senior school.' She was amused. Then she said: '*Your* father's a minister, isn't he? I think Barbara told me.'

I nodded my head.

She was thinking something. I asked her what it was.

'Well, only that ministers' sons either become ministers themselves,' she said, 'or go to the other extreme.'

'Oh!' I cried.

She blushed again and let her table-napkin fall on the floor. I felt as if my reputation must be on the floor in the moral sense.

'You don't know me,' I said.

'No,' said she, looking frightened.

A waiter came and picked up her napkin, and for a while we concentrated on our *hors d'oeuvres* — in my opinion, particularly good at the Carlos.

I reflected on the concept of marrying somebody whose social origins were approximately the same as my own. I was perfectly happy about it. In fact I had never really thought of marrying either above or below me. I supposed I might have thought of marrying above me, as ambitious men did — I *was* ambitious. But I was ambitious as a writer, as an artist. Had I been a publisher or a politician, it would of course have been a different matter: I had noted that politicians and publishers were great ones for marrying into the aristocracy. But I never saw how it could make me write better novels even if I married a Royal Princess. So why worry? I asked myself.

I looked at Elspeth — she happened to be eating a little
mound of shrimps in a curry-flavoured sauce that she had
been saving to the end — and thought there was no need
to worry at all. She was eating slowly and with pleasure.
Nice and relaxed, I thought. The right one for me. From
bending forward over her plate, a dark strand of hair had
fallen across her forehead.

'Well?' I said, when she had finished the shrimps.

'M'm,' she said.

'It's a nice place, this, isn't it?'

She said 'M'm' again.

While the wine-waiter took over, I looked approvingly and
proprietorially round the room. It was panelled in a brightish
wood that I took to be mahogany. On most of the tables
there were small lamps with old-fashioned pink shades and
tapering silver vases with daffodils in them. The curtains
were of some dark, unstirring colour. My glance was caught
by the flickering flame of a spirit lamp that rose up when a
chafing-dish was lifted off it.

When we had got started on our next course, I said:

'How do you come to be a friend of Barbara's?'

'We send some of our children to Barbara's clinic.'

'Oh,' I said. Nothing easier to understand after all.

'The L.C.C. always seem to send you a long way from
home.'

'What?' I was completely at sea, now. 'They send *you*?'
I was trying to work out all sorts of complicated inter-
pretations.

She said: 'No. Barbara.'

I laughed.

'They could perfectly well have found Barbara a job,' she
said, 'somewhere near to where she lives, instead of sending
her all the way down to our borough.'

I had no views on this. Judged by the heat with which
she spoke, Elspeth had.

I said: 'If the L.C.C. had found her a job near where

she lives, you would never have met her.' Anyway, no civil servant would be prepared to judge L.C.C. policy on one example.

'I shouldn't . . .'

I looked at her. 'And so you'd never have been at the party. . . .'

A smile showed at the corners of her mouth. She glanced away and drank some wine. We paused for a little while. Elspeth said:

'Barbara tells me you write novels.'

In the ordinary way I should have replied: 'Yes, have you read any of them?' in a tone which indicated that a negative answer would not be well received. (I never understood why people expected one to smile, if not actually to pat them on the back, when they disclosed that they had never read any of one's books.) I said:

'Yes.'

'I should like to read them.'

I had met this remark before: the correct riposte was, 'Well, what's stopping you?' I said:

'That's the spirit!'

'Actually,' she said, 'I've just finished ——' and she named a book I had brought out after the war.

'What did you think of it?'

She smiled shyly: 'I've never met an author before.'

I was interested by that but did not see how it answered my question. Elspeth said:

'I don't know the kind of thing to say about a book to its author.'

'I should just concentrate on praise,' I said. 'Sustained praise, with a touch here and there of flattery.' I recalled a friend, a woman, who, when I sent her a manuscript for her opinion, used to ask: 'Which do you want to hear, flattery or what I really think?'

Elspeth gave a laugh which seemed to absolve her from the need to reply. Encouraged, I said impetuously:

'The book I'm just about to bring out is much better than any of the others.'

'Oh, I shall get it!'

At that moment I thought of my reputation in her eyes. I have to say that the book I was encouraging her to read was on the same lines as this which you are now reading: it was about myself. Only it was about myself before I became a changed man. The moral tone of the book I was encouraging her to read was consequently nothing like so high as the moral tone of this book — after all, if you are behaving respectably, your moral tone cannot help being high, can it?

You see my point. I was sitting there in the Carlos with Elspeth, behaving in the most respectable manner imaginable, namely in the manner of a man who is taking a girl out to dinner with a view to matrimony. The book of mine which was going to come out in the following month was about a man who took his girl out to dinner with a view to *not* marrying her. A reprehensible view. A reprehensible man. I had difficulty in recognising the fact that it was me, even me before metamorphosis.

'What is it called?' Elspeth was asking.

I told her, wishing I had given it one of those American titles like *Now Yesterday* or *Here and Forever* that nobody can remember. Elspeth did not write the title down but I knew she would not forget it.

'I shall watch for the reviews,' she said.

People always said that, rather as if they had some idea that both they and I gained merit by it.

'They may be bad,' I said insincerely.

'I don't think they will.' For all her shyness Elspeth was giving me a sparkling look, quick but direct, appraising but admiring.

'Oh!' I cried. 'I'll let you read a proof copy if you like.'

Elspeth said she would like.

I grinned. 'I suppose you might as well know the worst.'

Elspeth looked down at her plate, which by now was empty, and I saw her forehead go pink. What a wonderful girl! I thought. Just right for me. . . . It only remained now for her to think my novel was the funniest, the wittiest, the most touching, the most truthful, and in some ways really the most profound book she had ever read.

'What would you like to eat next?' I asked, happy enough to buy her the most expensive *crêpes* on the menu or even a whole *bombe surprise* for herself.

Elspeth considered the alternatives and modestly chose to have some *marrons glacés*.

'I love chestnuts,' she said when the waiter had gone, 'but I've never tasted *marrons glacés*.' She smiled. 'We couldn't afford them.' She smiled. 'I still can't.'

I made the sort of tut-tutting noise that rich people make in the effort of trying not to hear what the poor are saying, and said:

'Well, they are pretty expensive.' I did not want her to think I could afford to dine at the Carlos every night, though I guessed she would have found somewhere not so grand less of a strain. 'Actually,' I said, 'I don't think I tasted them till the days when I was an undergraduate.' I had explained to her about my mother inheriting a little money which had enabled me to go up to Oxford — those were the days when only a grand slam, so to speak, of scholarships and grants enabled a boy to go up to Oxford without some other source of money. 'We were quite poor, you know. If there's anything poorer than a Methodist minister, I'd like to know what it is.'

'Yes, but you didn't have five brothers and sisters. I mean, your parents didn't have to bring up six children . . .'

'Six children!' I cried. 'They're not Roman Catholics, are they?' Though I no longer believed in God, I was still a hundred-per-cent Protestant. Generations of nonconformity had endowed me with a blood-pressure that rose at the mere thought of Papism. I could have married Elspeth if she were a Mormon or a Seventh Day Adventist, but not if she were R.C.

Elspeth shook her head. 'Of course not. Actually they were Baptists, though I'm not.' She grinned. 'They really wanted six children.'

'I see. . . . That's all right,' I said, though I was not sure I hoped Elspeth would want six children.

'We were very happy, really,' she said, 'though we had to go without lots of things that most children have.'

I saw the force of that.

'Do you know,' she said, 'that until I went to college I never had a dressing-gown.'

The fact she disclosed was poignant, but the portentous tone that came into her voice made me, I am sorry to say, want to laugh.

Elspeth was offended. I could see her saying to herself: 'I won't tell him anything else.' I realised that for me to say something even more poignant, such as 'Until I went up to Oxford, I never even had a pair of shoes,' would only make matters worse. And that would not have been in keeping with my parallel response to her remark, which was, 'I'll give you a wonderful dressing-gown. . . . You shall be warm, however chilly the night, for the rest of your life.' This was assuming, of course, that I did not lose my job as a civil servant and have all my manuscripts turned down by publishers.

'Here come your *marrons*,' I said.

Elspeth tried one and her expression melted. My absence of feeling had been shown to be only of the moment and possibly not characteristic. I ate some runny Camembert cheese and the meal ended in delicious harmony.

Afterwards, when we came out of the hotel, it was a dry night, and we walked up through Grosvenor Square to Bond Street Tube Station, where Elspeth went east and I west. On the station platform, before she got into the train, I took her hand again and kissed her goodnight.

Her train moved out. When I turned to go to the adjacent platform, I felt as if the image of her face, smiling as she waved to me through the window, were still lingering on my retinas. Sparkling eyes and a long mouth curled up at the corners: the right face for me. Was it, I asked myself in an effort to be detached about it, a beautiful face, the sort of face that could for instance launch a thousand ships? I supposed it was not. But that did not worry me. I had my doubts about such faces: I suspected that if I saw the face of Helen of Troy her nose would look to me as if it started out of the middle of her forehead. And furthermore I was not looking for a face that would launch a thousand ships. I was only looking for a face that would launch just my ship.

CHAPTER IV

## MISCELLANEOUS CONVERSATIONS

I TOLD Robert I had spent an entirely satisfactory evening with Elspeth.

'Who on earth's Elspeth?'

Robert's attitude towards the existence of anyone whom he had not discovered for himself was incredulity.

'The girl I met at Harry's party on New Year's Eve,' I said. 'You saw her. I told you I was going to take her out to dinner at the Carlos.'

'Was it a good dinner?'

'Very good.' I began to describe the dishes we had eaten, in detail as boring as I could make it.

In retaliation Robert gave me what we nowadays referred to, *vide* W. H. Sheldon, as a mesomorphic glare. Mesomorph is the name for the square, all-muscle type of man, and the glare is the blank unchanging expression you see on his face. (The word 'glare' is chosen because the emotion in which mesomorphs most readily express themselves is rage. Undiluted men of action, they burst into rage when action does not produce the desired result. The glare gives intimations of this.) Most of our colleagues in the Civil Service, like men of action in all walks of life, were predominantly mesomorphic, and as a private parlour game Robert and I used to give them marks out of ten for the impenetrability of their glares. Robert's large F.D.R.-like face rather untypically did not score more than about seven out of ten. And my own score was so much less that, in order to keep up in my Civil Service career, I practised my glare regularly in the mirror after shaving.

I said to Robert:

'You ought to pay attention when I mention Elspeth. Because I think it's possible I may marry her.'

Robert's glare disappeared instantly. He said with emotion:

'I hope you do.'

And while he said that his face fell into an expression which I readily identified — it was the expression into which both our faces fell when, for example, somebody whom we loved who had no literary talent announced that he or she was going to write a novel.

'You must meet her,' I said.

'I should like to,' he replied — in a tone with which we accepted the prospect of reading the first 10,000 words of manuscript.

I gave up.

In fact it turned out immediately afterwards in our conversation that Robert was preoccupied about something else. He had been called over to see Murray-Hamilton. One of the senior people at the research establishment at which I had done my staff-review had complained to Murray-Hamilton about something I had said.

'The snitch!' I cried, finding just the word I wanted from the vocabulary of my pupils when I was a schoolmaster.

Robert looked grave.

I asked who the man was.

Robert shrugged his shoulders. 'I don't know. As it was some deputy superintendent or other . . .'

I asked what I was supposed to have said.

'History in this case doesn't relate that.'

I was about to comment angrily when Robert went on: '*I* don't know what you're supposed to have said. I suppose Murray-Hamilton does, but that's not what concerns him. As he sees it, whether you said it or not, even whether you were provoked to it or not, you *offended* somebody.

Introduced friction into the machine. . . . That's something he takes seriously. He's bound to take it seriously.'

'Oh, blast!' I said. 'Why can't he take no notice for once?'

'He's not the sort of man who could, even if he approved of you in the first place. . . .'

That remark shut me up for quite a while.

I had a picture of Murray-Hamilton sitting in his office brooding and reflecting. A new thought crossed my mind. Could it be that what he was interminably brooding and reflecting upon was the awesome difference between Right and Wrong? A book, a large ledger, lay open in front of him. Then I saw Spinks, 'Stinker Spinks', come in — at that I discontinued thought in favour of speech — and I said to Robert:

'I wonder what I really did say.'

Robert had got up and gone to look glumly through the window. He said:

'Probably something sharp and bright.' He paused. 'But that's immaterial. . . . The fact of the matter is that you say things that set these people's teeth on edge. You make them feel you're getting at them.'

'Oh,' I said.

'Even your quips are not the sort they're used to — or even take to be quips, for that matter.' He turned on me. 'I've heard you, myself, invite people to think mesomorphic glares are funny, when they have mesomorphic glares themselves!'

'Oh,' I said again.

Robert turned away from me. 'You may have to pay for it, that's all.'

'What do you mean by that?' I asked quickly.

'I don't know,' he said.

That remark shut me up altogether.

Robert went on glumly staring out of the window. He had nothing else to say on the matter, either then, it appeared, or later.

During the next few weeks I had other, different things to think about.

The time came for me to invite Robert and Annette to meet Elspeth. I invited them to dinner with us at my flat. I bought some very expensive *pâté* and spent an additional ten shillings a bottle on the claret. The flat was central-heated and warm, and three hyacinths growing in a pot gave my living-room — I had two rooms — an agreeable smell. It was the first time Elspeth had been to my flat: I should have thought it quite improper to invite her alone. Robert and Annette seemed to me, though they might not have seemed to everyone, to constitute proper chaperonage.

After dinner Robert and Annette sat on the sofa and held hands, at least they began by holding hands. I thought it was a good thing for Elspeth to observe that a man as eminent and as lofty in general purpose as Robert, and a girl as high-minded in the philosophical sense as Annette, made no bones about liking — well, you had only to see them together to see what they liked.

And I must say that Robert knew how to play his part. He instructed both girls on how good a novelist I was. By this time Elspeth had read the proofs of my new novel and declared that she liked it. This, of course, was not enough for Robert. I listened to him with pleasure and satisfaction. Girls do not, more's the pity, want to sleep with a man because he writes good novels; but if they are not averse to the idea of sleeping with him in the first place, then hearing that he writes good novels sometimes appears to help things along. (For this reason the artist's life is not entirely composed of suffering and rejection.)

Robert did me proud. None of us were left in any doubt that my new book was a small masterpiece. Small? You may think that was not doing me as proud as all that. I recommend you to concentrate on the important thing. It is masterpieces that live, whatever the size. Better a tiny masterpiece than the most massive of potboilers. Robert said:

'He may even make a bit of money with it.'

I glanced at Elspeth. She was looking radiantly pretty, in the dark green dress which made her eyes look so blue. The same dark green dress — she probably had not got any other dress. . . . Money. I thought of making a bit of money in an entirely new light. How could two live on the income of one? By the earner taking a cut.

'How much?' I asked Robert, poignantly.

He mentioned a sum. Not enough. Nothing like enough! Elspeth's expression of general enthusiasm and amusement did not falter. No more did it need to. Nor did Annette's falter. No more did hers need to, either. Robert earned much more than me, and Annette never wore anything but the same jumper and skirt.

'Of course,' Robert was saying loftily about my novel, 'it's probably the most original book to come out since the war. And it may well be the progenitor of a whole series of similar books.'

'But the money?' I interrupted. 'What about the money?'

Robert shrugged his shoulders, as one does when a man of talent reveals a petty obsession — which happens to be pretty often, if it comes to that. Of course I wanted my book to be a masterpiece and a progenitor and all the rest of it. I wanted that first of all. But *after* that . . .

The following morning at the office, Robert came in and said:

'I think Elspeth's a nice girl. A very nice girl. Intelligent . . . and comparatively relaxed.' He nodded his head in agreement with his own description.

I nodded mine. I said:

'I need someone who's pretty relaxed. Someone to cushion my . . . fluctuations.'

Robert nodded his head again, probably not so much in agreement with my description of myself as in censure of what I was describing.

'Yes,' he said gravely. 'I think she'll do that for you.'

I was satisfied. In fact I was happy.

Annette, too, was approving, though on different grounds. Next time we met, she said to me:

'I knew I should like Elspeth. I admire her.'

I said: 'She admires you.' I thought that actually Elspeth admired above all Annette's First in Modern Greats.

Annette went on: 'I think I envy her really.'

I said with astonishment: 'What do you envy her for?'

'Her profession, of course.' Annette looked at me, smiling. 'It's a very useful one.'

I had forgotten for the moment that Elspeth was a school-teacher — possibly I was thinking chiefly about the time when she would cease to be one. And I had also forgotten that Annette was still doing nothing, apart from turning her D.Phil. thesis into the form of a publishable monograph and writing occasional reviews for professional journals.

'Oh,' I said. 'I didn't know you'd been talking to her about it.' Nor did I see why, with marriage imminent, Annette had been talking to Elspeth about it.

Annette laughed. 'I haven't.' She looked away and her hair swung girlishly. 'But I think I will,' she said, in a firm clear voice. And then she added, even more clearly and firmly: 'I must.'

CHAPTER V

## APPROACH TO MARRIAGE

M Y NOVEL came out in April. I have observed that it was a book on the same lines as this one you are now reading, so you can judge its quality by inference. Masterly? Oh well, have it your own way! Though I can tell you that *some* people said it was masterly. And what is more, they were paid for *their* critical efforts.

Robert and I followed the reviews with the sort of excitement with which one follows the results of a General Election. I had made a list of the days of the week on which novel reviews appeared, so I duly arrived at the office on any particular morning with a copy of the right paper. Robert, of course, had one as well. We hurried out of the office at lunch-times to buy the appropriate mid-day editions of the London evening papers, and after we came out of work in the afternoons we went up to our club and furled through magazines like *The Sphere* and *The Tatler*, for which, since they were inclined to lag behind in reviewing, we were not prepared to risk the outlay of ready money. And I had a press-cutting agency, which I used to telephone for reviews that Robert and I had missed but which watchful friends had seen in, say, *The Farmers' And Stockbreeders' Gazette*.

It was a thrilling time, more thrilling in my opinion than watching election results come out — though it would presumably not be so in the opinion of a political party leader.

'I think it's going to be all right,' Robert announced when the most important reviews were in.

So I settled back for 'the bit of money' to come in. My

publishers appeared to be settling back too, because the book went out of print three weeks after publication. Several weeks elapsed before it came into print again, but everybody said it did not affect my sales; at least, my publishers said that. I trusted the bit of money would come in.

While I was waiting and trusting, the time for Robert's marriage to Annette came near. Now that I was buoyed up by thinking I might manage to get married myself, I was freed from my disfiguring envy of Robert's good fortune. In fact I began to think he might envy me, who foresaw no trouble of any kind with my loved one. For signs of trouble, as far as Robert was concerned, were beginning to appear. They were trivial, of course. Signs of trouble always are to start with.

I sympathised with Annette. The first difference of opinion arose over whether the wedding was to be grand or not. I first heard of it one Sunday afternoon when Annette invited Elspeth and me to tea with her and Robert at her father's flat.

We were eating slices of bread and butter and marmalade. Annette gave Robert a clear-eyed look and said:

'Must I dress up?'

She was awaiting an answer Yes or No. Love and devotion for the person to whom she addressed the question seemed to shine from her face. At the time she asked it she was wearing the usual polo-necked jumper and some wrinkled navy-blue trousers — as it was getting towards summer I presumed it was a thinner jumper, but it looked the same. Her complexion had its delicious cleanly sheen and her bell of hair glistened as if she had just washed it.

'Dress up in what?' said Robert.

'In bridal white,' said Annette. 'You know I don't want to, darling.' She gave him an amused smile. 'I don't see myself as the central figure in a fertility rite.'

Robert burst into a laugh. 'That's just what you'll be, my girl!'

Annette smiled back at him, simply, without inhibition. I was reminded of Robert's observation, when he first got to know Annette and her philosopher friends, that they believed in their new brand of high-mindedness being accompanied by plenty of copulation. To Robert and me, who happened to have been brought up on a brand of high-mindedness that was accompanied by continence, this new combination was surprising. It made us ready to re-consider our former unfavourable judgement on high-mindedness.

'I'm on Annette's side,' I said. 'After all, neither of you have any religious beliefs.' And they had been sleeping with each other for months.

Elspeth said: 'Oh, I'm on Robert's side. It's something that only happens to one once in one's life.' She suddenly faltered and blushed. 'At least I hope it does. . . .' She looked down — I realised that I had not breathed a word about marriage to her.

'Exactly,' said Robert, and rewarded her with a dazzling look of friendship. He went on: 'Elspeth is right, you know. At certain points in one's life, the maximum ceremony may well be desirable.'

Annette said to Robert: 'I find ceremony embarrassing.' She looked at him. 'It really is embarrassing to me, you know. Can't we do without it?'

'If you can't bear it, of course we'll do without it,' he said, and gave her a quick, faintly mechanical smile.

Annette's father came into the room.

We had not heard him come into the flat and we were all surprised to see him. He did not usually come back from his house in the country till later on Sunday night. He looked round to see whom Annette was entertaining. It was a characteristic gesture, such as I had often seen grand people make — he was weighing up whether to stay with us or not. He said:

'I should like some tea if there's any left.' He spoke with a mixture of politeness and carelessness that amused me.

95

Annette's father was different from the Civil Service bosses in our part of the world. Our department had none of the social advantages of being, say, antique, like the Home Office, or chic, like the Foreign Office. In fact I had once caused a bit of trouble by remarking, innocently and truthfully, in what had turned out to be the wrong company, that our department, as far as cachet went, was one of the slums of the Civil Service. (You may ask how there can be such a thing as the wrong company for Innocence and Truth. Kindly address your question to Murray-Hamilton and Spinks!)

In the first place, Annette's father looked different from our bosses. He was tall and slender, whereas they were mainly of medium height and broad: he looked as if he might once have played badminton, whereas they looked as if they might have excelled, in fact most of them had excelled, at games where you run about all the time, knocking other people over. And of course his manner was different. Murray-Hamilton and Spinks, for instance, had a manner that was affable and jocular and rather commonplace, though in their different ways neither were commonplace men. Not so Annette's father — scholarly and *dégagé* were the words that sprang to my mind as I watched him.

Annette said to him: 'I'll make some fresh tea for you.' From the way she looked at him it was obvious that she was very fond of him.

He sat down, folding his long legs gracefully. He said: 'Don't, if it's any trouble to you.'

Somehow it made me think of the way he conducted his public life, of the cultivatedly diffuse sort of minute he wrote to his peers — 'Do you think X is a good name?' he would write of some Vice-Chancellor of a university. 'I met him in the Club and thought he might do for us, but you may think differently.' Annette's father, I thought, showed you how the power-game after all really flowered at the top; though I never quite understood, being convinced that in general it was active, opaque, heavily-muscled men who got to the top, what phenomenon was responsible for Annette's father flowering there. I used to speculate on two questions. One was, had the upper reaches of the Civil Service in the previous generation been more sheltered, more university-like? The other was, was Annette's father only about one-third as *dégagé* as he seemed?

Annette went out to make some fresh tea and her father said to Robert:

'Really I shall have to give up this house in the country. It's an extravagance I can't afford any more.'

He gave a brief circular glance at Elspeth and me, to make sure that we were taking it in. His eyes were somewhere between grey and hazel in colour, very bright without being specially humorous.

Robert nodded his head in statesmanlike agreement.

'On the other hand,' Annette's father went on, 'going down there is my only chance of getting away from the Civil Service. And doing some of the things I really want to do. . . .'

He was writing a book on Hellenistic art between two dates of wonderfully esoteric significance.

'But of course,' he went on again to Robert, 'I know I'm not telling you anything you don't know already.' He was referring to Robert's writing novels.

Robert was beginning to say something about senior civil servants having to work too hard when Annette came back with the tea. 'I'm sorry we've only got marmalade,' she said to her father. 'I forgot to go out and buy some jam.'

Her father began to eat a slice of bread and butter, without marmalade. 'I was talking to Robert about giving up the house.' Then he turned to Robert as if the idea had just struck him. 'I suppose you and Annette wouldn't care to live there, or perhaps it's too far out of London?'

Robert's cheeks went slightly pink. 'Clearly, we should have to think about it,' he said. 'I think we probably——'

Annette interrupted: 'Oh no, Father. I don't want a house at all.'

We all looked at her. I cannot say Annette looked in the least perturbed as a consequence. I glanced at Robert: he did.

Annette said: 'I don't want to have servants. It would embarrass me to have servants . . . I don't think we *ought* to have them.'

Suddenly Elspeth spoke for the first time since Annette's father had come in. 'All we ever had was a woman who came in once a week to do the washing.'

'What's that got to do with it?' I said to her.

Elspeth replied: 'I was just telling you.'

Annette said: 'I'm not laying down a principle for other people. It's a personal choice that I shouldn't think of presuming to impose on other people.' She smiled. 'Though I should try to convince them of it if they came to me for advice.'

Her father said: '*Do* they come to you for advice?'

Robert said: 'Yes, that's a good question.'

Annette just went on smiling. The result of that round — Two Civil Servants *v.* Annette — seemed to me a draw.

Robert said: 'It's going to be increasingly difficult to get servants anyway. So I suppose Annette's views may be regarded as bringing her into line with the times.' He said it humorously but he sounded distinctly huffy all the same.

Annette's father said: 'I can only hope the times won't move too fast for me. I shall have to have some servants to look after me when Annette leaves me.' He helped himself to another piece of bread and butter, without marmalade.

Annette said nothing. Nor did anybody else.

In the social class to which I, like Elspeth, had been born, the question of whether one had a woman in to do the washing was decided by whether one had the money to pay her or not.

Annette and the others remained silent for a long time. I had a distinct feeling that a moral choice was floating over our heads.

Moral choices, I thought, are a pain in the neck.

## CHAPTER VI

## APPROACH TO BED

I SHOULD have prophesied that Annette and Robert would be married in a registry office and then live in a big house. They were married in church and then lived in a smallish flat.

The flat where Annette and Robert went to live was the one which had formerly been occupied by Annette's father. He had sold the house in Berkshire and set up in a big flat at the back of Gorringe's, where he employed two servants. Annette employed none.

Robert said to me: 'We've been rather fortunate, as a matter of fact. This arrangement will mean we shall have a good deal more money in hand for entertaining.' He paused.

'Who's going to do all the cooking and so on?' I asked, feeling very unimaginative.

'Annette will do some. And we shall get people in, professionals, to do the rest.'

I said: 'I see.' I thought I did see. I suspected that Annette and her father were turning out to be distinctly richer than I — or Robert — had thought. And why not? I liked the idea of big dinner-parties, and of anybody I knew being richer than we had thought. The bigger the better. The richer the better!

At this point I have to say that I was not getting any richer myself. As far as making a fortune out of my new novel was concerned, I was still trusting. I had written a book, the most original novel since the war, the probable progenitor of many others like it — I had Robert's word for

all this — and yet . . . Furthermore some people who were
so revered as to be paid for writing their opinion had said
it was masterly, and yet . . . A dent must have been made on
the public's mind: what about that dent on the public's
pocket?

My desires, my expectations, were modest. For instance,
I was not expecting the traffic in Piccadilly Circus to come
to a standstill. All I desired was that a fraction of the total
public, a small fraction — just a few tens of thousands of
them — should go into their booksellers, even into their Free
Public Lending Libraries, and utter the title of my work.
But how many had done? I have been advised not, for my
own sake, to tell you.

'I have kept your book out of your father's way,' my
mother wrote to me, 'but I have read it. Shall I send it back
to you?'

I judged from his silence that my literary agent must be
in America, even though it was the season of the year when
American publishers streamed over to London, looking for
books. One morning Harry joined me as I strode down
Putney Hill to the bus-stop.

'I was having a drink with your agent last night,' he said.
'He'd got an American publisher with him. I asked him
if he'd read your book. Nice chap. He said he had.'

'What did he think of it?'

'Actually he said it was the funniest book he'd read in
years.'

'Is he going to buy it?' I looked at Harry.

Harry shook his head. 'I'm afraid not. He said it was too
British.'

We went on walking.

I considered the verdict. I looked at it from many angles.
First angle: how could it be too British when I *was* British,
when all my forbears, as far back as any records went, had
been British? What did he *expect* it to be? Second angle: the
implication seemed to be that Americans would not under-

stand my book, would not understand what it was about. This puzzled me even more. Were Americans unable to comprehend the situation of a young man who sleeps with his girl and does not want to marry her? I should have thought not. Certainly I should have thought not, when I recalled the situation of some of the young Americans whom I had got to know in London during the war. Too British, indeed. I liked that! Third angle: no, two are enough. . . .

By the end of the summer I thought it was time to start writing another book. Another book? Yes, another book.

I went to Norway for a holiday, thinking that if I could bring a Norwegian scene into this new book, I could get my holiday expenses off income tax. While I was away I wrote a long letter to Elspeth. I was delighted with the result. She wrote a long letter back. She said she had an idea that she wanted to discuss with me when I got back. I have to admit that the first thought, the first, imbecile, groundless thought that crossed my mind was that it might be marriage.

We met in a public-house in Soho, near to a restaurant where I was going to take her for dinner. With the possibility in view of two having to live on the income of one, I was beginning to consider the Carlos a hasty choice of rendezvous. As Elspeth was a bit shy of going into a public-house by herself, I got there early. It was an unusually hot September evening, sultry and airless. The doors of the public-house were wide open, and the resident smell of spirits was tinged with a visiting aroma of garlic and French cigarettes. On the opposite corner of the street there was a collection of swarthy little men wearing black suits and shirts without ties: they seemed to be doing nothing, as if perhaps they might be dreaming blankly about the eastern shores of the Mediterranean; but I had been told they were engaged with the machinery of betting. They turned slowly to gaze in the direction of my pub. Elspeth came in.

She was wearing a thin summer frock, prettily draped over her small breasts, swirling out across her not so small pelvis.

'Goodness, you're sunburnt,' I said, and kissed her enthusiastically.

She laughed. 'So are you.' There were small dots of perspiration on her upper lip — apart from using lipstick, she appeared to be copying Annette in going without make-up.

'I'm glad you asked me out straight away,' she said, 'before my sunburn fades.'

'Didn't you think I should?'

For an instant she looked me in the eye, and then the corners of her mouth went up. 'How was I to know?'

'You might have,' I said humourlessly, in fact slightly shaken. Marriage, indeed!

We sat down at a table by the door and she said she would like to drink some iced lager. When she took off her short pair of white gloves I noticed the trace of dark gleaming down, all the way up her arms. I wondered how soon I could ask what her idea was.

We drank some lager and put the tall glasses on the table. A huge bluebottle made a buzzing circuit of them and went its way towards some sandwiches under a glass dome on the counter.

'I liked your letter,' I said.

'Yours was very funny,' she said. 'It nearly scared me off replying at all.'

'That's ridiculous,' I said. 'Now yours even incorporated suspense.'

She looked astonished.

'I'm dying to know,' I said, 'what the idea was you were going to talk to me about.'

To my surprise she blushed. 'Oh, it was nothing. I mean, it was only just an idea. *You* know . . . I mean, well, I wondered if it might be a good idea if I changed my digs. I'm always coming up to Putney nowadays, to see you, and Barbara . . .' She broke off, and then suddenly she said: 'After all, you never come down to the Green.'

'You mean you're going to come and live in Putney?' I cried.

'If you think it's a good idea . . .'

With an effort I said: 'I think it's a marvellous idea.'

Elspeth drank some more iced lager. The colour remained rosily in her cheeks.

A marvellous idea. Marvellous or menacing? It transpired that she had already found somewhere suitable and was only waiting to give her new landlady the word that she was ready to move in.

I told Robert about it first thing next morning.

He said: 'It's an encircling movement, old boy.'

'You only say that because you've been caught yourself!'

'I don't think so, you know. I see no evidence for that presumption.' He paused in a dignified way. 'I should have said it was entirely my own doing.' From dignity he passed to moral initiative. 'Anyway,' he said, 'you've been encircled before, haven't you, and got away with ease?'

I regarded this comment as unhelpful.

Robert looked at me. 'And anyway,' he said, 'I thought you wanted to be caught this time, don't you?'

'Yes. I mean, no,' I said. 'Yes. No.'

Robert shrugged his shoulders.

Was it yes, or was it no? Or both? I tried to forget about it. Elspeth came to live in digs in Putney, and the immediate results were happy to say the least of it.

'You reproached me with not coming down to the Green,' I said to her one evening when we were out for a stroll after dinner. 'But it's rather nice to be up on the Heath.' We had an arm round each other's waist.

'You should see Victoria Park on a summer's evening.'

I asked myself what that could mean.

I thought things over. From the beginning I had felt that Elspeth was going along the same lines as me. And what did those lines lead to? An act of will. An act of *my* will.

I decided to ask Elspeth to go to bed with me. No, do

not misunderstand me! Above all, do not misunderstand
me! I argued that going to bed with her would make my
act of will easier. Do you see? In a way, I should be half-
way there.

I recalled an event of my young manhood that must have
impressed itself on me. One of my friends, son of a high-
minded, free-thinking, upper middle-class family, had been
sent away for a week-end with his fiancée by his mother —
to make sure everything was all right before they married.
As I recalled it now, I thought how, in spite of everything,
I was a child of my time, of those far-off early 'thirties when
any reasonable couple made sure that everything was all
right before they married. I was comforted by the thought
of myself as a child of my time.

However, when it came to the point, I felt very nervous.
How I envied that chap who had his mother to organise it
for him!

I broached the subject with Elspeth one evening when we
were lying on the sofa together.

'I've been thinking about us,' I said, trying to make it
sound as if 'us' were spelt with a capital U.

She lay still, with her head resting on my arm.

'If we're thinking of going on . . .' Shades of girls who
had used that phrase to *me* when they meant getting married,
as I did now! 'I mean,' I said, 'if we're thinking of getting
married . . .' I practically had palpitation at using that
word.

'M'm,' said Elspeth, still lying very still.

'Well,' I said, 'don't you think perhaps we ought to make
sure everything's all right, first of all.'

I waited.

Quietly Elspeth turned her head and kissed my cheek.

'Do you?' I said, joyously, getting up to look at her.

She whispered something that I could not hear.

I swore to myself there and then that if everything was all
right I would let nothing stop me asking her to marry

me. I lay down again, putting my arms round her more tightly.

'When?'

She whispered: 'Not now . . . Not to-night.'

'Oh, no, no,' I said. 'We don't want to rush it. Perhaps you ought to come and stay here. At the week-end?'

I thought she nodded her head.

So I found myself with four days to wait. In four days I should be half-way towards having my act of will made for me.

The following Friday evening Elspeth arrived at my flat. I had made it look neat and pleasant, flowers in both rooms, clean sheets on the bed — it was a double bed — all kinds of drink in the cupboard. She was wearing a dress I had not seen before, dark blue with a light blue pattern on it. Her hair smelt delicious when I kissed her.

'I'm sure the hall-porter saw my case,' she said, as she opened it to take out her sponge bag and dressing-gown.

'I don't see that that matters.'

We went and had dinner in the somewhat indifferent restaurant in the basement of the building. I doubt if we noticed what we were eating.

At last we got to bed, hugging each other closely because the clean sheets felt cold. We kissed each other prolongedly.

I said: 'I'm a bit nervous.'

'So am I,' she whispered, though I thought that hardly mattered so much.

This went on for some time.

'I'm very nervous,' I said.

She whispered: 'Never mind . . .'

I began to get very worried. 'This is bad,' I said.

Elspeth hugged me and caressed me.

Everything was not all right. It was not all right at all. My act of will! I was not half-way towards it — I was making a grotesque progress in the opposite direction! What can I do now? I thought. If everything is *not* all right, there is no point in asking her to marry me, even if my will would stand up to it. I turned away from her and looked at the light of the bedside lamp shining on the ceiling.

I waited. No sign. No sign. . . . I saw my hopes crumbling, my dreams come to nothing, my life recurring in the same empty pattern for ever. I turned back to her and buried my face in the curve between her ear and her shoulder.

'I'm no use,' I cried. 'I'm no use to you.'

'*You must never say that again!*'

Her voice rang out resonantly, firmly. As my lips were against her throat I could feel the resonance through them. I was startled. I was more than startled.

Looking back on it now, I know exactly how I felt. I felt as if I had suddenly thought: Why, there's somebody *else* in bed with me!

Until this moment I had been so preoccupied with myself, or rather with my self, that I had not really thought of Elspeth as a separate, independent person at all. She was the person at the other end of *my* problem, only seen by me so far as she affected *me* . . .

With one fine resonant speech, Elspeth had ended all that. I had got somebody else in bed with me, a living, whole, human person. I was too startled even to say 'Good gracious!' I felt that it was the biggest surprise in my life.

Well, one of the things about a surprise or a shock is that it is said to take one out of one's self. I lay there with my face against Elspeth's throat. The vibration of this shock went on tingling in my lips.

After a few seconds, I really did say: 'Good gracious!' I felt the blood beginning to bump in my pulses. I had been taken right out of my self, without a doubt — I was a different man!

'Darling,' I said.

Elspeth took her hand away and turned *her* face into the curve between *my* ear and *my* shoulder.

'Darling!' I said. I could not even hear what she replied.

I moved over.

So there it was. Everything was more or less all right. Not the performance of a lifetime, I admit, but you can tell whether everything is all right or not. It was.

After we had had a rest I got out of bed and said:

'I suppose you could do with a nice cup of tea, now?'

Elspeth, deliciously pink in the face, looked up at me — I could not think why she seemed surprised.

The fact was that I was feeling as if I could do with a nice cup of tea myself.

## CHAPTER VII

## A DECISION AND A CELEBRATION

Yᴏᴜ may wonder if I immediately asked Elspeth to marry me. Well, no, as a matter of fact, I did not. I had sworn to myself that if everything were all right I would make my act of will. But then, I asked myself, could I say yet that everything was all right? I mean, definitely? One swallow did not make a summer, though I conceded that most people would think it meant they could reasonably look forward to a spell of warm weather.

Elspeth came to stay with me every week-end.

'I miss you in the middle of the week,' she said, 'darling.'

The discussion which followed was about which night of the week was more nearly equidistant from the week-ends.

The weather, in my metaphorical sense, was getting pretty warm; and had my act of will not been hanging over my head all the time, I should have basked in it without restraint. Even as it was, I basked quite a lot.

In our leisure moments, Elspeth and I indulged ourselves in true lovers' speculations and reflections. 'Wouldn't it be dreadful,' she said one day, 'if one of us didn't like it?'

'Dreadful,' I said.

Her imagination took a Gothic turn. 'Wouldn't it be dreadful,' she said, 'if one got married and then found the other person didn't like it?'

'Horrible,' I said impetuously. 'Appalling!'

And then I came to. Married. . . . Had somebody said something about getting married?

I realised that Elspeth now saw no reason whatever why we should not get married. This exemplified to me one of the characteristics that most markedly differentiated women from men. Confronted with the prospect of being tied, of being trapped for life, women showed neither reluctance nor caution. How different from men! I thought. Or, to be precise, how different from me! Women's nature seemed to make them ready for the trap. Men had to steel themselves to it. I felt that in my nature the steely element was . . . well not very steely.

One evening when Elspeth arrived, she said: 'I'm sure the hall-porter knows why I come here.'

This seemed probable. He never did much work, but he kept a very efficient eye on everyone who came in and out. I said: 'Oh.' We had agreed not to tell our friends — in particular we wanted to tease Harry by keeping it from him — but I did not see that it mattered if the porter knew.

'He says "Good evening" in a particularly insolent tone.'

I was surprised. He was a tall, lounging fellow, with a full-cheeked, oval face that made me think of a rabbit's. I had never had any trouble with him.

'I don't see what I can do about it,' I said. 'I can't very well tick him off.'

'No,' said Elspeth, thoughtfully.

I could, of course, put her in such a position that she did not have to suffer this kind of thing. But could I? Could I?

As the weeks passed I had found that I was getting no nearer to my act of will. Half-way there, I had told myself when I asked Elspeth to put our relationship on a somewhat marital footing. I was certain now that Elspeth was the one for me, and I must say she gave me little basis for arguing that I was not the one for her — on the contrary. So why could I not bring myself to the point of asking her to marry me? As I did not like putting the question to myself, I decided to try putting it to Robert.

I told Robert one dull wintry afternoon when we were coming out of the tea-shop after lunch. I felt it was a crucial occasion in my life, a day I should always remember: the only thing I can remember now, apart from what we said, is that a little way ahead of us on the pavement there was a woman in a red coat exactly the same shade as the pillar-box she was just passing. Robert said: 'Annette and I thought you probably were.' He looked at me affectionately. 'I'm glad. You've been looking much better these last few weeks.'

'Better?' I said. 'Was I looking worse before?'

'A more regular life seems to suit you.'

We walked in silence for a few moments, threading our way between people walking two or three abreast. Robert bought a newspaper. I was reflecting on the favourable effect on me of a regular life. Marriage was a regular life.

'The question is,' I said, 'what to do next?'

'Are you going to ask her to marry you?'

'What do you think?'

'You could do worse, much worse.' Robert glanced at me. 'Come to think of it, you *have* done in the past.'

'Considering that was on *your* advice, too,' I said, 'I——'

Robert said: 'I think Elspeth's a very nice girl. Very suitable.' He paused. 'You're very lucky.'

I laughed. 'You make it sound as if my deserts were a broken-down hag aged fifty!'

'I meant you're lucky in the sense that I'd say I was lucky to have found Annette.' A tone of strong feeling came into his voice. 'Someone odd enough to interest you, and equable enough to make you a good wife.'

Actually I did not think Elspeth was at all odd.

We came to Trafalgar Square and waited for the traffic lights to let us cross the road.

'Are you going to marry her?' Robert asked, as buses whizzed past the ends of our noses.

'That's what I can't make up my mind about.'

'Do you want to?'

'Yes. I suppose I do.'

'Then why don't you? I'm sure she'd marry you.'

The lights changed and the buses lined up their radiators across the road. We went in front of them and walked along the south side of the square, dodging the pigeons.

We came to the next road-crossing. Robert said:

'Of course there's the possibility that *she*'ll settle it by marrying *you*.'

'She's much too young and too shy.'

Robert laughed. 'I shouldn't rely on that.'

I was shocked by his cynical tone. He did not seem to realise that I was in love with Elspeth. I sincerely did think that — sweet girl! — she was too young and too shy.

This was a crossing without lights: we got safely as far as the island.

Robert said, on a different tack: 'Well, I suppose you can go on as you are.'

'Don't you see, that would mean I've fallen into my recurring pattern again?'

'I do see that.'

There was a lull in the buses and taxis. 'Come on, jump for it!' I said. We got to the other pavement. Though we had not discussed our objective, I judged that we must be making for the London Library. We went on walking in silence.

Suddenly, 'I really *will* marry her!' I said loudly.

'Good,' said Robert. 'I hope you will.'

We had to cross another road.

'I take it you're going to the London Library?' said Robert.

'I thought you were.'

'I hadn't thought of it.'

'Nor had I. Apart from thinking that's where you were going.'

'I'm perfectly willing to go, if you want to.'

'So am I, if you are.'

'Let's go, then!'

We crossed the road and continued on our way.

My will had hardened. I am not pretending it was steely yet, but somehow I felt sure that from this point I was not going to slip back any more.

I felt so sure that I stopped dead in the middle of the pavement, making Robert stop to look at me with the maximum attention, and said to him again:

'I really *will* marry her.'

This time his expression was quite different. 'Good!' he said, and his large grey eyes shone with pleasure and belief.

As we started to walk on again, he said: 'We ought to have a drink to-night.'

'To celebrate my decision?' I said, grinning.

Robert grinned too, but looked away in order to avoid answering my question. He said: 'Why don't you drop into the club late-ish to-night and join me for a drink? I shall be there with Annette's father and Harold Johnson.'

I recognised this instantly as a real treat for me. Sir Harold Johnson, another high civil servant, had only recently come Robert's way and had made the greatest of impressions upon him. As I gathered it from Robert, Annette's father and Sir Harold Johnson were, as far as exercising power in the outward direction went, among the top half-dozen or so men in the Service. As far as having influence in the inward direction, among those top half-dozen or so men themselves, Sir Harold Johnson had the edge over Annette's father, hands down. The fullness of time was going to bring Sir Harold Johnson to even greater boss-hood.

But this was not all. As far as Robert and I had observed, there was something in the opinion of the general public that senior civil servants, able and admirable though they might be in their jobs, were in their personalities not very exciting. But when it came to the highest bosses of all, public opinion had got it quite wrong. Among the highest of bosses, with Sir Harold Johnson as a case in point, personality could proliferate to a degree that, in the eyes of Robert and me, qualified as grand eccentricity.

To be allowed to meet Sir Harold Johnson was a great treat for me. 'Why not?' I said, enthusiastically.

Dutifully following Robert's instructions I entered our club at half past ten that night. I made my way through its Piazza San Marco, where there were a few cheerful, but comparatively quiescent members, drinking and chatting. From the doorway of the bar, however, came trumpeting, hallooing noises. I went into the bar.

In the semi-darkness I saw about three groups of noisy men. The noisiest, standing beside the bar itself, consisted of Robert, Annette's father, Sir Harold Johnson and a couple more members of the club. Robert waved to me as I came up. 'Come and join us, Joe!' He and Annette's father and Sir Harold Johnson and the other two men were happily and obviously drunk. They were hallooing with drink — at least Robert and Sir Harold Johnson were.

Robert said, with a don't-careish effort at formality: 'I don't think you've met Sir Harold Johnson.'

Sir Harold Johnson shook hands with me. He was a tall, strong man, like an ex-rowing Blue.

As I looked at him for the first time closely, I was reminded of another public misconception about high bosses in the Civil Service, i.e., that they all look as if they have come from Eton and Balliol. Annette's father did, as a matter of fact. Sir Harold Johnson, I saw, did not. Definitely not. His face, long-jawed with fleshy-lidded bright blue eyes, could not have sprung from one of our oldest families. Though one might have seen its characteristic expression at a racecourse — the expression, with lids momentarily half-dropped and mouth drawn knowingly down at the corners, of a man just about to take a trick — it would not have been *inside* the Royal Enclosure. I took to him immediately.

Robert had obviously taken to him. Handing me a large glass of port that I had never asked for, Robert looked at him and said to me:

'You ought to know he's read all our novels. In fact he's read practically *all* novels.'

I looked at Sir Harold Johnson, staggered, and remained standing beside him.

He looked at Robert steadily.

'Very remarkable, very remarkable,' said Robert, having some trouble with his r's.

I drank some of my port.

Robert glanced at everybody else's glasses and turned to the bar to order some refills.

Sir Harold Johnson now looked steadily at me.

'I'm not going to talk to you about novels,' he said. 'I've talked enough about novels this evening.'

I nodded my head.

'I'm interested in your job,' he said. He nodded his head in the direction of Robert. 'You chaps must have a very interesting job. People! Seeing people.'

I began to nod again.

Suddenly his eyelids half-dropped and his mouth drew down at the corners. 'Seeing them as ectomorphs and mesomorphs!'

Robert's voice came over my shoulder. 'It's all right — he's picked *that* up from Huxley's *Perennial Philosophy*!'

Sir Harold Johnson was watching me as if he were waiting to see if I knew he had got endomorphs up his sleeve. I said: 'Yes.'

'Well?'

Another nod was out of the question. I said: 'I think there's something in it.'

His eyes remained steady for a moment, and then a smile seemed to spread slowly round his long jaw. 'What do you think of this?' he said, and, looking up in the air, recited:

'Let me have men about me who are thin,
    Rough-headed men and such as wake o'nights.
Yond Cassius has a fat and well-fed look.
He thinks too much — such men are dangerous.'

Everyone standing round laughed.

Triumphantly Sir Harold Johnson finished his port and handed his glass to Robert for some more. He swayed.

Annette's father, on whom drink appeared to have had a silencing effect, proposed that we should all sit down. He and the others moved towards some chairs. Sir Harold Johnson stayed waiting for his next drink. Looking down at me, with the cheerful expression of a man who has just taken a trick, he said:

'Was that quotation up your street?'

I said it was.

He did not move. Robert handed another glass of port to him — and another to me. Sir Harold Johnson went on staring down at me. At last he said:

'You know what *you* want to do?'

I shook my head, waiting . . .

'Get rid of your inhibitions!'

## CHAPTER VIII

## A SILVER RUPEE

I DID not say anything to Elspeth immediately about getting married, but I felt that she must sense my new internal stability. We spent a most enjoyable week-end. I had told her I was going to tell Robert about us, and she asked me what he said.

'He was very pleased,' I said. 'He told me I was lucky . . .'

Elspeth said, out of the blue as far as I was concerned: '*I* told Joan.'

Joan was Elspeth's friend on the staff of her school. I said: 'And what did *she* say?'

'Oh, I think *she* seemed pleased . . .'

The following evening I did a thing that I very rarely did. Instead of walking straight up the hill from the bus-stop, I dropped in at a public-house for a drink on my own. The saloon bar was large but at that time of day it was likely to be deserted. I was prepared to see a workman chatting over a pint of beer with a barmaid, or a couple munching pork pie and potato salad, and to hear the wireless playing what sounded unremittingly like the Light Programme. I glanced round — and saw Harry. He was sitting at a small table, opposite a man who had his back to me.

'Joe!' he called, in his high sweet voice. 'Come and join us!'

I went.

'This is a surprise for you,' said Harry, as I got to the table and his companion turned towards me.

His companion was our hall-porter.

'You know Jamie Gordon,' Harry went on with cheerful

117

effrontery. 'Jamie used to be a lab-attendant at the first anatomy lab I ever attended.'

I looked at Gordon — I had not recognised him at first because he was not in his uniform.

'It's my day off, sir,' he said, grinning. In ordinary clothes he looked slightly less like a big cheeky rabbit, but that was not saying much.

I pulled up a chair to the table. I looked at Harry, and then at our hall-porter. So much for Elspeth and me trying to keep Harry from knowing what we were up to!

'I ran into Jamie,' Harry explained, 'just outside the pub.'

I did not know what I was expected to say to that.

The wireless said: 'This is the Light Programme,' as if it were necessary.

However, when Harry went to the bar to buy a round of drinks, I could have sworn he set up slightly less whirling disturbance in the air.

And when I stood up to leave after we had finished the drinks, he said: 'Come in and see us soon,' in a slightly lower voice than usual.

I could not help smiling. I had caught a glimpse in Harry's small, inquisitive, brown eyes of something I had rarely seen there before — shame.

The next day I told Robert about the incident. Robert had for some time shown a peculiar passion for hearing about Harry's manoeuvres — I could only suspect he was thinking of someone like Harry as a character for his next novel. On this occasion, however, Robert's passion seemed to be less. He scarcely waited for me to finish before he said:

'Did you know that Elspeth had been talking to Annette about her career?'

'No,' I said. 'And I don't see what help Annette could be, anyway.'

'The situation, old boy, is the other way about. Elspeth has been seeing fit to give Annette help, if that's what you choose to call it.' He paused. 'Elspeth has been asking Annette why she, Annette, doesn't become a teacher.'

'What sort of a teacher?'

'The same sort of teacher,' Robert said crossly, 'as she, Elspeth, is.'

You will remember the emotion with which I first perceived that Elspeth was a person who existed in her own right outside the bounds of my egocentric cosmos, that she was a living, whole, human person — and what a delightful one, at that! — separate, independent, and so on. . . . Well, it is one thing to perceive that the girl at the other end of one's problem is a living, whole, human person, separate, independent, and so on: it is another to contemplate her taking separate, independent action in one's friends' affairs.

Robert had been taking it as settled, now that Annette was married to him, that she would give up exercising moral choice over careers and occupy herself with social duties on his behalf. His projected series of grand dinner-parties, I was happy to note, had already begun. Elspeth and I had been to one of them — wonderful food from Fortnum's and the men all in dinner-jackets. (Annette, somewhat startlingly, had worn her wedding-dress.)

'What are you going to do about it?' I asked him.

Robert shrugged his shoulders. 'I don't know.' He looked away. 'I think perhaps you might have a word with Elspeth.'

I thought perhaps I should have to.

In general I was convinced that 'speaking' to people was liable to do more harm than good. In this particular case, it suddenly occurred to me after I had left Robert, it might also bring worse things to light. Suppose that in their state of admiring and envying each other, these two girls had *exchanged* suggestions — suppose that in return for Elspeth's suggesting Annette should become a school-teacher, Annette had suggested that Elspeth should take a degree in philosophy. I saw myself married to a wife who kept going out every evening to lectures at a Polytechnic. What a thought!

What a marriage! I decided not to 'speak' to Elspeth. Undesirable ideas are best left unwatered by discussion.

And so Elspeth and I came to Christmas, nearly a year since we first met. We were each going to spend the holiday with our families — should I ask her before or after? I had not made up my mind. It was to be one or the other, anyway. I was now so certain that I was going to marry her that I had been to my tailor's and ordered a new overcoat and new evening-clothes, on the grounds that if I did not get them before I was married, I should never be able to afford them after.

On the last evening before we went away, Elspeth came to stay at my flat. She was just thinking it was time to start cooking the dinner when, to our embarrassment, the doorbell rang. We straightened ourselves up and went to the door. It was Harry.

We were surprised. Since the occasion when I had found him drinking with Gordon, the hall-porter, Harry had kept out of my way. Elspeth had seen Barbara from time to time down at Bethnal Green, but we had not been invited to their house.

'Can I come in?' Harry said.

'Of course.'

Harry's face looked less pink than usual. 'I've got something for you,' he said nervously. 'I expected I'd find Elspeth here too.' He was carrying a parcel. 'Just some Christmas presents for you both.'

The presents were a bottle of whisky for me and a bottle of scent for Elspeth. It was the brand of whisky I liked best and the most chic and expensive kind of scent. Both Elspeth and I were touched.

'Let's open the whisky!' I cried.

Elspeth laughed at me. 'Let's open the scent!'

While Elspeth took the scent into my bedroom, I poured out some large drinks. Harry was satisfied. He sat down fatly on the sofa, his face as pink again as ever.

'Barbara was sorry she couldn't come,' he said. 'She's gone to listen to somebody giving a paper at the P.M.A.'

If I knew anything about it, Barbara had never been consulted. 'M'm,' I said.

Elspeth came in and we smelt the scent. 'I'll sit by you,' she said to Harry. He sprang up politely, and a whirling gust of air set up.

We started to drink. Harry, in high spirits now, seemed determined to show us how affectionate and uninquisitive he was. I have to say that he succeeded. You see, for the present he really was affectionate and uninquisitive.

We invited him to stay for supper. He accepted. We had a huge dish of eggs and bacon. By the time we were drinking our coffee our rapprochement was complete, in fact perfect.

In a gust of boundless, selfless, uninquisitive concern for our happiness, Harry said to us:

'*When are you two going to get married?*'

I saw Elspeth blush, and my confusion was so unbearable that I looked down at the table and could scarcely form an intelligible reply. In fact I cannot remember what I did reply. Somehow we managed to pass the hiatus over. But I swore to myself that I would ask Elspeth to marry me *immediately* I got back from the holiday. 'I really can't let that happen again,' I kept saying to myself, not only that night but every time during the following week at home when I remembered it.

Actually Harry, when he left us that night, said to me while he was putting on his overcoat:

'I'm glad you didn't take it amiss when I said that.' He wagged his globe-shaped head with boyish satisfaction. 'I thought I'd chance my arm.'

At home my mother, though occasionally permitting herself an oblique reference to 'your Elspeth', made it clear that nothing would persuade her — not that she had any need to fear persuasion from me — to mention my marrying

Elspeth. With my father I had no private discussions. His clerical duties, i.e. preparing his sermons, delivering them and visiting his parishioners, resulted, as always, in his being either *incommunicado* or not.

I had resolved to ask Elspeth to marry me immediately I got back. I did.

Elspeth came round to my flat on the evening of our return to London. I still kept remembering Harry's kindly, hopeful, selfless, uninquisitive question. . . . We were washing up after dinner, or rather Elspeth was washing up while I changed the living-room back from dining-room to sitting-room. We were conversing while Elspeth stood at the sink and I moved to and fro. The emotion I was feeling!

We were supposed to be talking about our plans for the week-end. Above the rattle of crockery in the sink, Elspeth was shouting to me:

'I think we ought to stay in, just by ourselves, this week-end.'

'I think,' I shouted back, 'we ought to get married as quickly as possible, don't you?'

'*What?*' Something splashed into the water. She sounded amazed.

I felt amazed.

I went into the kitchen — it was a very small kitchen. 'I think,' I said, 'we ought to get married as quickly as possible, don't you?'

She had turned from the sink to look at me. Her pale complexion was suffused with carmine, her sparkling blue eyes seemed to have gone smaller. Looking at me she saw the truth of my generalisation, that when somebody says something and you cannot believe your ears, they certainly have said it.

Her lips were moving, the lines at the corners of her mouth flashed in and out. 'Well, yes . . .' I rushed to embrace her.

There was a flap, which came down from a cupboard to

form a table, that served as an obstacle between the door and the sink. 'My darling!' I cried, putting one hand on her waist and rubbing my hip with the other.

We kissed each other.

'My darling!' 'My darling!' We kissed each other again. She was fumbling to take off her rubber washing-up gloves.

'Darling, I love you,' I cried. 'I want us to be married as quickly as possible.'

She looked at me. Tears were coming into her eyes.

'For ever,' I said.

'Oh yes, that's what I want, too . . .'

I lifted the flap so that we could get past. 'Let's go and sit down!'

She managed to get the gloves off and left them on top of the refrigerator.

We went and sat on the sofa and kissed each other many times. 'Isn't it wonderful?' I said.

Elspeth nodded her head.

'I love you,' I said.

She touched my lips with the tip of her middle finger.

'I do so want us to be married.'

'Yes . . .' she whispered.

After a while she looked down at her lap. 'But you didn't ask me,' she said.

'Didn't ask you what?'

'Well, if I'd marry you.'

'Oh dear! I wanted to come to the point as quickly as possible.'

She looked back at me. The corners of her mouth showed a fleeting grin.

'I thought,' I said, 'you *would* marry me . . .'

She was smiling.

'Didn't you think I'd marry *you*?' I asked.

She stopped smiling. 'Yes, I did to begin with, but I began to wonder . . .'

'But I always meant to.' I took hold of her hand.

'Darling.'

This kind of conversation went on for some time, but gradually it became less romantic and more practical. I wanted to settle where and when we were to get married. I wanted to be married by a registrar.

'The alternative,' I said, 'if we were to be married in a church, would be to be married by my father. We should have to tell him, and he'd volunteer to do it. I really couldn't face that.'

Both Elspeth and I were unbelievers. If we asked my father to marry us, I knew he would conclude that somewhere in us lay the seed of belief. I did not like the idea of unbelievers taking advantage of believers any more than I liked the idea of believers taking advantage of unbelievers.

'At a registry office,' I said, squeezing Elspeth's hand, 'we can get married sooner.'

Elspeth squeezed my hand in return.

In the end we decided to get married at a registry office without telling anyone but the witnesses. An exciting, romantic atmosphere came back into the conversation. (Perhaps I ought to say that in our romantic excitement we innocently overlooked the construction that some people — I will not say what sort of people — put on marriages that take place in a hurry.)

Next morning I set about making arrangements to marry Elspeth. I had some surprises. When I asked the registrar how soon we could get married, I learnt that for £3 6s. 9d. I could get married in two days' time.

And then I took Elspeth to buy a wedding ring. Robert and I had a habit of looking in the windows of jewellers' shops. (I thought we were odd until I did a day's count of the relative numbers of men and women who were doing the same as us.) Robert had a particular taste for sapphires. I chose diamonds that were not pure white, especially pinkish ones. The rings we were used to staring at often cost thousands of pounds, though of course I knew there were presentable rings to be had for hundreds or even tens of pounds. I had no idea that wedding rings were to be had for units of pounds.

'It's incredible,' I said to Robert, 'you can get married in no time at all, for next to no money!'

'Society sees to it that getting married is made easy.'

'I'll say it does.' We used to entertain ourselves with the concept of The Pressure of Society. As far as getting married was concerned, it seemed to me now that you had only got to make the smallest first move, and the pressure of society rushed you through the next before you knew what you were doing. No wonder some bridegrooms looked white as a sheet on their wedding-day — finding themselves at the ceremony perhaps a good six months, perhaps a good six years, before they meant to.

Four days later Elspeth and I got married. I did not look specially white in the face nor did Elspeth. But Robert and Annette did.

Elspeth and I arrived at the registry office about ten minutes late, because we had begun our preparations by spending too long over titivating my flat for the reception. It was decorated with large branches of mimosa which we had been keeping cool in the bathroom till the last moment. There was a bottle of champagne and a luscious cake from a French shop in Soho. The guests, our witnesses, were Robert, Annette and Elspeth's schoolteacher friend, Joan.

Anyway, we arrived at the registry office, and there in the waiting-room we found Robert, Annette and Joan. I had never seen Joan before, and expecting her to be the plain partner in the alliance, was surprised to find her quite as pretty as Elspeth. We were ten minutes late. Annette looked pale. Robert looked chalky.

The ceremony seemed to be over in no time, and Elspeth and I were delighted with the result. The thin gold ring was on her finger — never, on any account, to be taken off, I told her. We got into a taxi and embraced each other all the way home. Married! Married for good! I got out of the taxi first, and while I was paying the driver saw Elspeth pause, before she got out, to pick something off the floor.

'Look what I've found!' she cried, holding out her palm for me to see what was in it.

It was a small coin, silver, stamped 1 *Rupee*.

The taxi drove away leaving us standing there, smiling with delight. It was an omen. It was too fantastic to be anything but an omen.

'Darling, keep it!'

'Of course I shall,' Elspeth said, putting it in her bag.

Hand in hand we went quickly to the lift, so as to get up to the flat before the others arrived. When we opened the door the smell of the mimosa was overpowering.

The reception was a success. The guests ate some of the cake and drank all the champagne, and then did not go away. It is difficult to know what to drink after champagne at five in the afternoon, if your host has not got more champagne: they all said they would like some tea. I did not hurry them, I was so happy. I was triumphant, if it comes to that. They had all said I could not get married, but I could. I had done it.

Suddenly, looking at Robert, I realised why he had looked chalky. When we were ten minutes late he must have thought I was not going to turn up. Silly fellow!

As soon as they were gone, Elspeth carried the telephone into the room and we began sending telegrams to our families and ringing up our friends. While Elspeth was talking on the telephone, I was drafting the notice of marriage for *The Times* and the *Daily Telegraph*. I felt in this case it ought to appear surrounded by a special border like that on a greetings telegram. Or possibly just encircled by a wreath of laurels. They had said that I could not get married, that I had missed the boat. Not a bit of it. I was on the boat. I looked at Elspeth. What a boat! My boat. . . .

Elspeth was ringing Harry and Barbara.

'It's Barbara,' she said, handing the receiver to me. 'She wants to congratulate you.'

'Well she may!' I whispered to Elspeth. Then I said: 'Hello, Barbara. What do you think of the news? Isn't it wonderful.'

'It really is. Congratulations, Joe.'

'I've pulled it off. What do you think of that?'

'Splendid,' she said.

'I've got married after all.'

At that I heard Barbara laugh. 'Yes, you have, Joe,' she said. 'But you have to remember *getting* married is very different from *being* married.'

'What!' I cried. And then added: 'Well, of course it is. I can see that all right.'

'You have my congratulations, all the same,' she said.

I handed the receiver back to Elspeth. 'It's your turn to talk to her now,' I said with my hand over the mouthpiece.

I did not listen to what Elspeth was saying to her. Of course there was a difference between *getting* married and *being* married. Or was there? What the hell did Barbara mean?

PART III

# CHAPTER I

## NEWLY-WED

WE AWOKE next morning before the alarm went off, and I stretched out to find the catch on top of the clock which prevented the bell from ringing. There was scarcely any light coming through the gap in the curtains. The air in the room seemed close and scented. I rolled quietly back into my place.

Elspeth was stirring. As it were in sleep, her hand came on to my waist and her breasts brushed across my chest. I kissed her on the eyelids.

'Darling,' she murmured.

'My wife.'

She stretched a little, away from me, and then came back. 'I feel so sleepy. . . .'

I whispered 'So do I', more not to disturb the warm drowsy atmosphere than to express the whole truth. In one way I felt sleepy: in another I was obviously not. Our first morning married. My thoughts drifted round the idea for a few moments, and then began to circle round another idea. I put my hand on the small of her back and pressed.

Everything was so quiet that I could hear the clock ticking. We stayed for a while, just touching each other. I kissed her again.

'I feel so sleepy,' she murmured in a different way.

I whispered: 'I'll go very, very gently. So that it won't wake you up.'

I felt her kiss my shoulder.

With Elspeth lying drowsily, I acted according to my stated intention; but of course the fallacy in it began to assert itself, and soon she could no longer seem to be asleep. As I did not suppose either of us had ever thought she could, I was not specially conscience-stricken — after all, what nicer way was there, I asked myself on her behalf, of coming awake.

In due course we both came fully awake. Our first morning married. . . . I had time now to consider it at leisure. When I thought I must be getting a bit heavy, I raised myself on my elbows and looked at Elspeth. She smiled at me. Her dark hair was strewn across her forehead and I caught a glimmer of light from her eyes. I thought of a quotation, something about on such a morning it being bliss to be alive, and kissed her enthusiastically under the chin from one ear to the other. Having read physics at Oxford and not English Literature, I was never able to lay my hands quickly and accurately on quotations; yet I never felt it held me back.

'Goodness, it's warm in here,' I said, pushing off the bed-clothes. I switched the light on.

Elspeth said: 'We forgot to take the flowers out of the room last night.'

This explained why the air smelt so scented to me when I woke up. I smelt it now. 'A good job, too,' I said.

Elspeth laughed and put her arm round my neck. 'I don't mind, darling,' she said. 'You can't be having baths all the time.'

All the time. I made no comment on the implications of that. 'Just think!' I said, looking into her eyes, 'you're here to stay. . . .'

Although I was looking into her eyes, I noticed she was yawning.

I exclaimed.

Elspeth blushed. 'It wasn't a yawn, really.'

'I'd like to know what else it was.'

She glanced away with an expression so melting, as if I had touched some secret she was keeping, that I kissed her again.

After that I said: 'Now I really must get up and have a bath. Do you realise what time it is?'

Though it was our first morning married, we had both got to go to work as usual. The alarm clock, with its bell put out of action, had given a frustrated click a quarter of an hour ago. I jumped out of bed, gave Elspeth a parting slap, and went to the bathroom. We were already late.

I was late getting to the office. I sent for Froggatt, in order to put the news of my changed status into the official grapevine. To my mind it was worthy of an office notice, being much more piquant than the records of transfer and promotion which formed the typical content of Froggatt's communications. Anyway, *I* was transferred, *I* was promoted. Transferred to respectability, promoted to the ranks of decent ordinary men. Married!

Froggatt looked at me with his drooping, bloodhound eyes and permitted his long face a momentary gleam of amusement.

'May I be the first person here to congratulate you?' he said, in the musical lugubrious tone wherein he combined to perfection that mixture of superficial deference and underlying opposite which characterises the Executive Class.

'You may,' I said. I was delighted to see his feeling for his status — 'the first person here' — peeping through his genuine congratulation. 'Thank you.'

'I take it you'll inform Accounts.'

'Accounts,' I said.

'You'll have a different code number for tax purposes now,' he said. 'As I'm sure you know.'

I tried to look as if I did know.

'In fact you'll get a rebate for the whole of the present tax-year, won't you? As from last April.'

I had often been irritated by Froggatt's getting at loggerheads with the inhabitants of the snake-pit, but at moments such as this I forgave him. This kind of support was just what an S.E.O. was for.

'If you like,' he said, 'I'll notify Accounts. Then they can get in touch with you.'

'Excellent.' In the past Accounts' getting into touch with me had usually meant they were going to try and disallow the taxi-fares on my claims for travel expenses.

When Froggatt had gone, I reflected on how my absence of interest in money had been shown up. Robert was always telling me that I did not think enough about money; and for Robert to tell was for Robert to reproach. Apropos income tax, I did know that the possibility of claiming a full year's rebate brought the national marriage rate to its peak in March, but I had never thought of taking advantage of it myself.

I felt deflated, even chastened. I saw that one of my many moral defects was now going to have greater significance. I liked money very much when it came to me. The trouble was that I never thought hard about how to make it come to me. With a wife to keep I had clearly got to think about how to make it come to me. How many times as cheaply could two live as one? I asked myself. Just under half was my estimate.

I rang up Accounts instead of waiting for them to ring me. After that I deliberately sat for five minutes trying to think hard about money. I wished it did not happen to be the day when Robert had seen fit to stay at home to correct the proofs of his new novel, because I could have done with his advice, despite its reproachful tone, on how to make money come to me. I reflected on the hastiness with which I had persuaded Elspeth to give up being a schoolteacher, not that she needed much persuasion or that I felt the least inclined to change my mind. I wanted no more of being roused by an alarm clock so that she could set out for Bethnal Green; and I wanted to come home in the evening certain of finding her there already, possibly already cooking something delicious for dinner. You may think it had not taken me long to accept the decent, ordinary man's idea of married life. That is what I thought.

It was clear to me that as a civil servant I could never make money come to me. Robert and I used to comment with surprise on the fact that we had never been offered any bribes, even during the war when we had in our gift, so to speak, civilian jobs for people who were liable for military service. The nearest we came to it was when Air Marshals came to see us about jobs for their sons which would, in the national interest of course, keep the boys away from flying. What was the bribe there? The mateyness of an Air Marshal's manner, the glances, as between equals, from his glaring *beaux yeux*. Not, as Robert would say, a bribe and a half, that.

I supposed there was promotion to be thought of. With Murray-Hamilton and Spinks in the saddle, not, as Eliza Doolittle said, likely. Anyway, I could not be promoted without doing a different job.

Which left me with my art as a source of money. I thought of the excellent press my last novel had got; and then I thought of my publisher's most recent half-yearly statement of royalties. Robert still insisted that the book was a minor masterpiece. My publisher's half-yearly statement of royalties insisted on a minor balance. Of course I consoled myself again with the fact that it is masterpieces, minor or not, that last. The difficulty, as I saw it now, was how was *I* to last? I was nearly at the end of another novel, in the same vein as the previous one. I was pretty happy about it. I had written just what I wanted to write, and I had hit off exactly what I wanted to say — that, in case anybody would like to know, is how original works are written. Robert had identified it as yet another minor masterpiece.

Now, what was to be done? I had been told often enough. I had plenty of friends who were willing to tell me, friends who were in a position, were I to do what they told me, to help produce the result I desired. By that I mean friends in the film industry and the magazine industry. They admired my talent. While having to say that my minor masterpieces were not the slightest use to them, they had not the slightest doubt that I had the talent to provide just what they were looking for. Now you see what I am getting at. What I was required to write was not just what *I* wanted to write, but just what *they* wanted me to write. In other words, crude words, I was required to prostitute my art.

With only the slightest change in tone, in attitude, in subject, I could provide just what was wanted — so ran the argument. With only the slightest change, I could be a prostitute. I was not surprised by the argument, since one of the underlying themes of women's magazine stories, and obviously one of the dearest themes to their readers, was that all women, with only the slightest change, could be prostitutes. Let them try it! was all I could say, speaking as their artistic counterpart.

Speaking as their artistic counterpart, I can only say I believe it is nothing like as easy as it sounds to prostitute oneself. One has to have the talent for it, and if one is born without that talent, one had better stick, so to speak, to monogamy. One's talent, be it for communicating truth or untruth, is nothing like so flexible as people think. I could not decide which people struck me as the more unrealistic, writers who were not born with the talent for pleasing all men planning to write best-sellers, or writers of best-sellers planning to go somewhere, such as a purifying island in the South Seas, to write a serious work of art. If only one could be born all things! I thought. I knew it was no use my setting out to prostitute my talent because my talent would not stretch that far. No, I repeat, it is not as easy to be a prostitute as everyone thinks. In fact, it is jolly difficult. When I saw those girls on the streets, I took off my hat to them. They were doing something I could not do.

My meditations on how to make money come to me were at an end. Robert was wrong in thinking I was incapable of thinking hard enough about it. What I was incapable of, to my regret, was thinking on the right lines. I felt very discouraged. I pressed the bell for my P.A. to bring in my morning's work. While I was waiting for her to come, I wrote on my scribbling pad: 'Go to bank.'

I needed some cash with which to take Harry and Barbara out to dinner. We had invited them earlier in the week, without telling them that by then we should be married. Our reasons were sentiment. We could never forget that it was under their roof that we had met for the first time — tenderest recollections moved us, of dancing at their New Year's Eve Party, of 'The Dark Town Strutters' Ball' in which I hauled Elspeth up from the floor and first looked into her eyes — 'This is the one for me!' And then later, supreme cause for our gratitude, Harry's crucial question, asked out of selfless, uninquisitive affection for us: '*When are you two going to get married?*' There was no argument between Elspeth and me about whom we should take out to dinner on our first day married. Thank goodness for Harry and Barbara! was how we expressed our feelings towards them in anticipation of seeing them.

It happened that before they arrived, Elspeth and I expressed our feelings towards each other. We mixed ourselves some martinis and then set about bathing and changing — a procedure fraught with the likelihood of expressing marital feeling. I was standing in my vest and shorts, getting a clean shirt out of a drawer, when Elspeth came from the bathroom, holding a towel in front of her. The towel gave her a delightful air of modesty and unconcern.

'That looks nice,' I said as she went past.

She pretended not to hear.

'It would be wonderful just to see a bit more,' I said, and kissed her on the shoulder.

She turned to look at me. Without make-up her complexion had a glossy sheen: there were damp curls of hair on her temples.

'Darling!' I put my arms round her.

'The towel's damp.'

137

I took it away.

Her cheeks went pink. 'Darling, you know what time it is?'

'Indeed I do.'

I pushed her quietly backwards to the bed. 'You're wonderful!' I whispered, leaning over her.

'Harry and Barbara'll be at the door at any moment.'

'I'm practically at it, now.'

'Darling!'

We had to be quick. At any moment the doorbell might ring and we could not pretend we were out. I began to sweat. A race against time. A race against time.

We won it.

'Oh!' I said.

Elspeth was quiet.

'Well . . .' I murmured. For a few moments we were both quiet.

I glanced at Elspeth — just at the moment to catch her yawning.

We burst into laughter.

'Good Heavens! Just look at the time!' On the chest of drawers I saw the remainder of the drink I had been carrying round with me while I got dressed. I drank it. I handed Elspeth hers and she sat up and drank it. We kissed each other; and then we began to rush into our clothes.

'They'll be here any minute.'

We saw each other in a mirror, looking pink in the face. I was knotting my tie.

The doorbell rang.

'There they are.' I put on my jacket, kissed Elspeth's bare arm, and ran to let in Barbara and Harry.

Harry and Barbara stared at me briefly: I suppose I stared briefly at them — after all, there was no reason why I should not. 'Come in!' I cried. 'You wonderful pair. . . .' I was still thinking Thank goodness for Harry and Barbara! I kissed

Barbara on the cheek and shook Harry's hand. They followed me into the living-room. They congratulated me again on my new status.

I was just pouring some drinks for them when Elspeth came in. All three of us now stared briefly at her. She looked sparkling — in my eyes her whole outline seemed to shimmer — and the moment I caught her glance I knew that our expression of marital feeling, in combination with a couple of martinis, had produced one of those bursts of hilarity-cum-elation that are impossible to hide.

'I'm afraid we've had a drink already,' I said, as I handed glasses to Harry and Barbara.

'So I see,' said Barbara with a smile.

Elspeth came and stood beside me and I felt her elbow brush against mine. Barbara saw it and went on smiling. There was nothing wrong with Barbara's smile, and yet somehow it contrasted with Elspeth's and mine. I looked at Harry, to see how he was reacting.

'Is that some of your new manuscript?' he said, with an artlessly innocent glance sideways at a sheaf of papers on the table.

'Yes,' I said.

Harry turned his head to look at it steadily and longingly. He was wearing a new very dark grey suit, and his great girth, encased in almost black and momentarily unrotating, seemed to have a faintly sinister quality that was missing when it was light and on the move.

'Yes,' I repeated, in a disinterested tone. 'That's the first draft of Part I.'

Harry waited. He waited for me to ask him if he would like to read it. I let him go on waiting. I had no intention of letting him read a word of it before publication.

'You do work hard,' said Barbara.

'Have to,' I said. 'If I don't work, I don't eat.'

Barbara finished her martini. Smiling, she handed me her glass.

'I suppose now I'm married,' I said, 'I can still go on eating if Elspeth works — happy thought. . . .'

'Is Elspeth going to go on working?'

Though my back was turned to her, I could tell this must be a key question in Barbara's catechism — I recognised the 'I-know-you-better-than-you-know-yourself' sort of tone. I swished the stirring rod vigorously in the jug so that the ice cubes clinked and clattered.

I turned back with Barbara's drink. With her left hand she was fingering her big topaz and diamond brooch. With her handsome topaz-and-diamond-coloured eyes she was giving Elspeth a look of friendly interest. As she took the drink from me she switched the look to me.

'I'm delighted that you've got married,' she began, 'and I hope you'll both be very happy — I'm sure you will — but I'm still not sure I quite understand. . . . Tell me, Joe, what did you get married *for*?'

I gave the contents of the jug a splendid swish and said: 'Whadda ya think?'

Barbara's expression did not change. On the other hand, Harry's did. I just happened to notice him give her an odd glance — he looked momentarily hunted . . . I thought I knew why. I guessed it. My answer did not go for his marriage. Poor old Harry!

Barbara tasted her drink. 'You've made this very dry.'

'You've got to catch up with us.' I glanced at Elspeth's complexion, which was now radiantly pink.

Barbara laughed. 'I doubt if we shall!'

We took them to a restaurant where we could dance. Elspeth and I danced together.

'I'm afraid we're in disgrace,' I said. 'They're rather cross with us.'

Elspeth giggled.

'I know we've not behaved in good taste, but between friends it oughtn't to matter. Look at the times when we've called on Robert and Annette, and they'd practically only just——'

Elspeth giggled again.

I went on — 'And we didn't take umbrage like this.' I thought about Robert and Annette. 'In fact I envied them. I wished it were us.'

Elspeth rubbed her cheek against mine. 'Never mind, darling, *I* don't think you've done the wrong thing.'

I laughed and looked at her. 'With a bit of luck I'll do it again before the night's out.'

Elspeth moved slightly away from me. 'Oh no . . .!'

'Poor old Harry and Barbara,' I said.

'"Tell me, Joe,"' said Elspeth, '"what did you get married *for*?"'

The music stopped and we returned to our places. I ordered another round of brandies. I was beginning to feel tired, and I noticed that shadows were beginning to appear under Elspeth's eyes. Harry and Barbara did not look tired.

Elspeth and Barbara began to talk to each other, and Harry talked to me. First of all he gave me a quick, bright glance, and then said:

'You must be thinking about your future, now.'

His baggy eyes were sparkling, I thought, as if he were in possession of some peculiarly private information. Looking inordinately shrewd, he said: 'Your long-term future.'

'Oh, I suppose you mean children . . .'

Harry grinned. 'I think some of your father's congregation think you've thought of that *already*. . . . So your mother tells me.'

'Really!' I said. 'Oh, oh, oh!'

Harry said, slightly unconcernedly now: 'I meant you must be deciding whether you're going to stay on with Robert or not.'

Just to lead him on, I said: 'Yes.'

Harry looked away, diffidently. I waited. He looked back. 'Are you going to move away?'

I said: 'I don't think so.'

Harry drank some brandy. I noticed that Elspeth and Barbara seemed to be getting on very well together. I said to Harry:

'Why do you ask?'

'I was just wondering.' He paused. 'It must be very difficult for you.'

'Why difficult?'

'Difficult to see what there is for you, if you stay on.'

I was just on the point of drinking some more brandy myself. I halted, angrily. And then I saw that Harry's expression was unreservedly friendly and thoughtful.

I did not reply. How in God's name, I asked myself, did he know about my relations with Murray-Hamilton and Spinks? Had he managed to get to know Spinks? And if he had heard something about my future, what?

Harry was waiting for me to comment. I said:

'As long as Robert stays on, everything remains static, and that suits me.'

'And if he goes?'

I did not say anything.

Harry nodded his head as if I had.

I glanced at Elspeth. My wife — another mouth to feed in the future. And children, we were hoping to have children. In the long-term future more and more mouths to feed. That was what the phrase long-term future meant to me.

Harry looked at me. 'Anyway, you've got plenty of friends to make useful suggestions.'

I was touched.

At that moment the band stopped. Harry looked at Barbara, and said it was time for them to go home.

Our celebratory party was at an end. At the last moment, when we saw them into a taxi, there was a recrudescence of our sentimental regard for them. Thank goodness for Harry and Barbara! A little later, when we called a taxi for ourselves, we suddenly felt the evening had been a success.

'Goodness, I'm tired,' said Elspeth, leaning her head on my shoulder.

'So am I.'

She giggled. 'I'm a bit drunk, too.'

We embraced.

'What a pity,' I said, thoughtfully. 'Too tired and too drunk. . . .'

Elspeth laughed.

When we got home we went straight to bed. We lay in each other's arms. My faintly regretful mood persisted. 'Too tired and too drunk. . . .'

'We'd better go to sleep,' Elspeth murmured.

I waited a little while and then I whispered: 'I don't think I *am* too tired and too drunk. . . .'

'I know. . . .'

My regretful mood dispersed in no time. 'Darling!' I said.

I was not too tired and too drunk. I was just at the point when fatigue and the effects of alcohol counterbalance each other in such a way that one can go on and on, as it seems, indefinitely. There is a tide in the affairs of a man, I kept thinking as I went on and on, which, if taken at just the right point, like this, leads to a remarkable fortune. I felt uplifted by it, exalted. I got more than a bit above myself.

'This,' I said to Elspeth, 'this, this is what I married you for.'

'Oh,' she said. 'Oh.'

At last, at long last, I had opportunity to think over what I had said. I felt that I had taken advantage of Elspeth's ignorance about the tide in the affairs of a man. And not a bad thing, at that, I decided.

Elspeth was asleep.

## CHAPTER II

## OIL-CLOTH ON THE TABLES

A<small>T THE</small> beginning of March I thought Robert was looking more pre-occupied than usual. It was always on the cards that Robert's looking pre-occupied in my presence was the result of further sniping from Spinks and Murray-Hamilton, but this time I judged that it could not be so. During the last few weeks I had not been to a meeting of any kind and had conducted no interviews.

Often when Robert was troubled by something he was provoked to confide it through being stirred by something else. In this case I happened to stir him by reporting a conversation between Elspeth and me. It was a conversation I thought Robert ought to know about. It had taken place the previous Sunday morning.

Elspeth and I had had an enjoyable breakfast in bed. We were lying side by side. I was thinking that I ought to be reading the Sunday newspapers. Elspeth yawned.

I raised myself on one elbow to look at her.

'Tired?' I said.

A look of amusement shone in her eyes.

'What?' I asked.

'You've got black circles.'

'They'll go when I get up.' I smiled at her.

'What are you smiling about?'

'I was just remembering the first book about Married Life that I managed to get hold of when I was a boy. It said one of the most important problems that faced a newly married couple was: "How often?"' I laughed.

Elspeth laughed.

'Ridiculous,' I said.

'M'm,' said Elspeth.

I went on laughing. 'As if you arrive at that sort of thing by argument!'

Elspeth went on laughing.

Then she said: 'How often did it say?'

I was still laughing till that moment.

'How often did it say?' she said again.

'I don't remember. I don't think it said. It couldn't, anyway.'

'Oh.' Elspeth looked up at the ceiling. 'I read something like that that did say. You know, what a bride ought to expect . . .'

'Good gracious!' I was so surprised as to be gormless enough to add: 'How many was it?'

Elspeth said: 'Once a night for the first year, twice for the first six months, and three times a night for . . . you know, just the beginning.'

'Oh! Oh!' I cried.

'What's the matter?'

'What's the matter? Why, it's mad. *What* a programme! It'd be killing!'

Elspeth was silent.

I looked at her. 'Is this what you were expecting from *me*?'

Elspeth blushed.

'Oh!' I cried again, and lay down.

Then I said: 'You must have read it in a woman's magazine.'

Elspeth said: 'I don't think I did . . .'

'Well, it must have been written by a woman. No man could possibly have written it.'

Elspeth had nothing to say.

For a little while I too had nothing to say.

I jumped out of bed. 'I know how to settle this.'

'What are you going to do?' Elspeth asked suspiciously.

'Look it up.'

'You can't,' I heard Elspeth saying, as I went to a book-shelf in the living-room. I took down a book which was the record of a statistical enquiry that had recently been pub-lished and that, at the time, was being much talked about. *Sexual Behaviour in the Adult Human Male.* To my mind it was a pretty satisfactory enquiry, since it disclosed principles that had always been obvious to me, namely that people's range of possible sexual behaviour was much wider than it was officially supposed to be, and that people did not do what they publicly said they did. I furled over the pages now for an equally truthful disclosure of detail.

'Here it is,' I said, taking it to show Elspeth. 'Total out-let, active population — age forty, that's me; average 2.3 times per week.' I was delighted with the information: I even felt I might claim a small pat on the back. I repeated loudly: '2.3 times a week!'

Elspeth looked nettled, and tried not to see the graph at which I was pointing.

'Now, let's see,' I went on. 'Robert's forty-five. 1.8. Think of that! Poor Annette. . . . Just think of one point eight per week!'

'I'm not going to,' said Elspeth. 'And I think you ought to stop thinking about it.'

I was sitting on the bed beside her, with the book in my lap. She raised herself and turned over a wad of pages before I could stop her.

'Thought-control,' I said.

She was not listening. She had caught sight of what was on the new page. 'I don't remember this bit,' she said, in a tone that was different.

'Two point three,' I said, slipping my arm round her back.

She pretended not to hear me. My attention was caught by the lobe of her ear, peeping between two dark curls. The hand with which she was holding the book was touching me.

Of course, deliberately, I only reported to Robert the first part of the conversation to begin with, up to 'once a night for the first year, twice for the first six months, and three times at the beginning'.

'Good God,' he said.

He was standing between the top corner of my desk and the window, where the leads from my telephone and buzzer dropped to the skirting.

'I thought you ought to know,' I said. 'I didn't want you to be living in a fool's paradise.'

'That's the most daunting piece of news I've heard for a long time,' he said, and moved heavily towards my easy chair, catching his feet in the wires and bringing the telephone and buzzer crashing to the floor. I picked them up and stood by the window while he sat down. I let him suffer for a little while.

'Extraordinarily daunting,' he muttered. And then: 'What did you say?'

'Oh,' I said, putting on the tone of loftiness and confidence in which he normally addressed me, 'I saw my way through it quite rapidly.'

'What did you do?' he asked, for once in the tone in which I normally addressed him.

'I checked it in the standard work of reference.'

'What in God's name is that?'

I went on with the account of my conversation with Elspeth. Robert agreed with me that it must have been written by a woman. 'Or a man who ought to be a woman,' he said, impatiently waiting for me to come to the figures.

I watched him when I came to the 1.8. Instantly his eyes flickered with a recognisable glint, secretive, prudish and triumphant.

I laughed without saying anything.

Robert laughed without saying anything.

We were both silent for a while. Our laughter died away, as did our feeling of being daunted. It was at this moment that Robert's mood changed over unpredictably. He suddenly came out with what had been troubling him.

'Annette's going on with this idea of taking Elspeth's job when Elspeth gives it up.'

I stared at him. Elspeth had been keeping it dark from me.

'You poor old thing,' I said.

Robert shook his head gloomily. 'It's a moral choice,' he said. 'She sees it as a moral choice.'

'You poor old thing,' I repeated.

When I got home that evening, I reproached Elspeth. She said:

'I did tell you once and it upset you. Anyway, nothing very much has happened. I shall have to finish out my term's notice — we couldn't work an exchange in the middle of term. Whether Annette will get my job isn't decided.' Elspeth paused. 'She still wants it. She's been going ahead to try to get it.'

I asked how far she had gone ahead.

'She's got on to the L.C.C. about it, and she's having an interview with the headmistress. There's a terrific shortage. They'll let her come "on supply", if not as a permanent member of the staff. She's having her interview with the headmistress next week.'

I decided to talk to Annette.

Elspeth arranged a meeting that she considered would look un-arranged. Sometimes when I had a light afternoon at the office I left early and met Elspeth out of school. I met her the afternoon Annette had an interview with the headmistress.

I arrived at the school gates just before Elspeth and Annette came out. It was a cold blustery afternoon with patches of icy drizzle carried in the wind. The darkness of the sky made the hour of the day seem later than it was. A few yards further down the road stood a man in white overalls holding a pole with a circular sign on top of it to stop the traffic while children crossed the road. The children, as far as I could see, were well-fed and warmly dressed; and the prams that some of their mothers were pushing looked as new and grand as anything one saw in Hyde Park.

Suddenly a burst of emotion took me unawares. The impetus to make the change from what I remembered from my boyhood, when my father worked in a working-class place where underfed mothers pushed their babies about in little carts made from orange-boxes mounted on broken wire-spoked wheels, had come from Socialists: and I *was* a Socialist. I had always felt that I was a Socialist by birth, by social origin. My burst of emotion — I may say it was as unusual to me as it was unexpected — came from feeling that I was *right* to be a Socialist. At the thought of feeling I was right to be anything whatsoever, I exclaimed 'Good gracious!'

I saw Elspeth and Annette come through the gates. I kissed Elspeth. And then I kissed Annette.

'Tea now,' I asked them, 'or when we get back?'

They glanced at the dark sky and hugged their overcoats round them. 'Now,' said Elspeth. 'Now,' said Annette.

I said: 'We'll go to a Lyons or an A.B.C.'

Elspeth said: 'We won't, darling. We don't have Lyonses or A.B.C's down here.'

I felt ashamed of my ignorance and Annette burst into laughter. 'Lead us somewhere!' I said to Elspeth.

As we walked along I said to Annette: 'How did things go with the headmistress?'

'Very well.'

'Do you mean she'll have you?'

Annette smiled. 'If I decide I want to go.'

So she had not decided? I advised myself to hold back from argument.

Elspeth led us to a café behind a large window that was too steamed-up for us to see what was inside. It turned out to be a big place, the inner half a step lower than the outer, filled with tables covered in old-fashioned oil-cloth. All the tables were made to take six persons at least.

The girls settled down and I went up to a counter with its back to the large window. There was a burly man in a white apron behind the counter: on a shelf to one side of him was a small wireless set, playing popular jazz. The tea cost twopence a cup less than the lowest price at which I had previously been led to believe it could be profitably served in a café. I thought the burly man in the white apron must be a good chap. I bought some solid-looking buns.

The girls, like all the girls I had ever known, ate heartily. 'What a nice place!' said Annette. 'If I come to work down here I shall come here for tea every day.'

'What on earth for?' I asked.

'I feel at home here.'

I said: 'It can't be very like any home *you*'ve been used to.'

Annette laughed. 'Not in the material sense. The material sense isn't important to me.'

'It would be to most of the people sitting at these other tables, if they were offered the chance of having their tea every day in the sort of surroundings you're used to.'

'Exactly. One makes one's choice for one's self.' Her tone was light but firm. I noticed, now that she had loosened her overcoat, that she had gone back to the dark knitted jumper she used to wear all the time before she married Robert. 'One makes it for one's self, not for anyone else. If I go on having my tea every day in the sort of surrounding I'm used to, I shall still be choosing to do it.' She bit a piece of bun.

'I see,' I said. I also saw that we were discussing a great deal more than choice of locale for tea-eating. 'And what about these people?' There were a couple of elderly men, dressed very shabbily, sitting at separate tables nearby. 'Don't you think they'd think they were lucky if they found themselves in a position to have any choice?'

'Yes.'

'In fact, if we get down to talking about things that really matter, isn't the kind of choice, in particular the moral choice, that pre-occupies you and your friends, one of the perks of the leisured classes?'

Before she could answer, I went on. 'In fact, really getting down to business and talking about the pattern of one's career, for example — do you think that I've ever felt I had much choice about what I was going to do next? Because I certainly haven't.' I glanced at Elspeth, rallyingly. 'Do you think Elspeth has, either? You may argue that I actually have done, but all I can say is that it's never seemed like that to me. The only option I have had was to take the one thing that was offered me or to starve. You may say, of course, that I had a choice there.'

Annette smiled: 'I suppose I should.'

'Well, I can tell you, that isn't how it seemed to me.'

We stopped arguing for a moment. The tea was good as well as cheap. The sound of the jazz was cheering.

'I wonder why those two poor old chaps are having their tea here, all by themselves,' I said.

Elspeth looked at them. 'I suppose their families have migrated to one of the new estates up the line, Hainault or Woodford, or somewhere. They're probably too old to move. . . . And yet I'd have thought somebody would have asked them in for a cup of tea.' She answered my question: 'I don't know.'

'The school seems crowded,' Annette said to her.

'Do you really think of coming to teach here?' I asked.

Annette looked at me. 'If I do I shall cease to be a member of the leisured classes, shan't I?' She laughed. 'At least I shall have no leisure.'

I did not like the sound of that. Poor old Robert! Poor old thing! Out of the corner of my eye, I saw Elspeth become more attentive. I said:

'You'll have made your choice, anyway.'

'And I shall feel, as a consequence, that I'm really doing something useful.'

'And that will satisfy you?'

'I shouldn't have put it that way — but yes . . .'

'At the expense of poor old Robert's feeling homeless?'

Annette was not piqued. 'At the expense of Robert's being a bit put out,' she said in her light firm tone.

'Sometimes when you talk about moral choice,' I said, 'you make me feel it's something I've missed. More than that, as if it's something I lack. As if my moral nature were coarse, and insensitive, or even as if I were in some way morally blind. At other times' — I paused — 'I feel it's something I'm just as well without. Exercise of moral choice is one of the perks of the leisured classes, for one thing. For another thing, it often seems, to people who aren't pre-occupied with it, to come pretty close to self-indulgence.'

Annette suddenly blushed. I went on. 'You mean your statement "One chooses for one's self" to be a scientific observation of what happens. But it often rings with a note of *approbation*, which makes it sound like the statement of someone who is exclusively pre-occupied with his or her *self*.' I shook my head. 'You see what I mean.'

'I do. And if it did, I should agree with you.'

'Are you sure,' I said, 'that you don't want to come and work down here in order to avoid what, for some reason I don't understand, would be the greater effort of running a house and home for Robert?'

'I don't think it's right to have servants,' Annette cried. 'And I don't want to have to do myself the things they do — I can do more valuable things.' She raised her voice a little. 'And some things *are* more valuable than others. Some ways of living are more valuable than others.' She paused. 'And value,' she went on, 'if it means anything means value here and now.'

I drew back. I had been lectured before on the super-significance of 'here and now'.

'The value of our way of living, here and now, arises from the personal choice we make, here and now,' Annette said.

'Ergo, the succession of here-and-nows,' said I sarcastically, 'is a succession of personal choices.' Which made the future, I thought, a poor look-out for Robert.

'I was not going to say that at all,' said Annette. 'I was going to say, ergo — if you commit me to ergo — our way of living is just as valuable as we succeed in making it. Our lives are what we put into them.'

'Cor!' I said, but it sounded unconvincing — which was no surprise to me, because I agreed with what she said. The concept of moral effort was as dear to me as it had been to my non-conformist forbears.

There was another pause. Elspeth was the first to speak. 'I suppose I'm going to do the opposite thing to Annette,' she said. 'It seems funny, doesn't it?' She glanced at me. 'It isn't going to make *me* feel immoral, darling, to live on your moral earnings.'

Annette laughed. I gave Elspeth a look of praise. That's the sort of girl you want to marry! I thought.

After a moment, Annette said: 'Perhaps I shall let Robert choose for me.'

I smiled at her. 'Perhaps . . .'

Annette moved her head suddenly, so that her bell of hair swung to and fro.

'I don't think I shall,' she said. 'Let's talk about something else!' She took off her overcoat, letting it fall across the back of her chair.

Elspeth said to me: 'I should like some more tea.'

I picked up our empty cups and went to the counter. As I walked away, Annette set her elbows on the oil-cloth and said animatedly to Elspeth: 'When you come here alone, do you talk to people sitting at the same table?'

Suddenly an idea that had been lurking at the back of my mind came to the front. I could have said: That's broken my dream! Annette, twenty years ago, would have become a Communist.

As I waited while the burly man in the white apron poured the tea, I gazed through the steamy window in the direction of the street; but I was back in the thirties, at Oxford . . . thinking of intelligent, upper-class girls, choosing to join The Party.

Those days had gone, and I was confronted with the difference. Annette was a Socialist of sorts. She had little use for the Labour Party, which she regarded as worn out. 'They've got no theory for *now*,' she had once informed me. 'They had a theory fifty years ago, but it's no use for now and they know it. They're just hoping to muddle through without.' And she had less use for the Communist Party: she was completely disillusioned with revolution.

'Oh dear!' I said to myself, as I carried the cups of tea back to them. I was confronted by the fact that I was a generation older than they were. Was that difference the root of my feeling irritated by Annette? When I remembered that I had been equally irritated by intelligent upper-class girls, especially pretty ones, choosing to join The Party, I thought not.

What irritated me was something that had irritated me throughout the whole of my life — the peculiar kind of self-concern that always seemed to go with the deliberate making of moral choices. I had never liked it. I never should. I thought of Robert, who liked it as little as I did.

'Poor old Robert,' I said to myself. 'He's had it.'

## CHAPTER III

# AN OFFICIAL VISITOR FROM AMERICA

O<small>NE</small> afternoon my P.A. rang me.

'I've got someone to speak to you, Mr. Lunn, who says he knows you. I think he's an American. Do you know a Mr. Thomas Malone? He says he met you in Washington. I've got him on the line now.'

I could not remember anyone named Thomas Malone, not anyone special, that is. It sounded the sort of name that a lot of people might have. I said:

'If he says he knows me, I suppose he must. Put him through to me.'

I heard her say 'Here's Mr. Lunn for you, Mr. Malone', and then a loud, exuberant, American voice said to me:

'Hello there! Is that Mr. Lunn? This is Tom Malone here. How are you?'

I said I was very well.

'Remember me?' he said. And then he announced the name of his office.

At that I remembered who he must be. Three years earlier I had been over to America on an official trip, and for one of the jobs I had to do he was my opposite number. Without being able to recall what he looked like, I did remember that we had got on well.

'Remember that night at the Statler?' he asked, even more exuberantly.

We must have got on very well. I had a weakness for hearty evenings, for being a man among men.

'Wish I could!' I said facetiously, while trying to think which one it was.

'That's the boy! I can hear you haven't changed.'

What is commonly called a warning instinct made me say quickly:

'Oh, but I have. Wait till you see me!' I thought I had better put him wise to my change of status as soon as possible. 'Since you last saw me I've got married.'

'Then you look better than ever, I guess.' He laughed. 'Am I going to have the pleasure of meeting Mrs. Lunn?'

'Certainly you are,' I said, recalling that on the evening of the party at the Statler I had not had the pleasure of meeting Mrs. Malone, very definitely not. I had gathered that Mrs. Malone was at home looking after their five children. I said: 'How long are you staying?'

He said he was planning on staying through Wednesday — to-day was Monday — when he was going to Paris. 'I've got to drop in on NATO and SHAPE.' He had also got his plans for London, these including an evening with me, and a morning looking round what he chose to call our 'outfit'. He wanted to meet our bosses — I may say that after his fashion he was quite a big shot, himself. 'I may even tell them how good you are at your job!'

To my chagrin Robert was not in London. It was just my luck, I thought, for Robert to be hearing about people with whom I had made a negative hit and then to be missing when I could produce somebody with whom I had made a positive one. Positive, I thought, and not afraid to say so!

Tom — I had to call him Tom, since Americans give one no alternative between calling them by their Christian names and calling them Mr. — had already got hold of Robert's name. Also of the name of Murray-Hamilton. He had not previously met either of them.

I was free to fit in with his plans. Elspeth and I would take him out to dinner that evening. The next day he could have a look round our outfit and meet Murray-Hamilton. I put down the telephone receiver and pressed the buzzer for my P.A. to come in so that I could tell her about it. I felt excited. The telephone seemed to have transmitted to me a gust of euphoria.

When Elspeth and I met Tom Malone that evening his state was clearly euphoric. I could not say whether I should have recognised him or not. He was short and stocky, about the same height as me and a stone and a half heavier — that stone and a half being composed of muscle, powerful active muscle — and he had the sort of square, snub-nosed, grinning Irish-American face that seems to be made for expressing a mixture of blarney and ruthlessness. It was obvious, from the moment we met, that he liked me. I could not for the life of me think why.

It was obvious that he liked Elspeth, too. Every glance he gave her was so filled with life and energy that I felt ashamed of lapsing from my duty as a host — the trouble was that since getting married my list of girls, from whom I might have rustled up one for an occasion such as this, seemed to have dispersed. So soon, I thought, so soon. . . . How sad I felt to have lost them! And yet, how cosy I felt to be just with Elspeth!

'You didn't tell me your wife was so young and pretty,' he said to me, while we were drinking some preliminary whiskies.

'Did I have to?'

'Well' — he gave Elspeth and me a vigorous, blarneying look — 'no!'

Elspeth blushed. I was delighted.

When we had settled at our table in the restaurant and were looking at the list of things to eat, Tom said:

'If you won't raise any objections, I'm going to buy the champagne.' He glanced at us to make sure he was carrying us. 'O.K.?'

'Champagne!' we cried enthusiastically, meaning that it was O.K. — actually it usually gave Elspeth and me stomach-ache.

I was amused. We had brought him to an expensive restaurant. Up to now I have omitted to tell you that Tom

Malone was both clever and quick in the uptake. I may also take this opening to observe that in my experience there is nobody like an American for summing up on the spot exactly how expensive a restaurant is. 'Lots of champagne!' he said.

I decided he should have caviare if he wanted it. He chose smoked salmon.

The evening was a great success, and I was pleased for more reasons than one. Honesty compels me to admit that in the first place I had felt relief at having Elspeth to get me out of spending another evening like the one at the Statler. Much as I had enjoyed it — it really was one of those nights when one cannot remember next morning what happened — I just did not want another. Not here. Not now.

'You take him out to-night on your own, darling,' Elspeth had said when I had first told her Tom Malone was here.

Let me explain why she said it. A few months earlier, just after we got married, I had happened to make, in passing and yet not unaware that she would pick it up, one of my favourite generalisations, that married men had a tamed look. Elspeth took it amiss. She took it touchily, I thought.

I did not start an argument with her about the truth of the generalisation: it stood up to the test of experiment to the extent of enabling me, when I was interviewing our scientists and engineers, to judge whether they were married or not and get the answer right eight times out of ten. I could never understand why people took it amiss. They would not have expected a man with a full belly to have the same look as one who did not know where his next meal was coming from.

In my opinion, based on observation, when a man was satisfactorily married a certain look went out of his eye. A certain, identifiable look. (Its disappearance had enabled me, only a few weeks earlier, to guess that a candidate who came up before an annual promotion board had got married since we saw him the previous year. When he asked me how

I guessed and I innocently told him, he said with a furious glare: 'I happen to be rather tired at the moment because we've just been moving house!') That tamed look. . . .

It was women who took the generalisation the most touchily.

'I suppose you think you'll look tamed?' Elspeth said.

'Why not?'

'You'll think it's my fault.'

'I shan't *notice* it. That's the point.'

'I don't like to think other people will.'

'*They* notice next to nothing.' I changed my tone. 'And anyway, darling, *I* think it's worth it. . . .'

At that Elspeth's tone changed. But not her intention. From then on she encouraged me to have hearty evenings out with my friends, to keep up my minor taste for games-playing, and so on.

So you can see how it came about that Elspeth asked me if I would like to take Tom Malone out for an evening on my own. And I am afraid you will also be able to see why I declined.

While we were eating some particularly succulent fillet steaks, I looked at Tom and wondered if he regretted the kind of evening we were having. Sybil! — I suddenly thought of Sybil. She would have been just the girl for this evening. She would have liked Tom Malone and Tom Malone would have liked her. I wondered where she was, and I felt glum. And ashamed of myself. . . . However cool and remote she was, I had no excuse for just quietly letting her go, with hardly a word, when I decided to get married. Dear Sybil, who had never done me a scrap of harm, in fact had always done me a power of good.

However, Tom Malone did not appear to be regretting the kind of evening. On the contrary.

Incidentally, just to finish off my case about being tamed, let me add that all men who are satisfactorily married — and most men are: I was astonished by the number of letters

I got from men from whom I would never have expected it, writing to congratulate me on my marriage, who said with obvious truthfulness: 'I can only hope you and Elspeth will be as happy as we have been' — all such men have a recognisable, tamed look; but this does not mean that they all do not have an eye for a pretty woman, far from it. A certain look, which identifies an unmarried man, goes out of their eyes. But other looks can come in. I would not have needed to glance twice at Tom Malone to know that he was a married man. I did not need to glance at him twice to know that, were I out of the way, he would have made a pass at Elspeth.

I thought Elspeth was looking remarkably pretty. She was pressing her knee against mine.

Tom said to me:

'Next time you come to Washington, you must bring your wife with you.' To Elspeth: 'Have you ever been to the States?'

Elspeth shook her head. As scarcely ever having been out of the country caused Elspeth exaggerated feelings of inferiority, I intervened quickly.

'I'm afraid the Civil Service don't pay for wives to go to Washington with their husbands.'

'Why shouldn't *we*, if we invite you? Why don't we do that? You did us a lot of good last time you came. It would be worth it to our outfit just as much as to yours.' Tom looked at us with blarney and ruthlessness in his bright blue, slightly bloodshot eyes. 'Come on, let's say we're gonna do it! O.K.?'

'O.K.!' we both cried, caught up by the spirit of the moment.

'As soon as I get back to Washington, I'll have us send an official invitation. Who do we send it to — Mr. Murray-Hamilton?'

'That would be correct,' I said. I could not subdue a wish that for once Murray-Hamilton should hear good of me,

even though I knew — Robert had told me often enough —
that I stood the best chance of survival in my job if Murray-
Hamilton heard nothing of me, neither ill nor good. (Why,
I asked myself, should people who think ill of one become
even worse disposed to one if they hear a good report?)

'Then that's as good as settled,' said Tom. 'Here's to
Mrs. Lunn in Washington!' And he finished his glass of
champagne.

I did not see it ever happening, but that did not stop me
finishing my glass.

'We need another bottle,' said Tom and beckoned the
wine waiter.

Elspeth now appeared to be blushing all the time.

By the time we left the restaurant it was nearly midnight.
We were all floating in euphoria. Tom and I went and
stood out in Jermyn Street while Elspeth got her coat: we
needed air.

'It's been a very, very swell evening,' he said. 'London's
a wonderful town. Wonderful people.'

'Glad you liked it.' I glanced up the street, thinking about taxis and home. 'Which way do you go from
here?'

'Got 'ny ideas?'

He was giving me a knowing, encouraging grin. How
could I possibly pretend to misunderstand him? I looked
round quickly for Elspeth to save me — she did.

'Ready?' she said, coming down the steps to us.

Tom burst into laughter. So did I. Elspeth said to
him:

'Are you coming back to have a drink with us?'

Tom said: 'Well, no, I'll stroll back to my hotel. It's only
just down Piccadilly.'

We said our goodnights, and then Elspeth and I got into
a taxi. I put my arm round her.

'What an extraordinary man!' Elspeth said. 'What do
you think he's going to do now?'

'I hate to think.'

I felt Elspeth kiss my cheek and I heard her whisper: '*I don't. . . .*'

She kissed my cheek again.

'Good gracious!' I whispered. 'Surely you don't mean in a taxi?' I knew that was just what she did mean; but I thought it well, now that I was married, to start being a bit stuffy about such matters.

'It's quite a long way to Putney,' she whispered.

On the following morning neither Elspeth nor I had stomach-ache from the champagne. 'You look very well,' she said to me. I was relieved. I did not want to take Tom Malone over to see Murray-Hamilton looking as if some of the things I was supposed to be accused of were true.

My P.A. had arranged for us to see Murray-Hamilton at eleven o'clock, and at a few minutes to eleven I got a telephone call from the policeman on the front door to say that Tom had arrived. I said I would go down to meet him, to save him coming up to my office first.

'Hello there!' The exuberant call rang through our foyer. Tom and I shook hands vigorously. He looked spruce and freshly shaven. 'All set?' he said.

We began to climb the staircase — Murray-Hamilton's office was on the first floor.

'Did you get home safely last night?' I asked.

'Fine,' he said. 'London's a wonderful town. Wonderful people.'

I glanced at him. He glanced at me, with his Irish grin — and caught his toe on the edge of the stair. 'Since I last saw you I haven't missed a minute of it.'

I glanced at him more closely. 'You don't mean,' I said, 'that you haven't been to bed?'

'Not to sleep,' he said. 'How do I look?'

I laughed. 'No different.' It was true. His blue, slightly bloodshot eyes looked bright and clear. His step was powerful and energetic. Looking at me, he laughed with satisfaction. A great gust of his breath came across to me. Brandy. Pure brandy. He was drunk.

'I'm looking forward to meeting your Mr. Murray-Hamilton,' he said.

I could well imagine that he was.

It embarrasses me to describe the meeting of Tom Malone and Murray-Hamilton. In fact I seem, presumably for the sake of my own peace of mind, to have forgotten a good deal of it. I remember crossing Murray-Hamilton's large room and seeing Murray-Hamilton sitting brooding and reflecting behind his huge mahogany desk. A particularly handsome Ministry·of Works picture glowed from the wall behind him. Our feet made no sound on the carpet.

'It certainly is a pleasure to meet you, Mr. Murray-Hamilton,' said Tom, striding forward to shake his hand. 'And I certainly consider myself fortunate to have Mr. Lunn here to introduce me to you.'

'Sit ye down,' said Murray-Hamilton, banishing his brooding look in favour of an affable smile. He handed Tom a cigarette, and then lit it for him — I wondered if the match would ignite Tom's breath.

They began to talk. They began to talk about Tom's work, and about ours. Tom talked loudly and forcefully and with sustained emotion. I tried to keep out of the conversation. Things could hardly be worse, I thought. The brooding, reflective look was creeping back into Murray-Hamilton's eyes.

In due course Tom referred to my last official trip to Washington. At that I realised things could be worse.

Loudly, forcefully, and with sustained emotion, Tom Malone told Murray-Hamilton how wonderfully I had represented our department, how wonderfully I had represented *him*, Murray-Hamilton. Do you wonder my memory begins to give out?

Tom paused — I wondered if I had ever seen a man so drunk.

Tom went on. He told Murray-Hamilton what a grasp I had of my job, and what a technique I had with which to do it. And he ended up by telling Murray-Hamilton I was the best interviewer of scientists and engineers in the United Kingdom.

I really do not remember anything else till I had got Tom Malone out of the room. I do not want to remember anything else.

When Tom and I got outside we went steadily down the staircase. At the turn we met Spinks, Stinker Spinks, going up. Spinks and Tom Malone turned to eye each other; Tom missed his footing, and with a succession of bursting laughs bumped down to the bottom of the staircase on his backside.

He was a damned good chap, Tom Malone.

## CHAPTER IV

## ROBERT'S TROUBLES

I DID not give Robert an account of Tom Malone's visit — for once I thought he might be allowed to preserve his disbelief in the existence of anyone whom he had not found for himself. I was haunted by my picture of Murray-Hamilton sitting at his desk, the ledger open before him . . . on opposite pages he recorded Right and Wrong.

Robert had a new novel coming out. Also he had Annette to cope with. In case you have not had the opportunity to study the artistic temperament, perhaps I ought to say that it was the former which occupied him the more.

Robert had a fit of gloom. He was always in a hyper-sensitive state just before a book came out — a state from which he was readily thrown into apprehension if not gloom. And this essential state appeared not to be seriously altered when, as the centre-piece of his excellent press, he had the middle page to himself in the *Times Literary Supplement*. Very useful, indeed. People do not appear to read it, but they do appear to know it is *there*. For instance, the *T.L.S.* circulates officially, along with *Nature*, *The Economist* and others, through the offices of the upper echelons of the Civil Service. Within a fortnight of Robert's getting the middle page, he had been invited out to lunch by first Murray-Hamilton and then Spinks.

'What did Stinker Spinks say to you?' I asked.

Robert was markedly offhand. 'Actually he was rather interesting, when off his normal beat. It appears that he's got quite an important collection of Roman coins. I didn't know about it. He talked quite interestingly about them.'

'Do you think he'll invite *me* out to lunch when *I* get a middle in the *T.L.S.*?'

Robert said: 'I think he might, you know. Murray-Hamilton definitely won't, I can tell you that. But Stinker might. There are moments when his desire to be near to success, even somebody else's, is even greater than his envy of it. I think he might ask you.' He paused. 'If you have this ambition, peculiar as it is, you ought to be warned that his club gives you a very poor lunch. An execrable lunch.'

When we went to our own club it was obvious that Robert in their opinion was doing well. No body of men responds more quickly to a change in the barometer of one's prestige than one's club, especially to an easily visible movement in the upward direction. Members who have not spoken to one before, speak to one: members who have spoken to one before, offer one a drink: members who have offered one drinks before, suggest one goes up to dinner with them: and members with whom one has dined for years say they are going to buy one's book. It is difficult not to let it go to one's head.

The first weeks after publication passed. And once again gloom, this time a different kind of gloom, supervened. The reviewers who had put Robert's book at the head of their columns were now, with equal hebdomadal panache, putting somebody else's book there. Robert came into my office and sat heavily on the corner of my table.

'I feel,' he said, 'as if I might just as well have dropped it into the sea.'

I understood how he was feeling.

Why worry? you may ask. How right you are — please go on! Why be a writer? Why be Robert or me? Why not be two other chaps? Robert and I sometimes considered your last suggestion as the one, true way out of our dilemma.

'I might just as well have dropped it into the sea,' Robert said again.

The poignance of the concept kept me silent. Attention,

attention . . . all artists are endlessly craving attention. A neurotic lot — not like everybody else.

Robert found little to console him in his domestic situation. Annette was still holding to her moral choice. Speculating on what he might do, I took it into my head that he might get Annette's father to take his side.

Then one day I happened to meet Annette's father. I called at Robert's flat on my way home from the office, to collect some of my manuscript which Annette had been reading. To my surprise, the door was opened by Annette's father.

'Come in,' he said cordially. 'I'm here on my own.' Tall and stork-like, he walked ahead of me down the corridor. 'I'm staying here while my flat is being re-decorated. It's rather more agreeable than getting a room at the Club.'

I was touched by his unusual cordiality. Tall and stork-like, he preceded me down the corridor — to the kitchen.

'I was just going to have a whisky,' he said, 'to save myself trouble, though I should prefer to have some tea. Perhaps as you're here we might make some tea?'

In the kitchen he turned to look at me with a sparkling, encouraging look in his eye. It was the most intimate sign of recognition he had ever given me. I felt that he was almost offering me his friendship. Actually, I realised, he was inviting me to make tea for him.

'The first step,' I said, 'is to put on the kettle.'

'I believe that is so,' he said, with an amused glance round the kitchen which indicated little intention of doing it himself. I filled the kettle and lit the stove.

'At least it is,' I said, 'for people of our class.' I did not see why he should not get something of what he was asking for. 'In schools for the lower classes,' I said, having picked up the information from Elspeth, 'the child's first instruction is, "First empty the pot!"' In case he did not follow, I added: 'The implication being that the pot has not been emptied after being used.'

To my surprise he bestirred himself to the extent of looking for Annette's tea-pot. It was on the window-ledge. He picked it up, weighing it, and then with a negligent gesture handed it to me.

It was full.

I burst into laughter. I could not help admiring him. I had demonstrated that I did not give a damn. No more did he. He smiled with sub-fusc satisfaction.

'I wonder where Annette empties it,' I said.

He stroked his moustache and gave me a swift glance from under his eyebrows — he had long eyebrows that curled outwards. 'She used to empty it in the lavatory — after we'd once suffered a slight contretemps after emptying it down the sink.' He took the tea-pot from me and went out of the room.

When he came back the kettle was boiling and I had got cups and saucers for us.

'Shall we have tea in here?' he said. 'It will save us trouble, won't it?'

'I think Annette and Robert have their tea in here,' I said.

'Very sensible of them.' He got a bottle of milk and some butter out of the refrigerator. 'There doesn't seem to be very much to eat,' he observed as he shut the door. 'We must be going out for dinner.'

I opened a bread bin and took out half a sliced loaf wrapped in waxed paper. We sat down at a small table and began our tea.

'I wonder where we're going for dinner,' he said. 'I know Annette's first choice of place to go out to for dinner is a coffee-stall in the Fulham Road.'

'I didn't know there was a coffee-stall in the Fulham Road.'

'They're getting harder to find,' he said, with a touch of gloom. 'We're always having to go a long way . . .'

I tried to find a happier topic.

'This is superior tea they have,' I said.

'Very good.'

He got up and looked in some of the cupboards.

When Annette and Robert moved into the flat they had had the kitchen completely done up by one of the classy kitchen firms that had made their appearance since the end of the war. The tops of the stove and sink and the benches of drawers were all on the same level, while the hanging cupboards also were perfectly aligned. Some of the cupboard doors and drawers were painted bright yellow, the rest white, while the benches and our table were covered with the latest thing in plastic surface materials. The kitchen was much envied by Elspeth.

Annette's father opened a hanging cupboard which, as far as I could see, was empty except for a small jar on the lower shelf. He brought the jar out.

'Marmite,' he said. 'Annette used to eat a lot of it when she was up at Oxford. She believes it to be highly nutritious.' He spread some on a slice of bread and butter, and then passed the jar to me. 'I don't know if you know it? I rather like it.'

I said: 'You'll need something pretty nutritious if you're going out to a coffee-stall for your evening meal.' I thought of the pork chops which Elspeth had ordered for us. What a satisfactory marriage mine was!

'That's what I thought,' he said.

I waited a moment and then said directly:

'What line are you taking over Annette's becoming a schoolteacher in Bethnal Green?'

'I would have thought she might find a teaching-post nearer home.'

We stared at each other.

After a pause he said: 'Of course, she's changing, you know. I mean, since her marriage.' He could see that I was expecting some revelatory comment. 'She dresses better, don't you think?'

'I suppose I do.' It occurred to me that at dinner-parties which succeeded the first one, when she had appeared in her wedding-dress, Annette had worn a black frock which Robert had chosen — Elspeth thought it was cut too low at the front, but I thought it was all right.

'I always thought when she was at Oxford,' her father said, 'she looked as if she had just landed by parachute.' He could not resist glancing at me slyly.

I laughed.

'Oh yes,' he said, pretending not to have heard me, 'I can see Robert's influence.' He gave me the same glance again; and this time I saw a gleam, light and clear, of malice.

I stopped laughing. The full measure of his detachment had for the first time really struck home to me. He was clever, cultivated, cordial and humane; he was unusually free from envy and stuffiness. He was also free, I thought, from serious concern with anyone but himself, dazzlingly free. . . .

And I had taken it into my head that Robert might be hoping for his intervention! I had made a frightful ass of myself. I knew Robert could not possibly have hoped for such a thing.

Annette's father spread some Marmite on a second slice of bread and butter. 'I do recommend this,' he said.

Out of sheer moral disadvantage I took some. A look of amusement was glimmering in his eyes.

'What do you think of Robert's new novel?' he said. 'You and he write very different kinds of novel, don't you?' He paused. 'I think it's very interesting that you should have such a high opinion of each other's books. It does you both credit.' He leaned forward a little. 'And it *interests* me.'

We engaged in literary conversation.

Meanwhile I was reflecting on a matter that had not occurred to me before. I knew that every shrewd man considered it was a good idea to marry his boss's daughter. To a really shrewd man it is so self-evident as not to require consideration — he just does it automatically. What I had not reflected on before was what the boss thought about it.

I kept thinking of the gleam of malice, light and clear, that Annette's father had let out of the corner of his eye.

## CHAPTER V

# SEVERAL POINTS ILLUMINATED

ANNETTE moved into Elspeth's job.

One day when I happened to see Barbara — it was a day when I was going to the office by Tube and we met on the station platform — I asked her how Annette was getting on at the school.

Barbara was going down to her Bethnal Green clinic. 'I suppose you see Annette quite often now,' I said.

'Yes, we're getting to be quite friends.'

'How's she doing?'

'Very well indeed.' Barbara looked down the railway line. It was a cold June morning and there was a drift of mist in the cutting. 'I think she's made an excellent adjustment.'

'That's fine,' I said. 'What has she adjusted?'

Barbara smiled. 'You know what I mean.'

'You mean she's adjusted herself to the children,' I said, modelling my tone on that employed by Robert on such an occasion — the tone of a bright boy successfully taking part in a guessing competition.

Barbara said: 'She's made an excellent *overall* adjustment.'

'Over all what?' I burst into laughter. 'All right. I won't go on. You mean that you think her "moral choice" has made her feel cheerful.'

'I do.'

'And what about poor old Robert?'

Barbara began to say something, but I did not hear it because the train came into the station. We got in and sat down side by side. After a while I could not resist teasing her.

'I suppose it was "adjustment" you had in mind when you warned me that it was easier to get married than to be married.'

She nodded her head.

'What does it mean,' I shouted, 'actually?'

She thought for a moment. We were crossing the river: it looked pretty in the morning light.

'Learning to live with each other. Making allowances for each other's different desires.'

'Most of the time we seem to have the same desires.'

Barbara looked at me. The train stopped in the next station.

'Do you really find that?' she said.

I thought about it. It was true. I said:

'I suppose we must be easy-going, that's all.'

Barbara was smoothing a crease in her skirt — she was wearing an expensive-looking dark grey suit. Just before the train started again she said:

'And you have no feeling that you're *missing* something?'

'Well, no. . . .' What could we be missing? Children? There was not time yet for us to have had any. I was at a loss. I said: 'Missing what?'

Barbara leaned towards me.

'Have you had many quarrels?'

'No.'

Instantly I knew that I had failed to recognise a key question, and as a consequence, worse still, had truthfully given the wrong answer.

'You mean,' I shouted, 'we ought to quarrel?'

'It's very unusual not to.'

'Why ought we to quarrel?' I put my ear close to her mouth to be sure of hearing her answer.

'It's one of the commonest ways of relieving the tensions of marriage.'

I was confronted with the possibility that my marriage had no proper tensions.

I was silent. I got out my newspaper. It was *The Times*. Since getting married I had started to take *The Times* and to wear a bowler hat. I felt that such a radical change in status as getting married ought to be marked in my case by an appropriate change in outward habit. Elspeth did not mind my taking *The Times*, but she hated the bowler hat, on the explicit grounds that it did not suit me. I suspected that implicitly she considered it was a symbol of tamedness. Actually I thought I looked ridiculous in it. (Come to that, I thought all other men looked ridiculous in bowler hats. Just think detachedly of a human face, and then of a bowler hat on top of it!)

Throughout the day I considered the fact that Elspeth and I did not quarrel. If there were tensions in our marriage we were not releasing them. And if there were no tensions there must be something seriously lacking. I meant to discuss it with Elspeth when I got home.

When I got home — delightful experience!... Elspeth was there — Elspeth opened the door for me. A delicious smell of cooking came out. I realised exactly, now, what it meant in romantic novels when it said 'He kissed her hungrily.' Elspeth, by a marvellous combination of instinct and intelligence, was turning herself into a first-rate cook. The time was just long enough after the war for food to be getting varied and plentiful again, even though some of it was still rationed. Publishers were racing each other to bring out new cookery-books: I used to give them to Elspeth as presents.

After dinner we sat on the sofa, enjoying the pleasures of digestion before we did the washing-up. I was holding her hand.

'Men are carnal,' I said, as a more highbrow way of expressing the fact that the way to a man's heart was through his belly.

Elspeth stroked my hand consolingly.

'I must say it's wonderful being married,' I said.

Elspeth gave me a quick look.

'It's specially wonderful being married to you.' Luck had come my way after all, and all at once.

Elspeth said: 'You never asked me.'

I was caught. I could not think what on earth she meant.

'You never asked me to marry you.'

'No more I did.'

She looked at me closely. 'Don't say you don't remember!'

I frequently got into trouble for not being able to remember cardinal events in our married life. 'Of course I do,' I said. 'You were washing-up, and I was in this room.'

She relaxed. 'Near enough. . . .'

I touched the wedding-ring on her finger. 'Ought I to have asked you?'

'Yes.'

'Didn't you know I was going to ask you?'

'I wasn't sure . . .' She faltered. And then she picked up. 'I thought it was getting time.'

I laughed and then kissed her.

I touched her wedding-ring again. 'Poor baby, you didn't get an engagement ring, either.'

She blushed.

'When I get the Book of The Month in America, I'll buy you a great big diamond.'

'I don't want a great big diamond.'

We were silent. Suddenly she laughed. I asked what was the matter.

'I just thought of you buying yourself all those new clothes before you got married.'

I thought the best thing I could do was to laugh.

And then *I* picked up. I kissed her cheek. 'You're not doing so badly.'

She turned quickly and kissed me.

We were silent again. 'It *is* wonderful . . .' she said.

175

At that moment I recalled my conversation with Barbara. *Was* it wonderful? *Was* it?

I said: 'Darling, do you think we ought to quarrel?'

Elspeth looked at me in some stupefaction. 'What for?'

I then reported my conversation with Barbara. Elspeth listened with attention, and at the end said:

'I don't agree.'

I was relieved. In fact I was pleased, terribly pleased. I confided:

'I don't like quarrelling.'

'Nor do I,' said Elspeth.

I said: 'I don't quarrel easily, and when I do, I mean it. Unfortunately I can't make up and forget it. I remember it.'

'I've hardly ever quarrelled with anyone. And when I did it upset me for months.'

I said: 'In that case, I think we'd better go on as we are. It seems all right to me.'

'I don't want to quarrel with you, darling, ever.'

I said: 'Then, don't let's!' I was very happy about this outcome.

Elspeth sat quietly, thinking about it. After a little while I became discursive. I explained to Elspeth a fact which had first occurred to me several years ago, that some people seem to need to quarrel. 'It seems to provide the friction, the stimulus,' I said, 'which makes them feel they've really been brought to life.' I recalled one of Robert's former loves — the one who hit him with the whisky bottle.

'In fact,' I wound up, 'it seems as if, for some people, a clash of wills is inseparable from sexual excitement.' I paused. 'I should have thought it must be very tiresome for them. And tiring. . . .'

We were silent. I was thinking that my generalisation was profound and that the tone in which I had stated it was admirable.

Elspeth said: 'I've remembered — I think that book was by an Indian . . .'

I was caught again. I simply could not work it out: I had to say 'Which book?'

Elspeth said: 'That one that gave you and Robert such a shock. What did he call it? Daunting?'

'An Indian!' I said. I suddenly thought of millions of bright-eyed, birdlike little Bengalis, perpetually on the boil. But I was not willing to give an inch. 'An Indian *woman*,' I said.

Elspeth laughed. She looked at me sideways. Her eyes were sparkling.

I jumped up. 'Come on!' I said. 'It's time to wash up.'

Elspeth got up. 'I've been waiting for you all this time.'

We went into the kitchen and did the washing-up. If our marriage was missing something, we still had plenty to keep us satisfied.

The following morning, whom should I meet, as if by chance, but Harry. I was sure he had been lying in wait for me somewhere on the route to my usual bus-stop. He fell into step with me.

'Lovely morning, Joe,' he said.

I agreed that it was. The lilacs and laburnums were in flower in people's gardens. It was some time since it had rained, and the dust on the road gave out a faint familiar scent — it reminded me of being somewhere abroad, where roads were always dry — the South of France on a dazzling spring morning, in the days long before the war. . . . Some little girls in purple blazers passed us.

Harry said: 'It's nice to see you again.'

I nodded my head.

It was difficult to say whose fault it was, that we had seen so little of each other recently.

Somehow Elspeth's and my getting married had estranged us from Harry and Barbara. 'You could scarcely think it really could be that, when it was they who brought us together,' Elspeth had said.

'The movements of the soul,' said I, 'are not necessarily to be explained mechanically.'

As this speech had a somewhat dowsing effect on Elspeth, I added: 'Actually, it's one thing to bring people together, and another to know how you're going to take the outcome.'

The light had come back into Elspeth's eyes.

So, when Harry said it was nice to see me again, I felt it as unintended reproach, and yet there was nothing I could do about it.

'Why don't we have lunch together?' I said, doubting if it would do any good. Harry and Barbara, in their married state, had looked at Elspeth and me in ours, and something had — well, made them turn their heads away.

'Yes, we will,' said Harry.

He swung along beside me — he walked with short steps, seeming, compared with me, to be balancing forwards on his toes.

'I hear you saw Barbara yesterday morning,' he said.

I smiled. 'Yes.' I wondered if it was to discuss this that he had waylaid me, and decided not. Harry was too innately wily to come straight to the point, even when there was not the slightest reason for not doing so.

'She's a strange girl,' he said, looking in front of him.

I was touched.

'I'm very attached to her,' he said.

I was touched again.

He turned his head — I was aware of an odd glance coming round his snub nose — and said: 'She has a good deal to put up with from me.'

I said mildly: 'Yes.' It seemed fair enough.

'Even if I didn't see myself as others see me, I should realise that,' he said. He seemed to be laughing.

'Yes,' I said again, now completely mystified.

Harry said nothing else. In a little while we came to the bus-stop.

We climbed to the upper deck of the bus and settled ourselves in two seats at the front.

'Well,' said Harry, speaking now in his high, fluent,

conversational tone. 'What do you think of Robert's new novel? I've scarcely seen you since it came out.'

The scales of mystification fell from my eyes. Though there had been a break in our conversation, and though Harry's tone was different, the subject was still the same. Before I could answer, he said:

'I enjoyed it tremendously.'

I knew what he had waylaid me for.

You may remember that although Robert did not see much of Harry — in my belief because he had not found Harry for himself — he used to question me about Harry with such interest that I suspected he must be thinking of someone like him as a character for a novel. Well, there was a character in Robert's new novel who resembled Harry in some important respects, in particular being globe-shaped, whirling, and impelled by curiosity — while differing in others, such as social origins, profession and so on.

'I enjoyed it tremendously,' Harry repeated, just to make sure the point had gone home.

I said nothing. I should have loved to question him about what he thought of Robert's character — it would have taught me a lot about Harry and a lot about literary art. For Robert's vision of Harry, as far as it actually was of Harry, was different from mine. I tended to see Harry as a sort of non-sexual voyeur, whose ferretting out of details about everybody's lives somehow fed his sense of power. Robert saw his own Harry-like character in a more Dostoievskian light, as wildly whirling in the flesh and pretty wildly whirling in the soul as well, held in control only by a strong will — a will stronger than I would at first sight have given Harry credit for. Yet every so often the will of Robert's character failed him, and an act of a most peculiar kind so to speak escaped him. It was an act of what Robert chose to name 'motiveless malice'.

The vision fascinated me, partly because I had seen nothing of such acts in Harry's conduct of recent years, partly because it evoked an extraordinary recollection from my boyhood. Harry had told a schoolgirl whom I was going out with that I was writing love-letters to another girl. It was untrue: there was no basis for it: Harry had absolutely nothing to gain. The girl dropped me, refusing to tell me why, and I was unhappy for weeks — during which time Harry had listened to my confidences and gone to great lengths to console me!

Such an act of 'motiveless malice' provided Robert with a dramatic turn — completely invented, of course, since in life his own path and Harry's scarcely ever crossed — in the central plot of his novel.

Suddenly I heard, to my stupefaction, Harry saying:

'I enjoyed it most of all for the portrait of that young economist.' This was the character I was thinking of.

'It was splendidly done,' Harry said. 'I know what it's like to be that sort of man.'

I turned to look at him and in his expression saw strong emotion. His eyes were shining. 'Yes,' he said. 'Robert understands us very well. . . .'

Then, just as suddenly, his mood changed. His shining glance shifted obliquely and his tone of voice went up.

'I think,' he said, 'Robert understands me better than you do, Joe.'

I looked through the bus window as if I had noticed something specially interesting about the traffic.

'Don't you?' he asked triumphantly.

'I think that's for you to say.' I went on looking through the window.

For a little while Harry looked through the window, too.

'Yes, Joe,' he said. 'Let's have lunch together — let's make it soon!''

## CHAPTER VI

## A SURPRISE AND A SHOCK

THROUGHOUT the next months I worked hard on my new novel. I was beginning to have the highest hopes of it. I had made a dent in the public's consciousness with my previous book. It seemed reasonable to believe that another small masterpiece, banging on the identical spot, would make the dent deeper. Why not? The public's consciousness is not like a tennis-ball.

'You're bound to make a bit of money sometime,' said Robert. 'I rather fancy it may well be this time.'

I was not, of course, expecting to make a similar impression in America. My sense of humour had not become the least bit un-British, as far as I could see, during the last year. When I read through my manuscript, it made me laugh. When Robert read through my manuscript, it made him laugh. But what was the good of that? *We* were British.

'One thing's certain,' Robert said, still in his optimistic mood. 'Courtenay will be delighted with it.'

Courtenay Chamberlain was my publisher.

I said: 'I think he will.'

This encouraged Robert still further. 'If you don't get an excellent press for this, I shall be very surprised. Very surprised indeed. And, well . . . you may well make a bit of money.' He grinned. 'And so will Courtenay.'

I grinned, but not quite so much.

Anyway, in October, having given the manuscript its last cuts and titivations, I sent it on its way to Courtenay. Another small masterpiece. (Actually, by now, I was getting a bit sick of reading it, but that did not make me feel any less inclined to accept Robert's opinion of its quality.) I registered the parcel.

Then Robert and I sat back to wait. In these days Robert seemed to be enjoying a remission from his gloomy, apprehensive, pre-occupied state of the last few months. For one thing my affairs were clearly going much better. For another his own affairs, I judged, were troubling him less. All the same, I was completely unprepared for what he said to me one morning when he came into my office.

Robert was sitting on the corner of my table, stirring a cup of tea which our P.A. had just brought in. We had been talking about a visit we were going to make to one of our research establishments, and he had lapsed into gazing idly through the window.

'By the way,' he said, turning to me, 'it looks as if Annette's going to have a baby.'

For a moment I was too surprised to think, and then, I am ashamed to say, I thought something unworthy about him.

'Good gracious!' I said. 'That's wonderful news.'

'It's not a hundred per cent certain yet, but I shall be very surprised if she isn't.'

I began: 'Did you — ?'

Robert gave me an authoritative look. 'It's unintentional as far as both of us are concerned.' He paused.

I paused. 'What does Annette think about it?'

'She seems very happy about it.'

'What about her doing a job? It will affect that.'

'I realise that.' Robert thought about it. 'In some ways it's a little awkward, happening at this particular point in time.' He glanced at me sideways. 'But she's quite certain that she wants to have it . . . And I don't need to tell you that I want her to have it.' He looked at me full face. 'I want it very much.'

I was moved by his emotion. 'Then I'm very, very glad indeed.'

'I think it will be all right.'

I laughed with relief. 'All women want to have babies, anyway.'

'Some less than others.'

We were thoughtful.

I told Elspeth that evening. 'You must admit it's a surprise,' I said.

She glanced at me oddly. 'Yes, darling.'

'What's the matter?'

She began to smile. 'It's a bit alarming, isn't it?' she said. 'Think about us . . .'

That point had not struck me. 'We shall be all right.' I hugged her. 'You're a wonderful wife.'

We were silent for a little while.

'It makes all the fuss about whether she ought or ought not to become a school-teacher look rather academic,' I said.

Elspeth said: 'Why?'

I said: 'Well, she won't be able to, now.'

'Not at all. She can have time off to have the baby and then go back again. Time off,' she repeated emphatically, 'with pay!'

I did not argue. That was as might be.

And then I thought: Suppose I made a bit of money with my new book, should Elspeth and I think about having some children? I began to long for that bit of money.

And that reminded me that it was time I heard from my publisher about my new small masterpiece.

Another fortnight elapsed, and then one morning I had a telephone call from my literary agent. Robert was in my office at the time, sitting on the corner of my table.

My agent was ringing me with news from Courtenay.

'What is it?' said Robert, beginning to turn pale.

I tried to listen to both him and my agent.

'Doesn't he like it?' Robert asked incredulously.

I put my hand over the mouthpiece. 'He thinks it's wonderful. But he can't publish it.'

'Why on earth not?'
My agent rang off.
I turned to Robert.
'He thinks it's too improper.'
Robert went on turning pale.

# PART IV

## CHAPTER I

## LEARNING THE LAW

Two days later I had lunch with Courtenay.

Courtenay was an excellent publisher. The discouraging thing about him was that there was a startling physical resemblance between him and me — discouraging to me because, though we looked startlingly alike, I was an artist and he was a businessman.

Let me give you an example. The first time we met, Courtenay asked me to have lunch with him at his club. Being young in those days and unused to clubs, I was pleased and impressed. We sat down at a table and ordered what we were going to eat.

'What would you like to drink?' Courtenay asked. 'A glass of beer or something?'

'Thank you,' I said shyly, 'I should like a glass of beer.'

Courtenay called the wine waiter and ordered a glass of beer for me and a bottle of wine for himself.

You see what I mean about being a businessman? And yet he was not insensitive, far from it. Later in the meal, when I was finishing my glass of beer and he his glass of wine, a rueful look came into his eyes, large, light-coloured eyes that Robert, with a more romantic vision than mine, used to refer to as sad and lemur-like. Courtenay put down his glass not quite empty and said to me consolingly:

'It was only cat-piss, really.'

We looked, I can tell you, surprisingly alike. He was the same size and shape as me; he had the same large rounded forehead as me and the same sort of curly hair, now turning grey like mine. He looked very lively and, worse still, he looked — painful though it is to say it, artistic integrity compels me — dapper . . . I looked at him and I thought of myself. I was an artist and he was a businessman. I wore a bow-tie; he wore a bow-tie and a carnation. One day, when we were washing our hands in a club lavatory, he suddenly looked intently into the mirror above his wash-basin, and said in a rueful tone:

'Joe, why do I look such a cad?'

Far was it from me to give him an answer.

He was an excellent publisher. To be an excellent publisher you have to be a businessman. I had no intention of leaving Courtenay.

On the other hand, the morning I met Courtenay for lunch I was not what my Civil Service colleagues might have called happy in my relationship with him. I felt amazed and injured. My small masterpiece *improper*? (Or, more accurately, perhaps too improper to be published.) It seemed to me incredible. It was no more improper — if you want to be able to judge for yourself — than this book you are now reading! (To be accurate, just about the same.) I went to Courtenay's club looking pale, I have no doubt, but feeling proud.

I was early and had to wait in the foyer. I meant to reproach Courtenay as soon as he came in, not to wait until after lunch. Businessmen, I had learnt, went in for lunch first, business afterwards, a form of etiquette that I, as an artist, found intolerably digestion-destroying. In the past I had put up with going through the whole lunch, with wine, waiting for Courtenay to say what he thought of my new manuscript. Nowadays I used to ask him before he got his overcoat off. Lunch first, business afterwards — O.K. But Art before either!

Through the glass doors I saw Courtenay coming vigorously up the steps. He was not wearing an overcoat. A carnation glowed in his smartly-cut lapel. He shook my hand.

188

'It's a very good book, Joe,' he said, warmly. 'Very good.'

I stared at him.

'But I can't risk publishing it.'

Before I could say anything he got me moving up the staircase to the bar.

Courtenay got some drinks and we settled down in a corner by ourselves.

'So you think it's improper?' I said.

Courtenay gave me a shrewd glance. 'Who said I said that?' Though his eyes might normally, according to Robert, look sad and lemur-like, they could give a shrewd glance that was positively levantine.

I told him my agent said he said that.

Courtenay then did look sad. 'How you both misunderstand me,' he said. He looked at me straight. 'Do you think I'm a prude, Joe? Do you honestly think I'm a prude?'

I said I did not think so.

'You, Joe, can write anything you like,' he said, 'and I should like it.' He began to smile. 'In fact, in this book you have . . .' He went on smiling. Then suddenly he stopped smiling. 'But if I print it, I shall have the Home Office down on me like a ton of bricks. It won't do, Joe. . . . Publishing's a business, you know. Something you artists sometimes don't fully understand. The firm's got to make money, not lose it. If I brought this book out I'd risk losing a hell of a lot of money.' Then he added. 'And it's not *my* money . . . It's the firm's money.'

I cannot say my heart was wrung as much as his by that thought. I said: 'But surely it's not as improper as all that? I've read books much *more* improper.'

'So you may have. So have I. They've been published and nothing has happened to them because the Home Office hasn't been interested in them.' He drank some of his gin-and-tonic and then gave me his levantinely shrewd look. 'But we've just heard that the Home Office is going to start getting interested.' He glanced round as if he might be making sure that nobody was eavesdropping. 'Apparently they're just about to open a new drive . . .' He paused. 'In case you should be thinking that some other publisher might be ready to publish your book, I'm afraid that won't be so. The word's going round . . .' He drank some more gin-and-tonic and said modestly: 'I just happened to be the first one to hear.'

This left me for some time with nothing to say.

'I suppose,' I said at last, 'I shall have to alter the book?'

'I sincerely hope you will,' he replied.

I remarked. 'You sound doubtful . . .'

'I am, Joe, I am. I don't know how much you'd have to alter it to make it pass.'

'There must be some standard of reference,' said I.

Courtenay shook his head. 'The Home Office, or the Director of Public Prosecutions, can set the standard more or less where they like. Since the war everybody's noticed that it's been going down. Now they're going to put it up. We shan't know how high they're going to put it' — he made a gesture with his hand — 'till they put it.' He rested his hand on my arm. 'It's got us publishers worried, Joe. Definitely worried.'

'No more worried than it's got one of us writers,' I observed.

'For instance,' said Courtenay, 'they could take *The Decameron* out of circulation tomorrow if they felt like it.'

'But you don't publish *The Decameron*.'

'No.'

'And I,' said I, 'am nothing like as improper as Boccaccio.'

'I know.' He patted my arm. 'Have another drink, Joe. I wish I could help you, old boy.'

With a lively step he went to the bar. When he came back with two more drinks, he said:

'Of course I'm not entirely without any suggestions for you, Joe. Don't think that! I want to publish that book, Joe. I believe in it.' He looked at me. 'My suggestion is that you should talk to our solicitor about it. I rely on him. Will you do that, Joe? He'll explain the law to you, and then even make some suggestions about how to . . . tone the thing down so as to get by with it. You just twist the book a bit' — he grinned — 'and we'll twist the Home Office.'

I said all right, I would see the firm's solicitor.

We drank the rest of our drinks without making any further headway. And I must say I did not feel very much like eating any lunch afterwards.

In his businesslike way, Courtenay arranged for me to see the solicitor on the next afternoon.

The solicitor had his chambers in an old rabbit-warrenish sort of building. However, the room in which he himself worked when I finally got to it reminded me agreeably of a tutor's room in a college. It was a square room with a tall sash-window that looked out on to a green stretch of grass. The walls were panelled and painted white — as in college rooms, they looked fairly dirty — and they were ornamented with old county maps in Hogarth frames. An electric fire was glowing in the fireplace.

When I entered the room the solicitor got up from his desk — I saw my manuscript on it — and smiled at me in a pleasantly composed way. He was tall, slender, nicely filled-out. I judged him to be about fifty. His neck was long and cylindrical, and he had a smooth oval face. His hair appeared to have gone white prematurely. Altogether he was a nice-looking man. Beautiful teeth, I noticed, when he smiled. Nice grey eyes.

'Ah,' he said, shaking my hand and speaking in a warm unaffected voice. 'I want to tell you how much I've enjoyed and admired your book.'

I must have looked startled.

'You see,' he said, giving me his pleasantly composed smile again, 'I want you to see right from the start, that I'm not pi.'

$\pi$? For a moment I was startled again. Then the language I had never spoken at a prep. school came back to me. 'Oh, pi,' I said, nodding my head. 'Yes, not pi . . .'

'H'm — h'm.' He sat down again.

Actually I would not have thought at first sight that he *was* pi — or not pi, for that matter.

I sat down in a big leather armchair beside his desk.

He clasped his hands beneath his chin and began.

'The first thing I have to explain to you, Mr. Lunn, is that the law relating to Obscene Libel is——'

'*Obscene Libel!*' I cried.

He smiled. 'Libel, in this case, does not mean what you think it means. The word derives from *libellus*, meaning "little book".'

Little book! That was just what I had written. A charming, attractive little book, a masterly little book!

'But obscene!' I still cried. 'That means repulsive, repellent. There's nothing repulsive or repellent about what I've written.'

'Not to you, clearly. Not to many people, I dare say.' He spoke slowly and evenly all the time. 'But that is not relevant, I'm sorry to say. One of the questions we have to ask ourselves in the first instance is: Might it seem repulsive, repellent, to the Director of Public Prosecutions?'

'How am I to know? I've never met him. Anyway, there's always *somebody* to whom *something* is repellent.'

'I was referring to the D.P.P. in his official role.' He smiled a little.

'What's that?'

'That of advising the police whether or not to take action over a particular book.' He paused. 'Though I must tell you the police are not bound to take his advice.'

'I see,' said I.

192

'Not,' he went on, 'that it need necessarily be the police who set the Act in motion in the first place. Any person, any private person, can set the Act in motion.' He paused again. 'But we are straying away from the point. I have to explain to you that in connection with the Act there is no definition of what is obscene.'

'Oh,' I said.

'Nor is the punishment for "publishing an obscene libel" anywhere defined or limited.'

'Oh,' I said again.

'Of course,' he went on, 'there are, as it were, *some* sign-posts.' He smiled at me.

'M'm?' I said.

'In the absence of a definition of obscenity, we have a test for obscenity. You probably know it? That of Chief Justice Cockburn in 1868.'

I shook my head. He nodded his.

'In any case, I should have felt bound to remind you of it,' he said. 'It goes thus: "The test of obscenity is whether the tendency of the matter charged as obscenity is to deprave and corrupt those whose minds are open to such immoral influences and into whose hands a publication of this sort may fall" . . . Let me anticipate' — he held up his hand in a pleasantly composed way — 'a claim that I'm sure you must be going to make, that you, as the author, had no intention to deprave and corrupt any of your readers.' He smiled at me, shaking his head. 'In the court, this is ignored. The intention is judged entirely from the book itself . . . I can go further. In the court the author has no *locus standi*, as we call it. He may neither give nor call evidence.'

It dawned on me that he must be the most composed person I had ever met.

'And lastly,' he went on, 'two final points, before we get down to work on your book, in which, I'm afraid, we shall have to make radical alterations if we are to meet the Home Office in its new mood — in what we have reason to believe will be its new mood — two final points. With reference to Chief Justice Cockburn's test. There is no certainty in *theory* as to the meaning of the words "deprave and corrupt" nor to which class of persons they apply.' He paused. 'Nor is there any certainty in *practice* either.'

There was a short silence.

'Well, thank you,' I said. 'It sounds to me as if you've covered the lot.'

'Thank you for saying so.' He turned slowly to look out of the window. The light glimmered on his beautiful teeth. The contrast between his white hair and smooth uniformly brownish complexion was striking. He turned back to me.

'In our work we shall have two signposts on which we can rely,' he said. 'The one, my knowledge of previous indictments. The other' — his voice became more resonant — 'our own good feelings.' He nodded his head. 'It is the latter which in the long run will make the more important signpost. Incomparably the more important. I'm confident that if we rely on our own good feelings, all will be well.'

Something made me feel inclined to reserve my judgment.

'Now,' he said, beginning to turn over the pages of my typescript. 'To begin with I think we'd better look for isolated passages that might cause us trouble.' He glanced up and smiled. 'I can reassure you. They are fewer than might be expected. If I may say so, that is a tribute to your talent.'

As he appeared to mean it, I smiled back.

'Here is the first point. I see here a word consisting of the letter "f" and three asterisks.'

'Good gracious,' I said. 'That word's printed in full, about ten times a page, in ——' I named an American war-novel that everybody had read.

'In that work,' he said, 'you will recall that the word was *mis-spelt* . . . I'm afraid your device leaves it open to the correct spelling, when no doubt might be left in the mind of the Home Office.' He held up his hand. 'Now, please don't think I'm being pi! I'm not suggesting you should remove it. Indeed, I'm not. We all know the word is sometimes used, even if we do not use it ourselves. What I'm suggesting is that you may keep the letter "f" and add four, or perhaps five asterisks.'

'That might certainly leave some doubt in the mind of the Home Office,' I said.

'With five asterisks we might have no trouble at all. And our good feelings would be spared.'

I said: 'I think I'll cut the whole remark out.'

'That would be meeting the Home Office more than half-way. I'm glad, Mr. Lunn.'

He went on turning over pages. 'And now,' he said, looking down, 'I have to notice that here you've mentioned a member . . .'

'Member?' I said, startled. 'Member of what?'

His head remained down. 'I was hoping you'd take my meaning without further explanation. I was using the word "member" in the sense of . . . "organ".'

'Oh dear,' I said. I felt as if I were going to blush. Then I said: 'Where have I mentioned it?' I went and looked over his shoulder at the manuscript. 'But I *haven't* mentioned it,' I said. 'Show me where!'

'Ah, that is merely a tribute to your literary skill. It is not mentioned by word, but I have no doubt that the Home Office would feel it was *there*.'

'If two people are making love,' I said, 'it's bound to be there! Home Office or no Home Office.'

'H'm, h'm,' he said thoughtfully. Then: 'Making love . . .' He looked up from the manuscript. 'I wonder if your good feelings tell you that kissing might serve your purpose just as well?'

'I can tell you,' I said, tapping the manuscript, 'it wouldn't serve *theirs*!'

There was a long pause.

I said: 'I suppose that scene will have to go out.'

'That's excellent, Mr. Lunn. I'm very glad indeed to hear you say that. I can see that ours is going to be a very fruitful partnership.'

There was a pause. He quietly turned back the pages of my manuscript, so that the book was closed.

'I see that I can now safely leave isolated passages to you, Mr. Lunn.' He smiled. 'I wish that were the end of our troubles. If the law were concerned only with isolated passages, I can assure you it would be. However, the law is so framed that there is no certainty as to whether the test of obscenity is an isolated passage or the book's dominant effect. We now have to consider the book's dominant effect.'

'The dominant effect,' I said with authority, 'is that of a work of art.'

He said: 'In declaring a book "obscene" according to the law, it is very doubtful if a judge or jury may take that into consideration.'

'Oh,' said I.

He smiled. 'I hope I'm not tiring you with so many explanations. I think I can make quite shortly the statements in the light of which we have to consider your book for the purpose of judging its dominant effect. Obscenity, as you know, has always been confined to matters related to sex or' — he completed the sentence hurriedly — 'the excremental functions. Furthermore, we say something is obscene, we know it to be obscene, if it arouses in us a feeling of shock, of outrage.'

I was really irritated.

'In your book there is a good deal about matters related to sex,' he went on. He smiled friendlily. 'Now didn't your good feelings tell you that the dominant effect of the way you had presented them might arouse a feeling of shock, of outrage, in some persons who might read it?'

'Not till there was some question of the book not being published.'

196

He shook his head in a way that signified composed disappointment in me. 'I'm afraid it may arouse that feeling. It well may. The characters in your book make love to each other. There appears to be no likelihood of their generating children thereby — in fact you go to no lengths to conceal from the reader that they are not married. What is the dominant effect of the passages in which these actions are recounted?' He answered the question himself, after first posing another one. 'Do we see them in a light of immodesty, of shame? . . . Undeniably we don't.' He paused. 'The dominant effect of these scenes is of pleasure.' His lips formed the word as if it were spelt with a capital P. 'Of undivided Pleasure! Of complete Enjoyment!'

'That was what I had in mind,' I conceded honestly.

He said: 'Suppose, then, a jury were directed to imagine a typical young person — tempted to sexual activity, and asking desperately "How do I stand?" and "Where do I go from here?" — searching for an answer to his problem in your book.' He paused. 'What answer do you think he'd find in your book?'

I did not say anything. He was making me feel shy again.

'The answer he'd find would be Yes, a thousand times Yes, wouldn't it?'

I said: 'I think a thousand's a bit much.'

'You may be right . . . But twice would be enough.' There was almost a tremor in his composure. 'Or even once, more's the pity!'

I looked out through the tall sash-window. The grass looked very green, the daylight very limpid. Not like his imagination, I thought.

'You now see what I mean by the dominant effect, Mr. Lunn.'

'Indeed I do,' I replied.

He smiled very composedly, very friendlily now. 'I'm glad you've been so understanding,' he said. 'Obscenity is a very difficult thing to make clear to authors. And the task of making it clear is specially difficult for anyone like myself, who, as you now see, is not in the least pi.'

I nodded my head.

He picked up my book to give it back to me. 'This is an excellent book, Mr. Lunn. When you are re-writing it, just let *good* feelings be your guide. Then the Home Office will let it go by. In affairs relating to sex, remember modesty, concern for the conventions, awareness of sin; above all don't give us a dominant effect of undivided pleasure, complete enjoyment, as you have done!' He smiled. 'Think of that typical young person whom the jury might be directed to imagine! . . . Keep him *clean*!'

He stood up, and I stood up. As he shook my hand he said:

'When I look into your face, Mr. Lunn, I can see that you *can*!'

## CHAPTER II

## WAS IT A HELP?

WHEN I bore the news back to Robert he was very distressed. By that time I was beginning to feel more than distressed.

'Altering isolated passages is child's play,' he said.

I nodded, thinking of the infallible device, i.e. excision, that I had already hit upon.

'But the dominant effect . . .' Robert shook his head.

'I don't see,' I said, 'how I can produce a different dominant effect with those characters and that story.'

At the thought of them Robert bowed his head. He was no doubt dwelling on undivided Pleasure, complete Enjoyment.

'The trouble is,' he said, 'that the dominant effect is . . . *you.*'

I did not quite like the sound of that.

'It's you,' he said, 'who shine through the whole book.'

Shine! That was better.

'If only,' I said, 'I could shine a bit more *cleanly*!'

'That,' said Robert, 'is the disability we've got to get round, somehow — the disability, I may say, *vis-à-vis* the Home Office. I personally don't agree with either Courtenay or his solicitor that the book is obscene, and I doubt if anybody we know would.' He paused. 'But it isn't anybody we know who's going to set the Act in motion; or anybody we know who's going to decide whether the Act shall take its course.'

'In some ways it would be a help in these circumstances,

I said, 'if you did think it was obscene, and then I could alter it so that you didn't.'

Robert glanced at me. 'Yes. I see that.'

'Or,' I said, 'if the dominant effect is *me*, I could ask *you* to re-write the book.'

'I think you can take it,' said Robert, in a slightly sharper, loftier tone, 'I should treat the subject rather differently.'

I had nothing to say to that. We remained silent. I was concentrating on how *I* might re-write the book so that, in the circumstances of there being no definition of what was obscene, it could in no circumstances be pronounced obscene.

Robert interrupted me.

'I wonder how this business started,' he said. 'I bet you when Courtenay first read this book he didn't think it was anything worse than mildly improper, in an amusing, amiable, acceptable way.'

'I didn't even think it was improper!' I cried. 'I just thought it was natural.'

Robert went on: 'Granted that, when he put it to this egregious solicitor you saw, he got the answer he did get, I still don't see why he sent it to the solicitor in the first place.'

'He heard the Home Office were going to start a new drive.'

'That's as may be. But I wonder what made him associate a prospective Home Office drive with your book . . .'

I shrugged my shoulders. I was too preoccupied with my own actual problems to be drawn into Robert's speculations. I was trying to think of the typical young person whom I was to try not to deprave and corrupt — remembering that nobody really knew, least of all cared to say, what being depraved and corrupted entailed.

'And I wonder how it's done, anyway,' Robert was saying. 'I suppose people at the Home Office get together with people in the Department of the Director of Public

Prosecutions, and then they tip off Chief Constables to start reading books.'

'*My* book!' I said, thinking of my innocent, natural, small masterpiece in the hands of a Chief Constable.

Robert said: 'I think I'll make it my business to have lunch with Courtenay. It can't do any harm to find out how he got the word from the Home Office, and it might do some good.'

There were occasions, it seemed to me, when Robert sounded more like a civil servant than an artist. However, I did not say anything.

Two days later Robert had lunch with Courtenay. When he got back, he came straight into my office. Without taking off his overcoat he sat on the corner of my table and said:

'I've found out how Courtenay heard the Home Office were going to start a new drive against books. He didn't hear direct. He was told by an intermediate person. And your book was specifically mentioned at the time . . . Who do you think that intermediate person was?'

I looked at him. Having declared our thoughts to each other continually over the last twenty years, there were occasions now when we just read them. I said instantly:

'Harry.'

Robert nodded.

'Good God!' I said.

Robert went on nodding.

'But why?' I said. 'And how?'

Robert paused and then said with heavy detachment — and very faint knowingness:

'I suppose "motiveless malice" . . .'

I pondered this.

'Incidentally,' said Robert, 'have you let Harry read the manuscript?'

'I have not.'

'How could he have read it?'

'He has a drink sometimes with my agent. I suppose he got a few pointers out of him, harmlessly enough, and then' — I thought of one of Harry's favourite phrases — 'pieced it together. . . . Nobody has more skill, or more practice, at piecing things together than Harry.'

We paused. Suddenly I had a new idea. I said:

'I suppose Harry didn't fabricate the rumour about the Home Office?'

Robert shook his head. 'That would be carrying motive-less malice to inconceivable lengths. No. I should think he did pick up something, probably from some bird in the Home Office who belongs to his club. It's very much a place for senior civil servants, especially youngish ones who're on the way up.' He continued my education by naming some of them.

I brought him back to Art. I said:

'But it doesn't follow that because Courtenay heard the Home Office were going to start a new drive that it was going to be directed against me for one.'

Robert shook his head.

There was a pause.

Robert said: 'I'm afraid the result of my researches isn't relevant to the immediate literary problem that confronts you.'

Now I shook my head. The result of his researches was not relevant to what I proposed to write; but it was relevant to what I proposed to do. I meant to see Harry without delay. I told my P.A. to ring him up.

Harry invited me to lunch at his club. It was not a club I liked at the best of times — like most men I cared only for my own. And this was far from the best of times.

In outward appearance Harry's club seemed to me to combine gloom with stodginess, its most imposing feature being a huge staircase of considerable grandeur and practically no illumination. And somehow my invariable recollection of the club was of having coffee, after a poor meal, in an alcove on this staircase. In fact there were no alcoves on the staircase itself, but that did not affect my invariable recollection. This was the club, as Robert observed, where senior civil servants had seen fit to swarm, as for instance bishops and vice-chancellors swarmed at the Athenæum, or men of unusual talent and exceptional good-will swarmed at mine.

When I arrived Harry and I went straight up to lunch — partly because we were late and partly because his club, like several others which prided themselves in not moving in an ungentlemanly way with the times, had no bar. (My invariable recollection of another club, much superior socially to Harry's, was of having to have drinks before meals standing up, more or less *under* the stairs.)

I dodged the club's soup by asking for potted shrimps, which were imported in blue cartons from a reliable contractor.

'I'm afraid,' said Harry, 'I don't belong to this club for its food.'

Not feeling called upon to express an opinion on that, I said:

'On the whole civil servants don't notice what they're eating. They're too busy thinking.'

Harry's eyes brightened. 'What are they thinking about?'

'What Action they ought to Take, of course.' I could never understand how the idea had got into circulation among the general public that civil servants were characterised by their capacity for doing nothing. The lower orders of the Civil Service may not get much of a chance, but the bosses are indomitable men of action. Confronted with a new fact, the first response of any moderately senior civil servant is to say 'What Action ought we to Take?' or of a boss as grand as Annette's father to ask 'Is there anything we ought to do about it?'

Harry laughed — a high-pitched, fluent laugh.

'By the way,' I said, 'did *you* tell Courtenay Chamberlain you had reason to believe the Home Office would object to my novel?'

'Yes,' Harry said immediately.

I looked at him. His small brown eyes looked at me unwaveringly. And yet he blushed. The whole of his face — which was quite a lot, I can tell you — was suffused with bright carmine. I do not think I had ever seen him blush so deeply before.

'Why?' I said.

'Because I did have reason to believe it,' said Harry. The blush was fading upwards into where the scalp showed through his thinning dark mouse-coloured hair.

'Will you explain to me how?'

'With pleasure, Joe.' He was trying to recover himself. 'You have a right to know.'

I gave him my mesomorphic glare.

'The Home Office are going to switch their policy,' he said, 'in the direction of cleaning things up. That's definite. I heard it from someone in this club who's in the Home Office. He didn't actually tell me in so many words, but I pieced it together.'

'I see no reason why he should not have told you in so many words.'

Harry jumped. 'I wanted to be discreeter than that,' he said.

'Discreeter?' said I.

The wine-waiter belatedly put two glasses of sherry in front of us. I drank some. Harry drank some — he had apparently given up abstention for this occasion.

'I immediately saw the danger to you,' he said.

'Danger?' I said. 'What danger?'

Harry drank a little more sherry to wet his lips.

'I knew this chap had read your previous books.' Harry tried to smile. 'He enjoyed the last one very much, thought it was very funny — *and* true.'

'Yes?'

'I wanted to find out what line the Home Office might take if you brought out another book that was . . . more so.'

'More what?'

Harry drank some more sherry.

I said: 'What reason have you to believe my next novel is what you choose to call "more so"?'

Harry looked at me brightly and blandly. 'Well, *isn't* it?'

'That,' I said, 'is a matter of opinion.'

'Exactly!' said Harry. 'Of course *I* haven't read it, so *I* don't know. . . . But why do you think your agent's so enthusiastic about it?'

'Because it's an excellent book.'

There was a pause while we finished our shrimps.

Then I said: 'So you wanted to find out what line the Home Office might take if I brought out another book that was more so?'

Harry looked menaced. 'I thought it would be interesting to know.'

'And what was the outcome?'

'He thought yours might well be the sort of book that a Chief Constable might pick on.'

I have to admit that my confidence fell.

'So you see, Joe . . .'

I said nothing for a moment. Harry looked round for the wine-waiter. He had ordered one of the best bottles the club stocked: there was no sign of it.

A waitress brought us some veal croquettes.

We began to eat. I said:

'So instead of telling me all this, you went and told Courtenay?'

Harry said: 'I happened to *see* Courtenay!' He gave me an unhappy look. 'I've seen so little of you recently. We don't seem to see as much of each other as we used.'

I glared at him.

'I can see you're angry with me,' he said.

'You weren't expecting me to be pleased with you, were you?'

'I *was*!' Harry cried. 'You've misjudged me!'

My glare changed, against my will, to a look of amazement.

'I thought I'd chance my arm for your sake,' Harry said. 'Suppose the book had come out and you'd been prosecuted.'

The wine-waiter poured out two glasses of claret at last. We waited for him to go away.

'I'd have told you if I'd seen you,' Harry went on. 'I can see you think I was trying to make trouble. You don't know how difficult things are for me.' He paused, his face bright with emotion. 'I know I've sometimes chanced my arm in the past and it's caused trouble. But this time it wasn't like that, Joe. If you're thinking it was what Robert calls motive-less malice, you're mistaken! I *had* a motive . . . And it was to *help* you!'

I felt as if my head were beginning to spin a little.

I proceeded to eat some more veal croquette with an unusually wet-looking brussel sprout.

'I'm not the sort of man you think I am,' said Harry.

I had never before felt so closely confronted with what is referred to as the mystery of personality. What for certain was at the core of spinning Harry? And how could I for certain tell, bearing in mind relativistic notions, if he set me spinning myself?

'Not quite, anyway,' he said. 'Not always.'

Something made me want to laugh.

Instantly there was a gleam in Harry's eye.

'Isn't this food awful?' he said. 'But the wine's good.' And he drank some wine.

I said: 'I'm in a hell of a mess over the book, Harry. I just don't know how to alter it. Courtenay's solicitor's opinion makes it simply impossible — and Courtenay won't publish unless his solicitor is satisfied.'

Harry nodded his head sympathetically. 'How's Elspeth taking it?'

'She's very upset.'

There was a pause while we finished our veal croquettes.

'Yes,' said Harry. 'That's a pity.' A look of special un-concern came into his face. 'Last time we saw her we thought how well she was looking.' He had picked up the menu card and was looking at the list of puddings.

He handed the card to me.

'She isn't going to have a baby, is she?'

I said: 'No,' with what I meant to be equal unconcern.

Harry smiled sweetly. 'It's all right, we were just won-dering.'

I said: 'Give us a chance! We've only been married a year.'

'Yes,' said Harry, pacifyingly. 'That's just what I said to your mother.'

'To my mother!'

I thought it would probably be difficult to estimate, now, which of our heads was spinning the faster.

'Now don't get me wrong, Joe!' Harry smiled shrewdly at me round his snub nose. 'Your mother doesn't necessarily think you ought to have started one yet. I think she's being got-at by members of your father's congregation.'

'Those old tabby-cats!' I said. 'When we got married they suspected Elspeth was going to have a baby and thought she ought *not* to. Now we've been married a year without having one, they think she *ought* to.'

Harry smiled. 'It's the way of the world.'

'Too damned symmetrical,' said I.

And yet I was wondering too. *Ought* we to be going to have a baby? I had not thought of it in that light before. Could it be that the pressure of society was getting me mobilised for the next step?

In due course Harry and I finished our meal and then, it seems to me in recollection, we drank some tepid black coffee in an alcove on the staircase.

Somehow Harry had composed our quarrel. There was

no doubt about it. I did not know if I could possibly believe what he had told me, and I was suddenly feeling more hideously got-down than ever by the prospect of changing my novel. Yet I was glad he was there.

In my reflections I heard him saying again:

'You don't know how difficult things are for me.'

## CHAPTER III

## DARK DAYS

I COMPLETED my work on the isolated passages — I found what I thought might be mistaken for several more. This kind of work was what Robert and I called literary carpentry, and we both enjoyed it. For example, it never failed to give me pleasure to see how, if one began using one's blue pencil at any point on the page of a manuscript and stopped at almost any other point, the thing still read on. (Would that more novelists, especially American naturalistic writers who produce 900 pages of 'total recall', would discover this innocent professional pleasure!) My pleasure in this case was mixed with a good deal of regret for some pleasing, natural scenes. And when I happened in my spare time to read a Deep South novel in which, as you might expect, there was printed a lavish description of a rape, my pleasure was mixed with a lot of bad temper.

However, I thought it wise to show my manuscript with its first alterations to Courtenay's solicitor. In the first place I felt that a pat on the head from him would be encouraging: in the second I had hopes that somehow the excision of isolated passages might have reduced the dominant effect.

Courtenay's solicitor was indeed pleased. I went to see him to collect the manuscript from him.

'This is a step in the right direction, Mr. Lunn. Surely a step in the right direction.' His smiling grey eyes and his shapely lips remained steady. 'I see that you've removed several major isolated passages that must surely have given the Home Office cause to think . . .'

'Cause to think? As if they didn't know!'

And then, thinking of the pleasing, natural, isolated passages that had gone, I thought of the passage in the Deep South novel that, in contrast, had been allowed to remain. My bad temper got the better of me. I pointed out the contrast to Courtenay's solicitor.

He nodded his white-haired head smoothly.

'But, Mr. Lunn, I don't think there'd be any harm in your writing about rape.'

At this my bad temper broke out. 'Thank you for nothing!' I cried. 'I don't want to write about rape. I couldn't anyway — I've no experience of it!'

I saw him looking faintly perturbed by my anger, so I changed my tone.

'Actually,' I said, 'I don't think I could get any experience of it. I'm rather shy, by nature. I like to be encouraged. . . .'

'I wasn't suggesting you should write about rape. I was only illustrating the major contention that you'll remember my putting to you last time we discussed this matter.'

'I see what you mean,' I said. 'I'm allowed to describe sexual activity if it's a crime. What I'm not allowed to describe is a simple, natural f***** that both parties enjoy.'

He nodded his head slowly, as if, for instance, I had at last seen that a straight line is the shortest distance between two points.

'Exactly. That is what I have been trying to put to you in essence. Though of course it's a question of degree. No one, not even the Home Office in its strictest mood, would expect an author not to refer to the phenomenon you mentioned. Refer to it, of course. But in describing it there must be limits to how far an author may go.'

I was reminded — I am sorry to say I was reminded — of a favourite recollection that Robert and I shared, of overhearing two office-girls sitting in front of us in a bus.

'I'm not going out with *him* any more. He wants to go too far,' said one.

To this the other said: 'I agree with you, I really do. If you let them go as far as they want, where would they stop?'

The concept of far-ness had exercised Robert's imagination ever since. What was too far? Or not far enough? And finally what was the farthest you could go?

'I think,' said Courtenay's solicitor, 'we should all agree that in this first draft you go a good deal too far for the Home Office.'

I said: 'I see.'

'That is what governs the dominant effect.' He handed me back my manuscript for the second time. 'I now look forward to reading this excellent book again when good feeling has kept you from going a fraction of an inch further than is absolutely necessary.'

I was dismissed. My alterations had clearly not altered the dominant effect at all. Far from feeling that I had been patted on the head, I felt that I had been kicked in the b**.

It took me some time to realise what the total effect of this interview had been. 'I just can't alter the dominant effect,' I said to Robert.

'I have to admit,' he said, 'that I can't see how the concept of far-ness can be applied to it in any way that would help you.'

'The only thing I can see for it is to scrap the book altogether.'

'I think that would be very foolish of you,' he said sharply.

I said nothing. I felt that Courtenay's solicitor, the Home Office, the Director of Public Prosecutions, and the typical young person into whose hands my book might fall, had between them got me down altogether.

I put the book aside.

'I'll come back to it in a little while,' I said to Elspeth, 'when I feel less persecuted.'

But I did not believe I could ever come back to it.

In the weeks that followed I concealed from Robert that I was not working on the book any more. I could not conceal it from Elspeth. She said nothing to me about it. I could see that she was taking it to heart in a way I had never bargained for. After all, was it not she who was the stable, relaxed person whom everybody had said would cushion my fluctuations of feeling?

I started to wake up in the middle of the night. In the first moment I would feel as if I had awakened naturally, and then suddenly, like a shutter dropping, the cause would come to me. My masterpiece, my small masterpiece . . . dropped into the sea, before it had ever been out in the air and light. I can't see how to alter it, I thought, I *can't* alter it.

One night I realised that Elspeth was awake too. I turned my head on the pillow, and I felt her hand take hold of mine.

'What is it?' I whispered.

Her fingers gripped mine.

'Tell me . . .!' I said.

'I'm worried for you. I know what it means' — she meant my book — 'to you.'

I squeezed her fingers in return. 'Please don't worry, darling. . . .'

There was a pause.

'It can't be helped,' I said.

Suddenly her whisper carried strong emotion. **'If only I could *help* you!'**

I smiled in the darkness. 'Darling, that isn't a thing to worry about. You couldn't be expected to re-write the damned thing.'

'If only I could!'

I whispered lightly, 'One novelist in the family's enough.'

She did not reply.

212

'Cheer up . . .!' I whispered, and to show that I was being playful I began to stroke her face.

I felt tears rolling down her cheeks.

I thought: Oh dear!

I went on stroking her face and then I began to kiss her. It suddenly struck me that it was difficult to know who was trying to comfort whom.

Those were indeed dark days. I simply did not see my way out of them. And my sufferings as an artist were not alleviated, I remember, by my current activities as a civil servant. Not only did I have to go to the office and behave as if there were nothing the matter: I had to put up with one of the chores I would most gladly have let Robert in for if I could. It was interviewing, for some temporary jobs in one of our explosives research establishments, a string of organic chemists.

Organic chemists had come to be my *bêtes noires* — they seemed to me to be characterised by a peculiar combination of narrowness and complacency, having changed neither their techniques nor their opinion of themselves since the days of World War I. Organic chemistry had seen some truly glorious days at the beginning of the century, and the 1914–18 war, with everybody thinking mostly about explosives and poison gas, had been a chemists' war. But after that had come the glorious days of atomic physics; and World War II, with everybody thinking mostly about first radar and then atomic bombs, was a physicists' war. To the sort of young men I had to see the point had not gone home. On they went, sticking together parts of molecules, by their crossword-puzzley techniques, to make big molecules: then, by more crossword-puzzley techniques, they verified that they had made what they thought they had made: and then they started all over again.

When asked if they used techniques nowadays invented and used by physicists, they said to me rebukefully:

'I rely on classical methods.'

And when invited to discuss the way their parts of molecules behaved in terms of electronic structure, they said very
rebukefully indeed:

'I'm afraid I'm not a theoretician.'

Some of them, it seemed to me when I got particularly
desperate, might never have heard the electron had been
discovered.

(In fairness I have to say that since then — I am writing
about 1951 and it is now 1960 — my opinion has changed.
Young organic chemists have changed, to the extent of
whipping at least one 'modern technique', nuclear magnetic
resonance, smartly out of the hands of the physicists.)

Anyway, it was in 1951 when I had to see a string of
rebukeful, classical, non-theoreticians, in a dark February
when I felt more like hiding in a corner and seeing nobody.
However, the chore at last came to an end.

One weekday morning I found myself, instead of interviewing anybody whatsoever, looking into the window of an
antique shop in Sloane Street. I had already stopped to look
into the window of several others, but I should have been hard
put to to say exactly what I had looked at. I was wander-
ing. There was nothing I wanted to do or, for that matter,
to look at. Elspeth had gone to stay for a few days with her
mother, who was ill, and I had taken a day off from the
office. I found it a consolation to be walking instead of
sitting still, and I had calculated that I could rely on the
contents of antique shops to have a slight but certain fascination for me — it was not often, I thought, you came across
a work of art that seduced you with its colour, symmetry
and balance, and at the same time offered you the opportunity to sit on it, eat off it, or keep things in it.

I lingered in front of the windows, hunched in my overcoat, though for February the morning was unusually sunny.
When there was too much reflection from the plate glass, I
put my face close to the pane and cupped my hands on
either side of my eyes; so that I could peer into the calm,

uninhabited depths of the shops, calm with the sheen of lamplight on velvet and brocade, uninhabited because all the things for sale were so expensive that nobody was inside buying anything.

On a small table at the side of one window there was a marquetry box that caught my eye. The door of the box was left open to reveal that it was a miniature chest of drawers. 'It couldn't be prettier,' I said half-aloud. I thought it would do for Elspeth to keep her jewellery in.

Suddenly I was pierced by superstition. If I bought Elspeth the box, we should both come out of our desolation. The gods would be placated. The Home Office would be placated. Elspeth would be happy again. I stared at the box. I pushed open the door of the shop.

The owner of the shop quietly but expeditiously brought the chest out of the window and set it down for me to see. I asked how much it was. Oh, oh, oh!

'It couldn't be prettier,' I heard myself saying. I should not have been surprised to hear myself telling him the whole of my story. I went on staring while he pulled out the drawers one by one, to show me that the bottoms were made of oak and had no worm-holes.

'As far as we know,' he said, courteously giving me what I took to be the old malarkey, 'it was made between 1750 and 1780. You might say it was a copy of the kind of cabinet that came in in the latter part of the seventeenth century.'

I managed to get out of the shop without buying it.

In the street again I was dazzled by the sunshine, and I stood still for a moment, recovering from the price.

I was startled when I heard someone say: 'Joe, what are *you* doing here?'

It was Annette. There she stood, in a tent-like overcoat.

'If it comes to that,' said I, 'what are *you*?'

'The school's shut for scarlet fever. I've just been shopping at MacFisheries.' There was one a few yards further down the street.

I said: 'Surely there's one nearer to where you live.' It seemed incredible that she had taken to shopping at all.

'I prefer this one.' Her tone was so indisputably that of a connoisseur of fish-shops that I did not argue.

I tried to raise a smile. 'I must say London's comforting. One's always running into people one knows.'

'When I first saw you, you were looking as if you were lost.'

I took hold of her elbow. 'Let's go and have some coffee!'

I knew where there was a Kenya café. When we were settled over our coffee and chocolate biscuits, I told her what I had just been doing when she met me.

'I think you ought to buy it,' she said.

I was not surprised by one woman's advising me to buy a present for another woman, as this was the recognised policy of what Robert and I usually referred to as the Trades Union of Women. I said:

'But it's sheer superstition! You can't act on superstition.'

'That's just what you can do,' said Annette. 'One doesn't take the gods seriously, but one does take mental states seriously.' She took off the head-scarf she was wearing and shook out her bell of hair.

I watched her, slightly mesmerised. Her clear light brown eyes seemed to shine with amusement. 'All choices aren't necessarily moral ones, you know.'

I was suddenly reminded of a conversation I had had with her and Elspeth in a steamy café in Bethnal Green. 'Oh, aren't they?' I said — was she taking the mickey out of me?

Annette said: 'I wish Robert's superstitious feelings could be bought off in a similar way.' Her light-eyed smile disappeared. 'He's terribly apprehensive lest anything should go wrong with me or the baby.' She looked at me earnestly.

'He's so persistent with his apprehensions that they become catching.'

'Don't I know that!' I calculated that her baby must be due in about four or five months.

'I hope Robert will get over it,' Annette went on. 'After all, I want to have at least three more.'

'Three more what?' I said. I could scarcely believe she meant babies.

She did mean babies.

'Good gracious!' I said. 'How you've changed!'

'I don't think so.'

I thought for a little while and then enquired with some diffidence: 'How have you fixed on four?'

'That isn't so interesting,' she said, 'as *why* we've fixed on four.'

'All right,' I said, willing to please. 'Tell me *why* have you fixed on four?'

'We think the degree of possessiveness we feel about each other will be less in a family of six than in a family of two.'

'I should think it couldn't help but be,' said I. But then I asked: 'What about your degree of love, though? In particular that of you and Robert for each other?'

In my opinion, loving people takes energy, takes time. If you start to love more people, those you already love have got to accept a cut.

Annette said: 'One has to make up one's mind whether it's worth it or not. I think it is.' She paused and then her tone suddenly changed. It became tender, almost shy — it reminded me of some other occasion, when she had seemed much younger. She said:

'I was never sure Robert wanted me, until he married me. And now I'm terribly possessive about him.'

I was touched. Then I asked:

'What about teaching? Do you intend to go on teaching as well?'

'Naturally.'

217

This really did give me something to think about. I guessed it must have given Robert something to think about, too.

Our waitress, seeing me apparently inactive, came over and asked me if we would like more biscuits or coffee.

Annette said to me: 'Of course, Barbara thinks I ought to go on teaching.' And she laughed to herself.

I laughed to myself.

'You know,' said Annette, 'that she's pregnant too?'

I did not know. 'Good gracious!' I said again. 'I thought they'd finished procreating.' Their youngest child, as far as I recalled, must be about seven.

'She and Harry thought they'd like to start again.'

I said nothing.

'I don't know if it was our example,' Annette said with a sort of comfortable amusement.

'I have a theory,' I said, 'that people's marriages interact when they come up against each other.'

Annette laughed. 'Everybody will be having babies!' She finished her coffee.

I suddenly thought: What about Elspeth and me? I felt, I have to admit it, that we were being left out of something. So much for that old Pressure of Society, dammit! I felt envious of Robert and Annette, envious of Harry and Barbara, envious of everybody who was going to have a baby.

Annette put on her head-scarf and then picked up a string bag in which there was a parcel of what I presumed to be fish. I noticed that her face looked thinner, as if the flesh were drawn down from her chin. She said thoughtfully:

'I shall have to get a taxi.'

We went out into the street. The morning was still calm and sunny, and there was a faint smell of wood-smoke diffusing from where a gardener must have been burning leaves in Cadogan Place.

'It's like spring,' Annette murmured. I thought of my book, unprinted; of Elspeth, unable to help. . . .

Two stringy superior-looking women who were passing glanced with distaste at Annette's head-scarf — they were hatless, their grey hair being beautifully arranged and dyed, in one case purple and in the other steely blue. They got into a large Rolls. I stopped a taxi for Annette.

'You go and buy that chest for Elspeth!' she said happily, and drove away.

I stood alone again on the pavement.

I went back to the shop. You may think I was in the grip of neurosis. Maybe — but not quite so far in the grip of neurosis as not to reflect that, if I were going to try and buy off the gods, I was not necessarily bound to pay Sloane Street prices.

The box was back in the window. Compulsively I pushed open the shop door. Courteously the owner made his appearance from the depths of the shop, and, when he saw that it was me, got the box out of the window again and placed it in front of me. I stared at it.

I admired it, said how much I should like to have it, and observed how costly I thought it was. Then I uttered the formula:

'Is that the lowest you'll let it go for?'

'Let it go' was a dealer's expression. What an expression! I thought as I waited to hear this dealer reply. Two things might now happen. He might say Yes. Or he might say — you think he might say No? Then you have not bothered to learn the ritual. The alternative to Yes is the antiphonal formula: 'I'll go and look in my book, and see what I gave for it.'

With a thrill I heard him utter the antiphonal formula. While he retired to wherever he kept his book, I waited patiently, quietly opening and shutting the drawers of the chest.

He was willing to 'let it go' for £8 10s. 0d. less than he had originally asked. I bought it.

Afterwards I stood outside the shop, holding the chest in

my arms while I waited for a taxi, and feeling a peculiar emotion. The price I had paid for it was enough to make anyone feel peculiar, yet it was not the price that caused me to feel so peculiar.

In my arms I was holding a present. A present for Elspeth, a present for the gods, a present for the Home Office . . . ? I scarcely knew which. I only knew that somehow the dark days had reached a turning-point. Whether they were going to turn lighter or even darker was a different matter.

## CHAPTER IV

## THE TURNING-POINT?

ELSPETH was due to come home. The present was awaiting her. Now that I came to consider it with detachment, I was not sure whether I liked it or not.

And yet, as I moved round the flat, making everything look tidy in readiness for her, I thought I did like it. With a large gin-and-tonic in my hand I sat on the edge of the bed and looked at it, on top of the chest-of-drawers. In the shaded lighting from behind me the scrolly patterns of acanthus leaves, composed of golden-brown woods splashed with malachite and mother-of-pearl, seemed to glisten with some inner radiance of their own.

'It couldn't be prettier,' I said to myself. 'Elspeth will love it.'

You can see from this that I was not certain about something. I was not certain that the gods would love it. I had not seen my way yet through my literary difficulties. My manuscript remained in the cupboard where I had put it on its most recent return from Courtenay's solicitor.

Superstition, neurosis. . . . Not for nothing was I the son of a nonconformist clergyman, I thought. Behind the words superstition and neurosis, in my mind, lurked the word self-indulgence.

'I shall be glad when Elspeth comes,' I said to the warm, empty room.

Elspeth came. I told her about the present for her, but not about the superstition and neurosis. I told her it was to put her jewellery in.

'It's beautiful!' she cried. 'Oh darling . . .' She kissed me and thanked me.

It did look beautiful.

We sat down side by side on the edge of the bed with our arms round each other. After a while she said:

'But I haven't got any jewellery to put in it.'

I smiled into her eyes. 'You shall have, my darling.'

I noticed that her eyes looked tired. At the same time they seemed to be searching in mine. I knew what she was thinking. The dark days. . . . The marquetry box had not diverted her.

'Buying it was a turning-point,' I said. 'I felt sure it marked a turning-point.'

She looked down at her lap.

I noticed the thin gold wedding-ring on her finger. I touched it.

She put her head on my shoulder.

We began to talk about other things. I tried to keep my spirits up and I could tell she was trying to do the same.

In the middle of the night I woke up. The shutter suddenly dropped. Nothing had changed.

I lay very still. Nothing had changed at all.

'Darling . . .' Elspeth whispered.

I did not reply.

Elspeth could tell I was awake. 'Darling,' she whispered, 'speak to me.'

I turned and put my arms round her but I could not speak.

'I wakened every night while I was away,' she said, 'wishing I could help you.'

'My darling,' I said. 'This is where we were the other night.'

'But it's *where I am*!' she cried.

I did not say anything.

'When two people are married to each other,' she said, 'they should be a help to each other. You're a help to me, but I'm not to you. . . .'

I held her more tightly. 'That's silly,' I said gently.

'We've been married a year and I'm no use to you.'

A sudden recollection came to me that was too poignant to be borne. *You must never say that again* — I heard her voice. Before I could manage to get any words out she said:

'You must wish you'd never married me!'

I was staggered by the incredibleness of the remark, of the *situation*. . . . It had never occurred to me that she might feel like this. My discoveries in our married life had been first that she was a living, independently existing person, and next that she was a living, independently acting person. Love, contrary to a lot of what is said about it, does not teach you to know everything about the loved-one. It makes you more sharply aware of some things, but it definitely makes you miss others. I ought not to have missed this. I was deeply ashamed of myself for not having seen it.

'My darling,' I said, 'I love you. I shall always love you. You're my wife. I wouldn't have it any different . . . I couldn't imagine it any different now. . . .'

I felt tears coming into my eyes.

I went on talking to her. I was speaking to her from the bottom of my heart. As the things that lie at the bottom of one's heart are few in number and very simple, I suppose I must have become somewhat repetitious. I would not have had my life any different: I could not imagine it any different now. I loved her. I wanted to give her confidence, unshakeable for the rest of our lives. And she listened to me.

Had things been such that the question could have been put to me at the time, I should have answered that I was thinking only of her soul and mine, that I was expressing truly spiritual love. I think I was. I was genuinely surprised, after a while, by being reminded that the soul and the body are one. I had not noticed the body, but it was clearly there.

When we next started to talk we had the light on.

I was looking at Elspeth's face. 'My darling . . .'

'Yes?' She did not smile at me.

There was a pause. I heard my watch ticking on the bed-side table.

'What are you going to do about your book?' She still wanted to know.

I looked at her. 'I've thought what to do,' I said. 'While I was in the bathroom.'

Her blue eyes looked at me steadily.

'My life,' I said, 'is obviously a series of acts of will. So I've just got to make another. Tomorrow I'll start writing the whole thing again, and then *not* send it to Courtenay's egregious solicitor. I'm going to ask Harry to get his Home Office friend to read it instead. With a bit of luck that could settle it.'

Her glance wavered, and suddenly, hesitantly, she smiled.

I remained bending over her, looking at her. The liberating idea actually had come to me in the bathroom.

But now I began to say something else to her — and until I had begun it I had no idea I was going to say it.

'My darling,' I whispered. 'I love you. . . . You're my wife. I shall always love you. I want us to have——' I did not finish the sentence. Instead I blurted out: 'I want you to make me a dad. As soon as possible!'

With a quick movement she turned her head away on the pillow. I heard her breath drawn in, and she burst into tears.

'What is it?' I cried, trying to see her face.

'Darling . . . *Yes* . . .'

At last she turned back to me. I got my handkerchief from under the pillow and dried her face.

'You'd better dry yours,' she said.

I stroked her hair for a long time while she looked up at me. Again I heard my watch ticking.

'Fancy all this happening in the middle of the night,' I said.

She appeared not to have heard me. Suddenly I noticed a faint flicker at the corners of her mouth.

'What are you thinking?' I said.

'I was thinking if only you'd said what you've just said half an hour ago . . .'

I burst into laughter.

We both laughed. And then went quiet again. Somehow we found ourselves staring at the marquetry cabinet, which seemed to be glistening radiantly at us.

'Like the flowers that bloom in the spring,' I said, 'it obviously had nothing to do with the case.'

'It's beautiful,' Elspeth said firmly. 'I shall always be fond of it. Thank you for it, darling.'

## CHAPTER V

## THE STREAM OF LIFE

WHEN I told Robert that Elspeth was pregnant, he was stirred, I could see, to strong emotion.

'I'm very, very glad,' he said. 'That's the best news we've had for a long time.' Startlingly he shook me by the hand.

'I think it's pretty good news too,' I said. (I must say it did strike me that fertility must be the predominant state in which the human race existed — hence, when you come to think about it, its history.)

Robert was also stirred to strong generalisation.

'There's no doubt that having children,' he said, 'does make one feel part of the Stream of Mankind, in a way that one wouldn't otherwise.' He nodded his head loftily in agreement with himself.

To one who was classed MISC/INEL for the Stream of Mankind this came as a most poignant, hope-giving thought.

I nodded my head vigorously in poignant hopeful agreement with him.

'It's a very good thing,' Robert went on in the same tone, 'for a writer.'

'Anything that's good for a writer will be good for me,' I said, trying to please.

Robert's eyes glinted. 'Though it's fair to say that the majority of writers have achieved it without its having done their books any noticeable good.'

The moment I laughed he switched to lofty seriousness again.

I said nothing. In fact, thinking of my own small master-piece no longer caused me such pain as it had in the days when I saw no way out of the dilemma presented to me by Courtenay's solicitor. I had spoken to Harry.

We had met again, for lunch yet again at Harry's club. Harry had insisted. There were not veal croquettes this time. There were chicken croquettes.

I put my proposition to Harry. I said: 'Presumably the chap who let you know the Home Office were going to start a fresh drive must be pretty close to the policy-making machine.' I saw a hunted look come into Harry's eyes. 'If you ask him to read my book, when I've re-written it, he ought to be able to let us have some sort of authoritative opinion.'

'I see that,' said Harry. The hunted look was disappearing.

'We could then tell Courtenay, and that would eliminate the necessity of having to get it approved of by his egreg-iously pi solicitor — which seems to me next door to impossible . . .'

Harry's small bright eyes became even brighter.

'You think I might,' he said, 'chance my arm . . .?'

I had never thought I should live to see the day when I would hear Harry refer to 'chancing his arm' with a frisson of pleasure.

'That's what I should like you to do, if you will, Harry.'

Harry gave me a look which indicated that he had a good idea what I was thinking. However, he was prevented from saying anything by an interruption. Two men were passing our table and we both happened to look up. One of them was Harry's boss.

Harry's boss stopped, gave us a shark-like smile, and then, glancing from me to Harry and back, said in his croaking voice:

'Hello, Lunn. I've just been reading your last book.'

And at that he moved on.

'A man of action,' I said to Harry, 'but not of comment.'

Harry grinned.

We went on with our chicken croquettes.

'Of course we know,' Harry said, 'my chap in the Home Office definitely did like your last book.'

I nodded my head.

'Joe, I *will* chance my arm! I'm sure I can manipulate it. I'll get him to read the manuscript and let us know if the Home Office would be likely to do anything about it or not. He wouldn't need to tell me in so many words.' A light came into his eyes. 'I could piece it together.'

'I'm sure he wouldn't,' I said.

'There's only one other thing . . .'

I looked at him, wondering what on earth that could be.

'There'd be no objection,' Harry said diffidently, 'to my reading it first?'

I burst into laughter. 'None at all, my dear Harry!'

I felt liberated. I knew I could get down to work again on the book with the prospect of getting a sensible opinion on it from an authoritative person. Thank goodness, I thought, for the Civil Service.

And so life had perked up again.

Soon after that Elspeth had told me her own liberating news.

As Robert remarked, there was reason for feeling part of the Stream of Mankind. Indeed calling it the Stream of Mankind seemed to me putting it in too abstract a form. I felt there was a sort of clubbiness in the air: Robert and Annette were due to have their baby in the late summer, Harry and Barbara in the autumn, and Elspeth and I at the end of the year. We were all in it together.

I happened to say to Barbara that as far as we were concerned, the Stream of Mankind was in no way to drying up.

'Parents,' she said firmly, 'have to have two children merely to replace themselves, and three to make a positive contribution.' She smiled. 'My dear Joe, you've got a long way to go yet . . .' All the same, her voice sounded softer. I noticed it was distinctly musical. I wondered why I had never noticed that before.

'Do you see me,' I said, 'having three children?'

'I don't see why not.'

I smiled at her without answering. And well I might! How things had changed!

Congratulating myself on my saintliness, in not pointing this out, I asked playfully:

'Or even four?'

'I expect Elspeth'll have some views on that,' she replied, smiling away the underlying Trades Union of Women tone.

'Naturally,' I said, like a well-trained member of the federation of employers.

After a few months the sort of clubbiness that had come into the air surrounding our close friends and us became even more clubby.

In the past I had been unequivocally in favour of the State running a free medical service, without considering whether I in particular stood to gain a great deal from it. If I, who happened to be well most of the time, helped to subsidise people who were ill, it seemed to me fair enough. Elspeth, a sterner Socialist than I, had come out even more strongly on this side of the argument: a free National Health Service was her idea of doing good; and given the opportunity of doing good or doing bad, she inevitably chose to do good.

One day, apropos of having the baby, she said to me:

'Of course I shall have it on the N.H.S.'

I said: 'Of course.'

And we discovered that she had been enrolled into one of the most gigantic, engulfing clubs in the country, that of mothers having babies on the N.H.S. At first Elspeth quailed, but conscience kept her to it, and soon she was overwhelmed. Month after month she had check-ups, did exercises, went to classes, and brought home vitamin pills and orange-juice. The effect of it all became so hypnotic that I began to feel like a co-opted member of the club myself. Elspeth told me some prospective fathers had sympathetic morning sickness. As I felt very well in the mornings, I offered to show willing by joining in the relaxation exercises.

At the time predicted, Annette had her baby. Robert, after going about for a few days so pale as to look green, turned up at the office looking as pink as if he had drunk half a bottle of brandy. The child was a boy, perfect in all respects, and Annette was extraordinarily well.

'Of course, having a child makes one feel part of the Stream of Mankind,' he said, too inflated to remember that he had said it to me before, 'in a way that one doesn't otherwise.'

Who was I to deflate him?

His speech sounded wonderfully lofty and detached, but I had intimations — and I was pretty sure he had intimations — that he was going to be an absurdly devoted father. Strongly affectionate and subtly power-loving, he was just cut out for it. Furthermore, if Annette's theories about the size of his family won the day, there was going to be plenty of scope for him.

It was a little while after this incident at the office that another, rather different one, occurred. I was chatting with my P.A. when she happened to say:

'I wonder if we're going to see you going to America later on in the year.'

'Oh?' I said.

She saw my surprise. 'I thought you knew . . .' She blushed at the thought of her indiscretion and explained: 'It's that Mr. Malone who came to see you that time, you remember him——'

'Indeed I do!'

'He's written to Mr. Murray-Hamilton about a conference they're going to have in Washington. And I *thought* he'd mentioned your name to go to represent the ministry.'

It was clear that she did more than think that Tom Malone

had mentioned my name — the grapevine must have told her. I did not press her for further indiscretion.

About three weeks later Robert was discussing our annual Staff Promotion Review.

'I'm afraid I may have to leave you to cope with the last part of it single-handed,' he said, and paused. 'I shall probably have to go to Washington.'

'*You?*'

He looked at me. I told him why I had said '*You?*'

Robert was apologetic. He admitted that Tom Malone actually had mentioned my name. 'As a possibility, but no more,' he said. 'He knows as well as you know that he can't formally ask for a particular individual to be sent.'

I saw that.

Robert said: 'Anyway, Murray-Hamilton couldn't be induced by me or anyone else to send *you*.' He paused and softened his tone. 'I didn't tell you all this because I thought there was no point in worrying you more than was necessary.'

So that was that. The incident, unlike the ledger for Right and Wrong, was closed.

I turned my mind to other things. The stream of life was carrying me on.

## CHAPTER VI

## STILL DARKER DAYS

A T the predicted time Barbara had her baby. Harry confided to me:

'You know, I adore very young babies.'

'Good gracious!' I said. I thought I should adore mine the more the older they got.

Harry looked knowing. 'There are quite a lot of men who do, you know.'

This had never occurred to me before. It seemed to me incredible that I must constantly be passing quite ordinary-looking men in the street, in Oxford Street for instance, whose natures were stirred to the depths by the sight of newly-born infants.

On the day of their child's christening Harry and Barbara gave a large party. Elspeth and I went.

'There'll be no jiving this time,' I said. She was getting quite large.

Elspeth grinned affectionately. 'I think it'll be all right, provided you don't throw me on to the floor again.'

I grinned affectionately back. *The Dark Town Strutters' Ball.* 'This is the right one for me! . . .' I remembered that statement which had expressed for me the poetic climax in human experience, falling in love. The fact of the matter was that, utterly flat as the statement was, I still had nothing whatsoever to add to it.

'Well, even so, we're not going to,' I said finally.

Elspeth smiled in a complacent way.

Everybody was of the opinion that her child was going to be a boy. Her doctor, her mother, the woman at the clinic, and even Barbara, committed themselves with a single practised glance to this opinion — the woman who came to clean our flat said: 'I can tell by where you carry it, dear. That's a boy, mark my words.' Talk about clubbiness! I, now thoroughly enclubbed, went along with the rest.

We enjoyed the party, even though we did not jive. I had just finished re-writing my novel, and that had brought me temporarily to a state of invulnerable high spirits. In the sense that the dominant effect was *me*, the book remained of course the same. In the sense that the dominant effect derived from specific expressions of feeling that might bring a blush to the cheek of a young policeman, it was toned down — rather skilfully, I thought. I handed the manuscript over to Harry on the day after the party. I then had to wait.

Immediately after that the Promotion Review began. Robert went to Washington.

The Promotion Review went on. Robert found official reasons for staying in America.

The Promotion Review ended. And then, late one afternoon, my P.A. came in and said:

'I've just heard from Mr. Murray-Hamilton's P.A. that there's a Parliamentary Question on the way over. Mr. Spinks has told her to mark it first to Mr. Froggatt, and then to you.'

I presumed it to be a question addressed by some Member of Parliament to our minister about something he thought was wrong. P.Q.s were a rare occurrence in our office. (Far be it from me to say that this was because we rarely did anything wrong. It was just that our work was not the sort that immediately evoked grievances among the public.) I regretted that Robert was not there to cope with it, and said:

'Tell Mr. Froggatt to bring it in as soon as it arrives.'

Actually this order was unnecessary, as everybody dropped whatever he was doing when a P.Q. came in — anyone who thinks civil servants are not sensitive to what is

said about them in Parliament does not know anything
about it.

It was next morning before Froggatt came in with the
file.

'It's the usual thing,' he said lugubriously. 'If you don't
get what you want, kick the civil servant whom you think's to
blame.' He looked at me in a thoughtful way. 'I don't
know what the public would do if they hadn't got us as
scapegoats.'

Suddenly his long fiddle face and large slightly aggrieved-
looking eyes struck me as exactly what you would expect to
see actually on a scapegoat.

I nodded my head sympathetically.

'I think you'll find all the relevant papers are there,' he
said.

The file began with a short letter from the Right Honourable Mr. Adalbert Tiarks, M.P., to our minister, saying he
would like our minister to advise him on the reply to a letter,
which he enclosed, from one of his constituents. This is what
the letter said:

Dear Mr. Tiarks,

   I do not expect you will remember me though I remember you, as I was the office-boy when you gained
your first post with our firm as Assistant Sales Manager,
North-West Sub-Region. In these circumstances I trust
you will not think I am presuming to write to you. It is
about my son Wilfred. I trust when you hear the facts
that you will agree that it is a case of injustice as I do.

   My son Wilfred has got his B.Sc. in chemistry with
honours and has just taken his Doctor of Philosophy. Thus
he is a highly-trained scientist. He read an advertisement
for highly-trained scientists to work for the Government
and applied for it. He got his letter for interview at the
Ministry and went up with high hopes, as he is always
reading in the newspapers that there is a grave shortage

234

of highly-trained scientists. He told me when he came home that he thought he had failed. He had.

The reason my son thought he had failed was the unfairness of the chairman of his interview. The chairman told my son that he was not a chemist himself and asked in a manner which upset my son if my son knew something about electrons which Wilfred says do not come into his studies, as he has been making chemical substances that have never been made before. My son is convinced that if he had been interviewed by a highly-qualified chemist like his professor he would have got through with flying colours. Instead of that, because of the Ministry's chairman, he is debarred from working for his country and may have to have his call-up for the Army.

I trust you will pardon this letter for being so long, for I do feel it is a case of injustice that it is only right to write to you about it. It has been a great strain to his mother and me to keep Wilfred at college, and so it is a great blow to us when his hopes are shattered thus. Is it therefore the Government's intention that a boy like my son, who has got his Doctor of Philosophy, should be debarred from serving his country through the unfairness of a Civil Servant?

Yours truly,<br>
R. T. Longstaff (Mr.)

P.S. I have not mentioned that I am writing this letter to Wilfred.

The letter was touching, but I have to admit that my predominant response to it was not sympathy for a father. It was a peculiarly unwelcome kind of concern for myself.

The file had been marked first to Froggatt so that he could attach all the relevant papers. There they were, attached. An application from W. Longstaff for a post as Temporary Scientific Officer; a couple of professional references, one from his professor and the other from his, supervisor of research; a copy of a letter from us calling him for interview and another saying that we had no appointment to offer; and on top, the last object to be attached by my P.A. — a rectangular index-card covered with my own handwriting.

While I was checking them, there was a telephone call. It was from Spinks, Stinker Spinks.

'About that P.Q. you should have on your desk at the present moment——'

'Yes,' I said. 'I have it.'

'Murray-Hamilton will be in Glasgow till the end of the week. I've just telephoned him. He'll want a suggested draft reply from you on his desk without fail next Monday morning.'

I said: 'Yes.' *Suggested* . . . anybody but Spinks would just have said a draft reply. I put down the receiver and looked at the index-card. It was filled up with notes about W. Longstaff made by me during the course of his interview.

'Tallish stringy white-faced schizoid-looking individual with unusually handsome eyes. $2:3\frac{1}{2}:5$. Got a II(i) chem, took to organic "because it's more orderly". Ph.D. without a single fresh idea of his own but has given satisfn to his prof classical synthesis. Not the sort of soma for creative energy. Tight constrained meagre temperament. Thoroughly second-rate but will prob get on through nagging persistence. Passionately anxious to come to us thereby avoid military service. Proposing get married — "prefers cycling". Reads *Daily Tel* "because it's unbiassed". Cripes! P.T.O.'

I read it with sarcastic ill-humour. The aim of my notes was to recreate the man for me when I read them. Reading these notes I remembered W. Longstaff. He was awful.

I turned the card over.

'Board more unanimous not to have him at any price than I'd expected. P.H.S. wanted us to send protest to D.S.I.R. about his being given Ph.D. Grant in the first place. Cripes again.'

I must say I read that side with a diminution in ill-humour. W. Longstaff was awful, but it did not follow that my colleagues would inevitably see his awfulness. They had! And furthermore P.H.S. was one of our cleverest, toughest, youngish organic chemists.

The telephone rang again. It was Stinker again.

'A letter has just come in for Murray-Hamilton from W. Longstaff's professor. I'm sending it over by hand.'

'Thanks,' I said.

'Also I've just heard from the Minister's principal private secretary — the Minister's personally interested in this case.'

'Perhaps *he* remembers R. T. Longstaff as an office-boy.'

Stinker laughed. He at least had a sense of humour — but nothing, let me repeat, nothing else.

I sat waiting for the professor's letter, not surprised by the fact that, in the Civil Service, it never rains but it pours. The Civil Service is devised, rightly, to provide an elaborate system of cross-checks and cross-references: let there be a break at some point or other in the network and switches are tripped all over the place.

The professor's letter, I thought when I got it, was designed to trip me. It was from W. Longstaff's professor of organic chemistry to Murray-Hamilton, and it began characteristically 'Dear Sir, I am at a loss to understand why, etc. . . .'

I could have made his loss good in no time at all, I reflected. Unfortunately that was not what I was officially required to do. I was required to draft a reply from Murray-Hamilton to the Right Honourable Mr. Adalbert Tiarks, M.P. I wished Robert were at home to draft it instead of me.

I knew, of course, exactly what line the department should take — it was perfectly obvious, not to say laid down in the rubric anyway.

Justice to W. Longstaff had been done. Murray-Hamilton would accept that without much trouble. Justice to W.

237

Longstaff must now be seen to be done. W. Longstaff must be interviewed again by a board, (i) whose chairman did not ask him any unkind questions about the electronic structure of the molecules he synthesised and (ii) whose constitution was such that his professor was not at a loss to understand how it arrived at its verdict.

To settle (i) make Robert the chairman.

To settle (ii) co-opt the professor on the board, so that he would be a party to the decision.

It was perfectly simple, perfectly straightforward.

(And W. Longstaff, being awful, would be turned down again.)

Why, you may ask, did I find it so hard to draft a reply for Murray-Hamilton? Why did I wish Robert were at home to draft it instead of me? What inhibited me?

Every time I put my pen to paper I thought of Murray-Hamilton, brooding, reflecting. No matter what I wrote on my minute paper, I knew what was written on the great ledger . . . I had done Wrong.

Of course I managed to write something in the end. And I thought it wise to send Robert a letter by airmail, saying what was going on.

On the following Monday morning, when Murray-Hamilton must have been studying what I had finally managed to write, the door of my office suddenly opened and Robert came in.

His face was white. 'I got your letter and caught the over-night plane back,' he said.

His face was white but not white from fatigue.

'Gawd, do you think it's as bad as that?' My spirits were plunging so fast that I could not keep up with them.

Robert flopped down on my table.

'If I judge the situation aright,' he said, 'it's probably worse.'

I stared at him. He had fallen into one of those moods of heavy silence that always indicated despair.

At last he roused himself.

'Look,' he said, 'I shall have to tell you this. I haven't told you before because I didn't want to worry you unnecessarily. I thought you'd got enough on your hands, with your book sub judice and Elspeth pregnant. . . . For some time now Murray-Hamilton has been proposing to eliminate this directorate altogether, or rather "roll it up", as he calls it, with the establishments division. . . . They'll find something else for me to do, probably with wider scope, where they can give me my head a bit more. . . . But there was absolutely nothing I could do to make him change his mind about you. He wanted the changes to eliminate you altogether.'

I could not say anything.

Robert gave an odd wry smile to himself as he went on. 'He's a very pertinacious man. But so am I. Also he's a humane man — outside keeping you in the Civil Service he'd do anything to help you. But I told him his humaneness wasn't much use. . . . Anyway, before I went to Washington I thought I'd just about argued him into the position of letting you have some sort of rôle in the new organisation. . . .'

He stopped. He did not need to tell me anything else.

In the end he stood up and said, not looking at me:

'I suppose you've not had any news about your book yet?'

I shook my head.

He went towards the door. 'I'd better go over and tell Murray-Hamilton I'm back.'

## CHAPTER VII

## HELP

THAT evening I had to tell Elspeth.

'What is it, darling?' she said when I came into the flat.

'You'd better sit down while I tell you,' I said.

As she already knew about *l'affaire* Longstaff, there was not much more in quantity to be said.

We sat side by side on the sofa. The flat seemed absolutely silent. There was a faint smell in the air of the dinner cooking, possibly burning.

'So there it is,' I said.

Elspeth put her arm round me.

'Try not to worry, darling . . .' she said. 'We shall be all right. . . .'

I looked down at my hands. All right — you and I and the little one! I thought bitterly.

'We shall be all right,' she repeated. 'I can help you, darling.'

I looked at her.

'We can earn a living together,' she said. 'You can write. And I'll go back to teaching. I can work. I can help.'

I could not speak.

'So you see . . .' she said.

I put my arm round her and pressed my face against the side of her throat. 'My darling, my darling,' I kept on saying.

We remained like that for what seemed like hours. I cannot tell you if the smell of burning got stronger. I noticed nothing.

The telephone rang.

'What's that?' I said.

'The telephone,' said Elspeth.

I got up and staggered across the room to answer it.

A light, high voice said gaily:

'The coast's clear!'

'What?' said I.

There was a hiatus. The voice said: 'Is that you, Joe?'

'Yes, it is.'

'This is Harry. The coast's clear!'

'What coast?'

Harry laughed. 'Were you drunk, or fast asleep or something? I'm talking about your novel. The coast's clear. I've just heard . . . You can go ahead. Have it printed. It's O.K. by the Home Office.'

'Good God!' I said.

'And may I say,' said Harry, 'I think it's excellent, Joe. It's your best book.'

At last I understood. By this time Elspeth was trying to share the earpiece with me.

Harry said: 'I don't know what you and Elspeth are up to — you sound *non compos* to me . . . I'm going to ring off, and you can ring me back when you feel up to it.'

With an especially fluent, honeyed, triumphant Goodbye he rang off.

'Well!' I looked at Elspeth.

Her eyes were shining. 'Ring up Annette and Robert!' she said.

We rang up Annette and Robert.

And then we stood, facing each other. I put out my arms and Elspeth moved towards me.

'Whoops!' She put her hand on her stomach.

'What on earth?'

'It's all right. Just the baby moved.'

'The darling baby, the darling you!' I embraced both.

Then we noticed the smell of burning.

After we had eaten our dinner, we thought about Murray-Hamilton and the Civil Service again. We spent the night in each other's arms, not sleeping much because of the strange combination of misery and joy.

Next morning Robert came straight into my office to hear all over again such detail as I had heard from Harry.

'It couldn't be better,' he said. 'I wasn't able to do anything at all with Murray-Hamilton. Incidentally you'll be interested to know that in the new organisation there's going to be no place for your old enemy Stinker Spinks. He's a permanent, so he can't be sacked, but I think you'll find he's moved off into distinctly outer darkness.'

'Well, poor old Stinker!' I cried. Detestable though he was, at that moment I really did feel sorry for him.

Robert looked at me. 'I wasn't able to do anything with Murray-Hamilton; but it occurred to me, last night after your news had cheered me up, that we're not entirely without resources. You could appeal, of course; but as a temporary you wouldn't really stand a chance. No. I think we've got to try to circumvent Murray-Hamilton. There are higher bosses than him, and they haven't all consigned you to the wrong side of the ledger.' He paused. 'I'm going to talk to Harold Johnson about you. I know him better now. . . . In fact some little time ago, with you in mind, I got him on the subject of temporaries.' Robert's eyes sparkled momentarily. 'As usual with him, when you press the button you get a powerful — and possibly surprising — response. He took my point. And characteristically observed there's no reason why temporaries should be treated like dogs.' Robert paused again. 'I think I'm going to talk to him again. I don't know why I shouldn't tell him that *I* think you're doing good work and these people are trying to *get* you.'

I said: 'I shouldn't think he could reasonably intervene.'

'There you're wrong,' said Robert. 'Justice is an absolute fetish with all these people. If it struck him in that way, he could perfectly well, as a personal matter, have a look at the papers.'

In spite of my anxiety I could not help thinking of Sir Harold Johnson. 'You know what *you* want to do?' Pause. 'Get rid of your inhibitions!' Suppose, though, he did send for the papers and saw the record of what happened when my control over my inhibitions momentarily lapsed, what then?

Robert decided. 'I'm going to try it, anyway. Something tells me the tide has turned.'

Well, Robert tried it.

I am now at the stage in my story where you do not want another long scene in which Robert told me the result of his trying it. Sir Harold Johnson did not send for me, of course, so I did not have a scene with him. He sent, of course, for the papers.

We had some anxious days of waiting. And then Robert came into my office and I read the look on his face. I shall never forget it, because, just as he was about to speak, two men came into the room. Both were wearing raincoats, and one was wearing a bowler hat. The one who was not wearing the bowler hat was carrying a surveyor's tape-measure.

Neither of them said a word to us or to each other. I recognised them at once as from the Ministry of Works. They had a way of setting about their business, as if nobody else were in the room, at which I never ceased to marvel. It was utterly beyond reproach. I could only imagine that in training them for this kind of activity the Ministry of Works put them through a most rigorous assault-course from which only star recruits ever passed out. Dazzlingly oblivious of us, the one with the tape-measure measured my carpet, and the one without the tape-measure watched him. They went out again.

My fate. I was to be moved to another department, well away from Murray-Hamilton, to what was an Assistant Secretary's post. I was to hold this particular post in my present rank, with the prospect of taking on the rank of the job in a year's time.

'He's a fair-minded man,' said Robert magisterially, 'and used to doing as he sees fit to do.'

'I don't feel I can say anything impartial,' said I.

'What I don't understand,' said Robert simply archiepiscopally, 'is that somehow or other you must have made a favourable impression on him.'

'You \* \* \* \* \* \*!' I cried.

Robert only said: 'I'm inclined to think your troubles are now over.'

## CHAPTER VIII

## SCENE FROM MARRIED LIFE

I RANG up the hospital — it was just after midnight — and an Irish nurse told me the news.

'You've got a beautiful little durl.'

'Little what?'

'A beautiful little durl.'

I realised she must mean a beautiful little girl. A little *girl*? They had *all* said we were going to have a boy.

'Are you sure?' I asked. 'My wife's name is Lunn. Mrs. Lunn.'

'That's right, Mr. Lunn. You've got a beautiful little durl.' From her tone I could tell she was now thinking me as stupid as I was thinking her.

'How are they?' I said, playing for time.

'They're both fine.'

If I was going to ask her to make sure they had not made a mistake with the babies, I must do it now, I thought. I felt embarrassed.

'If you're quite sure . . .' I began.

'Sure, an' I'm sure. That's right, Mr. Lunn.' She wanted to get off the line. 'You can come and see them to-morrow night. Now you can have a good night's sleep, Mr. Lunn. Cheerio.'

I put down the receiver and burst into happy laughter. Of course we had got a beautiful little girl. I was delighted. I got back into bed again, but I was much too excited to begin a good night's sleep. For one thing I had to adjust myself to a new idea — as, in due course, would all those know-alls. Yet the new idea was entrancing. A beautiful little girl. . . . Fathers had made fools of themselves over daughters since the beginning of time, and I found myself ready to make a start.

The following morning I enjoyed sending telegrams to relations and advertisements to *The Times* and the *Daily Telegraph*. I thought of the people who would read them — how many of them would remember that as little as two years ago they had written me off as far as getting married was concerned? How many of them, now that they could be seen to have been wrong, would realise they had been wrong?

None.

Time had passed. Like Communists whom we had seen reverse their attitudes at regular intervals, they had never been wrong: what they had believed at any particular point in time was a historical necessity for that particular point in time — and therefore right. Happy persons! Fortunate human beings! However, do not think I bore them any ill-will. I felt too happy a person, too fortunate a human being myself — deserved though my fortune might be! In the New Year I was going to move to a better job, away from Murray-Hamilton and Spinks. And in the spring my second little masterpiece was going to come out after all.

That evening I went to see Elspeth and the baby. It was the first time I had visited a maternity ward. I, and all the other fathers, were collected in the hospital corridor till the clock struck seven, when we all charged along to the door of the maternity ward — and then slowed up. The floor was softly polished; the beds looked white and fresh; the air was warm; there were flowers on a big table in the middle of the room; and in all the beds round the walls were women looking radiant.

I found Elspeth and skidded across the floor to her.

'You look wonderful!' I cried. Her dark hair, which she had had cut specially short for the occasion, was brushed over her forehead; her eyes shone; the brackets at the corners of her mouth were flickering. I kissed her and the smell of lime flowers wafted into my nose. 'You really do look wonderful, darling.'

'Why not?'

I looked at her. 'Where's the baby?'

'There, all the time.' She pointed to a small box, which I had not noticed, hooked on the end of the bed.

I looked at my first-born child.

Then I looked at Elspeth. 'She looks like your mother,' I said.

'I,' said Elspeth, 'thought she looked like yours.'

I stood looking at the child for a long time. Her eyes were shut, and I thought she was breathing terribly fast — I did not know all babies breathe terribly fast. I touched her hand and she opened her eyes. I caught a glimpse of deep violet-blue. . . .

'Oh, she's going to be pretty!' I cried, and tears came into my eyes. I glanced at Elspeth and saw that she was smiling with some satisfaction.

I went and sat down beside Elspeth and held her hand. I stroked her wrist. I began to kiss her wrist.

'Is this allowed?' I whispered.

She glanced around the room and I did the same. In all the white beds were women looking radiant, and beside them dark-clothed men were sitting holding their hands, intently whispering to them. I heard Elspeth breathing.

'Good gracious!' I whispered.

She shook her head in a way that signified 'I know . . .' I swallowed.

Elspeth put her hand on my hair. 'It's understandable.'

I looked up at her. 'Now I come to think of it, I suppose it is.' I glanced again at the dark-clothed men, intently whispering. 'All those poor bastards must be feeling the same.'

'Sh! . . . Don't use that word here!'

I began to laugh but was checked by one of the babies

beginning to cry. Elspeth said: 'It's all right. It's not ours.'

The first baby started off the others. A posse of nurses came and whisked the boxes containing the offenders out of the room. I went and had another look at ours.

She still had her eyes shut. She was still breathing terribly fast. After all, I thought, I am going to be able to feed this darling little mouth. I touched her again, and she opened her eyes.

I went back to Elspeth feeling very strange emotion. Elspeth said:

'While I think of it — will you leave me some small change before you go? I've got nothing to pay for my newspapers with.'

I got some money out of my pocket. She pointed to where her handbag was and asked me to put the money in her purse.

I opened the purse. Inside it was a bank-note and something folded in tissue paper.

'What's this in the tissue paper?' I said.

'Can't you guess?' She smiled quietly. 'Open it!'

I undid the paper. It contained the silver rupee we had found in the taxi on our wedding-day.

I sat down beside her. 'Have you carried it about with you all the time?'

'Of course,' she whispered.

I held it in the open palm of my hand, so that the light shone on it.

'It was for luck,' I said.

I could only just hear her — 'That's what it's brought us, darling. . . .'

I looked at her. 'It *has*. . . .'

We went on looking at each other. Then I touched it to my lips and carefully folded it back again in its tissue paper. Very carefully.

In a little while it was time for me to go.

'Fathers,' enunciated a clear, authoritative, feminine voice from the doorway, 'not able to come in in the evening, may come in for a quarter of an hour at nine o'clock in the morning!'

When I got outside I started to walk instead of catching a bus. The night seemed very dark, but not exceptionally cold — like the night, I thought, of human ignorance. I was pleased with the concept as a simile, but could not see any special application for it at the moment. I felt illuminated, myself. I was in possession of the most important piece of knowledge, which seemed to energise my whole being with light and warmth. It sent my body striding along the twilit street, and my imagination circulating among the peaks of Art. I could have seen it written in stars across the night sky. . . .

You want to know what it was? It was:

## MARRIED LIFE IS WONDERFUL

I dropped into an unfamiliar public-house for a glass of beer. A man standing beside me at the deserted bar said: 'You don't belong round here, do you?'

I told him what brought me there.

'Is it your first?' he asked.

I said it was.

He gave me a long look. 'Then *your* life is just beginning,' he said.

On the point of saying 'Then I can't think what I've been doing up to now', I said:

'I expect it is.'

At that moment, for no reason that I could find, I suddenly thought again of the official letter telling me I was MISC/INEL. What nobody knew, except me, was the effort I put into trying to be EL. That, I thought, was the theme of my life. MISC/INEL, trying to be EL. In this simple statement was embodied the poetry, the dynamism, the suffering of one man's existence.

I finished my beer and left the pub.

Next morning, in the lift on the way up to my office, I met Froggatt.

'I hear we have good reasons to congratulate you on a certain matter,' he said in his leisurely tempo. He was smiling.

I said he had.

He asked me if we were still living in a flat.

I said we were.

'Ah,' said Froggatt, as the lift came to a stop, 'then you'll be looking for a house, now.'

Now I am not intending to make anything of this incident. But when I got to my office and thought about it, I saw it, as Froggatt might have said, in a certain light.

I had got a wife; I had got a baby; and now it appeared that I had got to get a house. . . .

I sat in my chair and expressed myself in a phrase everybody was using in those days. 'Can you *beat* it?'

Instead of ringing for my P.A. I meditated. The conclusion I reached was that this side the grave there is simply no end to anything. Simply no end.

Well, so be it.